## The Div

"*The Diva Takes the Cake* does just that—takes the cake."
—*The Romance Readers Connection*

"Davis has devised a delightful romp, with engaging characters and a nicely crafted setting in which to place them. The author sets just the right tone to match her diva's perfect centerpieces, tablescapes, and lighting effects." —*Shine*

## The Diva Runs Out of Thyme

"[A] tricky whodunit laced with delectable food . . . [and] stuffed with suspects—and a reminder that nobody's Thanksgiving is perfect." —*The Richmond Times-Dispatch*

"[A] fun romp into the world of food, murder, and mayhem."
—*Armchair Interviews*

"Filled with humor, delicious recipes, and holiday decorating tips, *The Diva Runs Out of Thyme* is . . . a must-read to prepare for the holiday season." —*The Romance Readers Connection*

"*The Diva Runs Out of Thyme* is as much comedy as mystery . . . A really good book . . . A series worth watching."
—*Mysterious Reviews*

"An entertaining mystery novel with charming characters. The plot of the mystery is well drawn out . . . Davis is an excellent mystery author." —MyShelf.com

"Delivers a plethora of useful household tips and mouthwatering recipes immersed with a keep-you-guessing plot filled with suspicious-acting characters, and twists and turns around every corner. Davis's smart writing style and engaging characters are sure to garner fans anxious to read future books in the series." —AuthorsDen.com

"The beginning of a good culinary cozy series with some interesting and different characters." —*Gumshoe Review*

*Berkley Prime Crime titles by Krista Davis*

THE DIVA RUNS OUT OF THYME
THE DIVA TAKES THE CAKE
THE DIVA PAINTS THE TOWN

# *The Diva Paints the Town*

KRISTA DAVIS

BERKLEY PRIME CRIME, NEW YORK

**THE BERKLEY PUBLISHING GROUP**
**Published by the Penguin Group**
**Penguin Group (USA) Inc.**
**375 Hudson Street, New York, New York 10014, USA**
Penguin Group (Canada), 90 Eglinton Avenue East, Suite 700, Toronto, Ontario M4P 2Y3, Canada
(a division of Pearson Penguin Canada Inc.)
Penguin Books Ltd., 80 Strand, London WC2R 0RL, England
Penguin Group Ireland, 25 St. Stephen's Green, Dublin 2, Ireland (a division of Penguin Books Ltd.)
Penguin Group (Australia), 250 Camberwell Road, Camberwell, Victoria 3124, Australia
(a division of Pearson Australia Group Pty. Ltd.)
Penguin Books India Pvt. Ltd., 11 Community Centre, Panchsheel Park, New Delhi—110 017, India
Penguin Group (NZ), 67 Apollo Drive, Rosedale, North Shore 0632, New Zealand
(a division of Pearson New Zealand Ltd.)
Penguin Books (South Africa) (Pty.) Ltd., 24 Sturdee Avenue, Rosebank, Johannesburg 2196, South Africa

Penguin Books Ltd., Registered Offices: 80 Strand, London WC2R 0RL, England



THE DIVA PAINTS THE TOWN

A Berkley Prime Crime Book / published by arrangement with the author

PRINTING HISTORY
Berkley Prime Crime mass-market edition / February 2010


Cover illustration by Teresa Fasolino.
Cover design by Diana Kolsky.
Interior text design by Laura K. Corless.


For information, address: The Berkley Publishing Group,
a division of Penguin Group (USA) Inc.,
375 Hudson Street, New York, New York 10014.

ISBN: 978-0-425-23344-3

BERKLEY® PRIME CRIME
Berkley Prime Crime Books are published by The Berkley Publishing Group,
a division of Penguin Group (USA) Inc.,
375 Hudson Street, New York, New York 10014.
BERKLEY® PRIME CRIME and the PRIME CRIME logo are trademarks of Penguin Group (USA) Inc.

PRINTED IN THE UNITED STATES OF AMERICA

10 9 8 7 6 5 4 3 2 1

*For my dad, Anatol.*

*He would have been very pleased.*

# ACKNOWLEDGMENTS

Many thanks to my wonderful critique partners, Janet Bolin and Daryl Wood Gerber, who not only are delightful friends, but keep me on track with humor and sage advice. I owe special thanks to my mom, Marianne, who patiently reads first drafts and offers astute suggestions.

I am eternally grateful to my cheerful and understanding editor, Sandra Harding. I would be lost without her expertise. Thanks also to my agent, Jacky Sach, for all her help. And a special note of appreciation to talented Teresa Fasolino, who continues to create such gorgeous covers for the divas.

I'm also very appreciative of my writing colleagues in The Guppies. Especially Anna Castle, Heidi Noroozy, Kathleen Marsh, Theresa de Valence, and Cathy Rogers, who, along with my dear friend, Betsy Strickland, helped me with Mordecai's Latin. Special thanks to

Christie Harris for helping me with an interior design term. Any errors are my own.

Finally, thanks to Amy Wheeler, who sparked the idea for this plot and to Susan Erba, who patiently tested recipes and gave me a great hint for sweetening daiquiris!

# GUEST LIST

*Guests Invited to Mordecai's Bequest Soiree*

Nolan DuPont
Kurt Finkel
Mike Osmanski
Posey Powell
Ted Wilcox

*Show House Officials*

Camille DuPont—Chairperson of the Design Guild
Natasha—Co-chair of the Show House
Iris Ledbetter—Co-chair of the Show House

*Team Natasha*

Natasha
Beth Ford
~~Kurt Finkel~~
Ted Wilcox
Mike Osmanski

### *Team Iris*

Iris Ledbetter
Bedelia Ledbetter

### *Team Sophie*

Sophie Winston
Bernie Frei
Mars Winston
Nina Reid Norwood
Francie Vanderhoosen
Humphrey Brown

# ONE

**From** "The Good Life" :

Dear Sophie,

My miserable cousins have been pawing through Grandpa's house, claiming they're there to spruce it up. Granted, the house does need painting, but I don't see any improvements. How do I get them out of Grandpa's hair?

—Steamed in Frostproof

Dear Steamed,

With Grandpa's consent, throw a painting party. Gather funky old hats to wear (maybe from Grandpa's attic?), make fun drinks with umbrellas in them, and hand all the cousins paint brushes and rollers. Either they'll leave, or they'll paint.

—Sophie

I momentarily forgot about the icy February rain when a light flashed in a dormer window of Mordecai Artemus's house. In the many years I'd lived in Old Town, I'd never seen an inside light on. But the glimmer didn't last long, and seconds later, I wondered if it could have been some kind of reflection. Droplets of water ran from my face down my neck. I shivered, huddled under my coat again, and hurried toward my home, thinking about poor old Mordecai.

When he died two days ago, there were no hushed mentions of what a fine man he was or how much he would be missed. All anyone could talk about was getting into his mansion. I paused for a second and looked back, wondering if someone had managed to do just that. But the rambling house was still and dark in the night.

Shaking off my thoughts, I continued on my way. I had worked late at Rooms and Blooms, Old Town Alexandria's annual home and garden expo where two hundred builders, landscapers, interior designers, and companies selling home products had set up booths in the convention hall of a local hotel. It had been in full swing for a few days and would be winding down in a couple more, culminating with an awards banquet. I was glad for the work, but it was strenuous, and right now all I wanted was a mug of hot tea and to put my feet up.

Mochie, my spunky Ocicat, met me at the door, mewing complaints about being left alone. He rubbed against my legs but aborted that maneuver quickly once he realized I was wet, and retreated to wash his coat with indignation.

I hung my sopping clothes in the bathroom and slipped into a fuzzy bathrobe to warm up. Even though it was late, I lit a fire in the kitchen fireplace.

But when I poured water into the kettle and looked out the window over the sink, I couldn't help leaning forward to look at Mordecai's house again. Long a recluse, he had kept the drapes closed downstairs, and if he had ever ventured upstairs, I didn't know about it. I shut off the tap and stared at the dark dormer window, barely visible in the attic of his mansard roof. Had I imagined the light? The house looked as it always had at night—a giant, elegant ship of a house, faintly outlined by the streetlights.

Mochie watched me with knowing eyes, waiting for the moment when I would settle down and he could jump into my lap. "Soon," I assured him, filling his dish with food.

But Mochie showed no interest in his food. His golden green eyes wide, he stared over my shoulder and semi-crouched, his muscles tense as though ready to flee.

I looked around slowly, wondering what was agitating him. A gaunt face stared at us through the window of the kitchen door. Wet hair plastered the head of the man outside, and in the dark his head looked more like a skull than a living person. Raindrops on the glass distorted the image. A scream rose through my throat, drowned out by the shrill whistle of the kettle.

My heart thundered as I realized it was too late to turn off the lights and pretend no one was home. Grabbing my cell phone off the table, I started backing away.

"Sophie! Let me in out of the rain." I felt a total fool when I recognized Humphrey's voice.

I took a closer look before I opened the door. "I'm sorry, Humphrey, I didn't recognize you."

He stopped just inside, and water dripped off his black raincoat into a major puddle. But before I managed to shut the door, Nina Reid Norwood, my neighbor and best friend, barged past him, demanding, "Where have you been?"

I retrieved towels and handed one to Humphrey.

After I sopped up the water on the floor, I reached for his raincoat and stifled a laugh. Thin, pale Humphrey usually looked meek, but after being towel dried, his silvery blond hair stood up in spikes and he resembled a deranged punk rocker.

Nina didn't remove her coat. "I'm not that wet."

I hung Humphrey's coat in the bathroom, and when I returned, I thought Mochie was stalking him. Low to the floor, he stretched out one foot slowly, like a panther.

*Awwk.* A green head with a bright yellow patch on the back of its neck emerged from Nina's coat. "She's a witch!" the bird screamed at Mochie, who drew back in alarm.

Nina shrugged off her coat and let the bird climb onto her shoulder. "Meet Hank."

Humphrey shrank back, as appalled as Mochie. "Hank?"

"He sings Hank Williams songs. Someone found him on a park bench on King Street, and I'm fostering him because we're not set up for big birds at the shelter. He's a yellow-naped Amazon parrot. Apparently they're big talkers."

"You're keeping him in your home?" Humphrey didn't disguise his distaste. "Birds are so dirty. How do you know he's not carrying a disease?"

Who knew Humphrey would be so finicky about a bird? "Excuse me, but as a mortician, don't you embalm people who died from diseases?"

"That's entirely different. Birds belong in the wild."

"Someone must be looking for Hank," I said. "There can't be too many birds who sing country songs."

"That's what I think." Nina settled at the table, Hank still on her shoulder, Mochie eyeing him warily. "So where have you been? Why aren't you answering your phone? Do you have any cheese pretzels? I need something comforting to eat—you will *not* believe what happened!"

"I've been at Rooms and Blooms. Cell phones don't work in the convention center of the hotel. Something about the steel and the way it's constructed." I poured soothing lavender chamomile tea into mugs and found a stash of my homemade pretzels in the freezer. After starting the oven, I placed the mugs on the table and noted that Humphrey sat as far away from Hank as he could.

As I sliced strips of Asiago cheese, I glanced from Nina to Humphrey. It was closing in on eleven. What were they doing here, anyway? What was so important?

Nina leaned forward. "I am *so* furious."

"She's a witch! A witch!" cawed Hank.

"Last fall my husband testified on a murder case involving insulin that made the news every day. As a result, he was asked to go on a cruise as an instructor." She waved a hand carelessly. "I didn't go because it's business—he's teaching a class to doctors. But I just found out that the woman who organized the course used to work with him and had the hots for him—and she's on the ship!"

"She's a witch," Hank announced.

"She *is* a witch," confirmed Nina.

"He already picked that up from you? You better be careful what you say around that bird." I popped the pretzels into the oven and sat down.

Humphrey's eyebrows raised, and I had a bad feeling he was assessing Nina as though she were now available. "You don't think she set it up that way on purpose?"

"Of course I do! He's clearly the one who got away."

"Can you join the cruise somewhere?" I asked.

"I thought about that. But there's no one else to take care of Hank, and the cruise is in Asia. By the time I got there, it would almost be over."

"Are you really worried?" I asked. "You trust your husband, don't you?"

"I don't trust *her*. If she'd go so far as to arrange this convenient cruise rendezvous, over Valentine's Day no less, imagine what else she might do."

Humphrey cocked his head. "If I were married to

someone like you, I would never be tempted by a conniving seductress."

Nina froze, and I was about to burst out laughing, so I quickly changed the topic. "And what are you doing out in this weather, Humphrey?"

A flush of red rose in his cheeks. "I had some . . . business up this way. I hope you don't mind. I saw you coming home." He shivered. "It's dismal outside."

Business? I glanced out the window for his hearse. "You don't have a body out there, do you?"

"Personal business."

"Did you happen to notice a light on in Mordecai's house?"

He frowned at me. "You do know he's dead?"

"That's why the light caught my attention." I got up to put the cheese on the pretzels. News of Mordecai's death two days before had spread rapidly through Old Town. "No foul play, though, right?"

"He died from natural causes. Nothing sinister about it," Humphrey assured me.

I laid the savory cheese slices on top of the pretzels and slid the tray back into the hot oven.

"Maybe relatives have arrived and are staying there," said Nina.

A plausible theory.

Humphrey rose, stood in front of the fire, and rubbed his hands together. "Sophie, do you remember Hannah's wedding?"

Of course. Who could forget that nightmare? There had even been a moment of attraction between my sister and Humphrey. I wondered if he still held a flame for her. If he could just meet someone who would return his attention. . . . A wave of apprehension swept over me as I suddenly knew where he was going with his question. At the wedding, I had promised to help him meet women. More specifically—a girlfriend. During our high school days, Humphrey had a crush on me. I hadn't noticed, no doubt busy with my own teen angst. Unfortunately, my mother brought him back into my life, and he promptly pursued me in his own awkward way, then turned his interest to my sister, who, thank goodness, was now safely 150 miles away.

"Humphrey," I said gently, "I completely forgot about finding a girlfriend for you."

He straightened up, flushed from the warmth of the fire. "You don't have to. I've found her."

Relief washed over me. I wouldn't have to dodge poor Humphrey anymore. "That's great! I'm so happy for you." I clinked tea mugs with him in celebration. But then why was he here? "When can I meet her?"

"First I need you to introduce her to me."

I nearly spewed my tea.

"You haven't met her?" asked Nina, her expression incredulous.

"Please, Sophie?"

I wanted to tell him to grow a spine. But I didn't have the heart. He regarded me with a pathetic hangdog expression. "Humphrey, you're an adult. You pay taxes and a mortgage, you . . . you"—I searched for something adventurous to say—"you embalm people. It's time you had the courage to ask a woman for a date."

He hung his head and stared into his mug. His neck jutted forward and he reminded me of a huge blond vulture. It was hopeless, unless, of course, he'd chosen someone as meek as he was. I removed the pretzels from the oven, and Nina grabbed one even though they should have cooled a little bit first.

"This is exactly what I needed," she said. "I eat when I'm upset."

Nina believed in ordering out. With her husband away, as usual, I guessed her refrigerator was empty.

Humphrey watched as she tore the steaming pretzel and a dollop of melted cheese dragged loose. "Not me." He nibbled the edge of a pretzel as if he wanted to taste test it first. "If I'm upset or excited, I can't eat a thing."

I should have such problems. But since I was wrapped in a big bathrobe with no tight waistband cutting into me, I reached for a pretzel and bit into the warm cheese.

Unfortunately, Mochie chose that moment to jump onto the table and stretch a curious paw toward Hank. Hank screamed and flew to the seat of the bay window, Mochie leaping after him.

The big bird backed up, emitting horrendous, ear-splitting screeches that deterred Mochie from launching himself at Hank.

I grabbed Mochie, and Nina, holding her pretzel between her teeth, reached for Hank.

Behind us, Humphrey quietly said, "Look."

The three of us paused to stare out the window at Mordecai's house. Raindrops ran down the glass of my window, but there was no mistaking the dim light that shone in a second-floor window. It flashed brightly, then disappeared altogether.

# TWO

From *Natasha Online*:

*Find inspiration for your own home by visiting a decorator show house. The best interior designers in your area know that show houses are the place to display their creative ideas. Study the rooms you like and take home fresh ideas to make your own castle gorgeous.*

"Maybe a relative did arrive," said Humphrey.

"With a flashlight? Wouldn't a relative turn on a light?" I said.

No one bothered with coats. We flew out the door and across the street to Mordecai's. I ran up the front steps to the covered porch and tried the doorknob. The door was locked.

Humphrey rang the bell.

"What are you doing?"

"It's only polite. What if someone is staying here? It would be the height of impropriety to burst in on them."

After giving him an impatient look, I dashed down to the street, where Nina waited.

"I can't run with the bird, and I couldn't leave him with Mochie," she complained.

"I'm going around back."

Rain pelted me as I jogged along the sidewalk. In the distance a figure vanished into the darkness. The gate to Mordecai's backyard and garage was unlocked. I swung it open and cautiously stole toward the back door, fearful that someone might burst through it. I paused to look up at the house. The sudden appearance of a light surprised me, but as it dawned on me that the light was reflecting on the glass of the window rather than shining through from inside the house, a woman's voice behind me said, "Stop right there."

I didn't, of course. I turned around to see who held the flashlight. It wasn't easy to make the person out against the beam of light trained on me, but I could see a police hat with a rain cover on it.

I shielded my eyes by raising a hand in front of my face. "I'm a neighbor. We saw a light inside and thought someone might have broken in. The owner just died."

I must not have appeared too menacing in my bathrobe, with my hair plastered to my head, because she walked past me and tried the back door. "It's secure. Do you realize that you're trespassing?"

"Well, no. I'm being neighborly."

"Go on, now."

"But we saw a light."

"Thank you for letting me know. I'll keep an eye on the place."

She closed the gate firmly behind me and waited for me to walk away.

I caught up with Nina and Humphrey, who huddled out of the rain on Mordecai's front porch, and told them what had happened.

Satisfied that we'd done all we could, Nina hurried home to get Hank out of the cold, wet weather. Humphrey returned to collect his coat, but left quickly after I finally offered to host a dinner party and invite his new friend.

I tamped out the fire, locked the doors, and took a long, hot shower to warm up before going to bed.

⁂

Morning came too early the next day, but I reminded myself how lucky I was to be working. Too many companies had cut back on their events, and a lot of event planners were taking on other jobs to make ends meet. Still, being the coordinator of Rooms and Blooms was a demanding job. I was on my feet all day solving problems. After a few glitches setting up, the first days we were open to the public had gone well, considering the number of people involved, and I hoped things would continue to go smoothly.

The rain had stopped and the sun shone, but the trees in my backyard swayed in a strong wind. I opted for simple khakis and a coral sweater set, not too fancy because Rooms and Blooms sometimes required me to crawl around on my knees or scoop up spilled dirt. I fed Mochie while I swilled a mug of coffee. By the time I left, he had stretched out on the brick floor of the sunroom, already warm from the sun, and was snoozing.

⁂

Natasha waited for me at the entrance to Rooms and Blooms, chatting with the security guard. She and I had grown up together in a small town in Virginia. We'd competed at everything, pushing each other to try harder. Except I'd avoided the beauty pageants that Natasha loved so much. She'd parlayed her looks and driving work ethic into a domestic diva TV show on a local cable channel, but she aspired to greater fame. Sometimes I wondered if anything could stop her. And now she'd had the nerve to move into my neighborhood, which seemed to guarantee her presence in my life. I had come to terms with her, but Natasha still thought she was always right about everything, which irritated me no end.

The security guard nodded at me, collected a couple of candy wrappers, and left.

Natasha's dark hair framed her face as though she'd just left a salon. How could anyone look perfectly put together so early in the morning? A knit dress of robin's egg blue glided over her figure. On me it would have shown every lump and bump. She looked at her watch and said, "Don't you think the latte people should open when the exhibitors arrive?"

"I'm sure they'll be here soon."

"I'm giving a talk this morning, and I need a coffee jolt to get me going."

I couldn't resist. "What? You didn't whip up eggs Benedict for breakfast before you came?"

"Mars had a breakfast meeting, and I wanted to get here in plenty of time to set up." She grabbed my arm. "Sophie, you know all the exhibitors. I could use some help in winning Best in Show. It carries such weight with the Design Guild, and I'm in the running for their annual award."

The Design Guild had been around for decades. In fact, under a different name, Rooms and Blooms had originally been a Design Guild project. Years ago Guild members ran the home show outdoors in the spring, and instituted the Best in Show awards to encourage exhibitors to create fancy booths. As the show grew in size, they added categories and more prizes, and the Best in Show winner scored major points toward the Design Guild's prestigious annual award to the designer who had made the biggest contribution that year.

But Natasha already had her own TV show about all things domestic. Why would the Design Guild Award be so important to her? It wasn't like she owned an interior design business that would get a boost from the award and publicity. "All the visitors get to vote for their favorite booth. It's not up to me."

"But the exhibitors get to vote, too. Couldn't you put in a good word for me?"

"Don't you think each exhibitor feels the way you do?"

She drew back as though I'd said something rude and ugly. "I thought I could count on your support."

"Natasha, I'm running the show. It wouldn't be appropriate to be biased."

"In that case, don't expect any favors from me!"

She stalked off in a huff, and I wished my day had started better. Fortunately, work drew my attention and I didn't give her another thought until I took a midmorning break with a bottle of black currant juice. I sat on a concrete garden bench near a family of ceramic geese marching through a small field of soft pink Angelique tulips. In the springlike panorama of the hotel's convention hall, it was hard to imagine that a blustery winter wind blew outside.

"No one has seen the interior of Professor Mordecai's house in years, but his wife was a decorator and I've heard it's fantastic." I didn't mean to eavesdrop, but I couldn't help recognizing the perky voice of Iris Ledbetter, rumored to be the one to beat for the coveted Best in Show award for her design booth. In spite of her penchant for boxy clothes with busy patterns, at thirty-five Iris was making a name for her interior design business through her lavish use of sumptuous fabrics. Although she lived in nearby Del Ray, I was told the Ledbetter name was well known in Old Town decorating circles.

Camille DuPont, chairwoman of the Design Guild, said, "Mordecai's wife is the only person who ever won the Design Guild's Award two years running. But the house creeps me out a little bit. They say he hid a corpse in there. I've heard he used to go out at night and wander the streets of Old Town in the dark."

"The corpse is his wife," Iris responded. "My grandmother, Bedelia, knew them because she lived on their block. It was common knowledge."

"I thought you looked familiar."

That was a voice I knew well. I craned my neck to see my elderly neighbor, Francie, squinting at Iris. A longtime resident of Old Town, Francie was the epitome of a sturdy Southern outdoorswoman. Years of sun exposure from working in her garden and hours of hiking and birdwatching had left her skin deeply wrinkled. I'd heard people call her crabby, but the stocky little widow had weaseled her way into my heart by speaking her mind. "Is your grandmother Bedelia Ledbetter?" asked Francie.

"Yes! Do you know my Nana?"

"I never met a bigger busybody. Apparently, you're as daft as she was. Mordecai didn't kill his wife. She ran off with your grandfather."

I craned my neck to get a better look. Iris's eyes flew wide and she took a step back. Apparently she hadn't known about that bit of impropriety by her grandfather. And she clearly didn't know what to make of crusty Francie, who spoke her mind and didn't much care about being polite, a cardinal sin in Southern social circles. It wasn't beneath Francie to fib, though, as evidenced by the presence of her golden retriever, Duke. She must have invented some kind of assistance dog story at the door to get him inside.

After an awkward pause, Iris said coolly, "I'm certain that you're mistaken." She continued to gaze at Francie, and I had a suspicion that Francie had met her match. But Natasha marched up and declared, "You'd think that someone in this town would be willing to let the Design Guild redecorate their home as a Show Home. Honestly, if we don't land something soon, there's no way we'll have it ready in time for the statewide Spring Home and Garden tour. It would be an enormous embarrassment if the Guild didn't have a Show Home this year for the statewide program."

Iris must have decided to overlook Francie's slight, because she chimed in, "I know what you mean. People act like their houses have been professionally decorated when they're a mishmash of worn furniture and garage sale knickknacks."

"Sophie," said Natasha, "you have those horrible green and black bathrooms from another century."

Duke nudged me from behind, so I swung my legs around and bent forward to pet him. Natasha was right about my bathrooms. All one and a half of them. I needed a second full bathroom, and I'd been itching to shed the green and black tiles for years. But there was no way I was letting her impose *her* design ideas on me. "No, thanks."

"The best kitchen designer in town is willing to help, Sophie."

"I *like* my kitchen."

Francie frowned at her. "You're not on your game today, are you, Natasha? What about Mordecai's house?"

Natasha stared at her, momentarily speechless. "That's

perfect. Everyone is dying to get inside, and I'm sure it needs sprucing up. We could call it Natasha's Dream House, and I could shoot the progress for my show."

"Hold it, Princess. I'm not doing a room in a house with your name on it." Iris glared at Natasha.

"It *has* always been called the Design Guild Show House," Camille pointed out. "It has cachet. People look for that name, because they know it means excellence in design."

"But if we put my name on it, there will be brand recognition." As far as I could tell, Natasha wasn't convincing Iris and Camille. "How about—The Design Guild Presents Natasha's Dream House?"

Iris crossed her arms over her chest defiantly. "You're not even a professional decorator. I don't see why you're involved at all."

*Uh-oh.* I waited for Natasha to explode. Her mouth flapped open, but then, sweet as sugar, she said, "I'm a threat to you, aren't I, Iris?"

Iris had a broad face and features to fill it. When she crossed her arms defiantly, her jaw went as rigid as a bulldog's, and I caught a glimpse of a menacing side.

"We don't even know if we can use Mordecai's house yet." Camille spoke softly but with authority. "The first thing we have to do is find out who's representing the estate." In a split second, the three of them were off at a fast walk, gabbing like crazy.

Francie tucked her strawlike hair under a knit cap. "Boy, the apple doesn't fall from the addled grandmother tree, does it? Bedelia Ledbetter, Iris's grandmother, was one of those phony-baloney women who wanted to think she was better than everybody else. You know the type, talked incessantly about the house in Palm Beach, which I happen to know is a one-bedroom condo. You'd think she would have figured out that the ones with real money don't brag about it, like that Camille DuPont."

Camille's husband owned an antiques store in the heart of Old Town that was so expensive I was afraid to step inside. "They certainly have high prices at their store."

"That's just a hobby. Camille is the real deal—a bona fide heiress. She inherited a fortune from her grandfather's pipe and steel company."

On the petite side, with ash blond hair as perfectly coifed as Natasha's, Camille was nice to everyone. She sat on several boards, and was always the first to volunteer her time for a worthy cause—unlike her husband, Nolan, who had elevated snootiness to new heights.

"So their money came from Camille's family? I thought they were related to the famous DuPonts."

"Nolan certainly works at giving that impression, but DuPont is a common surname in France. It means 'of the bridge,' not exactly the name of nobility. I met his father once. He's a very down-to-earth pharmacist. Nothing like his pompous son. I'm telling you, it's always the ones without money who want you to think they're loaded." Francie was chuckling as she and Duke left.

By noon, I was ready to bail and leave any crises to my staff, at least long enough to grab lunch. Originally, Design Guild members ran Rooms and Blooms, but after one particularly nasty incident of sabotage involving Guild members in the eighties that resulted in a fire and a lawsuit, they wisely decided to hire professionals to organize the event. The general cutback in fancy parties had put a lot of event professionals out of business, so it hadn't been hard to put together a competent team. Besides, I would only be a block away at The Laughing Hound, the restaurant my friend Bernie ran. I would be close enough to hurry back in an emergency.

I found my ex-husband, Mars, short for Marshall, and our friend Bernie chowing down in the bar lounge near the humongous fireplace. I ordered hot English breakfast tea and roast beef au jus at the bar, told the waitress I'd be with Bernie, and gladly collapsed into the cushy sofa next to him.

Bernie shot me a quizzical look. "I was beginning to think you were avoiding me. How come you're not answering your phone?"

I explained about cell phones not working at Rooms and Blooms. "What's up?"

"Mordecai's lawyer wants us to spread the word to be on the lookout for Emmaline."

"Mordecai's Pomeranian?" I'd been so busy that I'd forgotten about the little dog. "Who's taking care of her?"

Mars groaned. "That's the problem. When Mordecai died, Natasha let her run out the door, and no one knows where she is."

Poor Emmaline. She'd been treated as a precious lapdog all her life. She must be traumatized to have lost Mordecai and be alone, outside in the frigid weather.

"Bernie is the one who found Mordecai," said Mars.

Bernie flushed and held up his hands in protest. In his unmistakable British accent, he said, "Twice a day I sent someone by with a meal for Mordecai, and when he didn't answer the door, I knew something was amiss."

"I had no idea you were so close." His kindness to the old man made me feel guilty. Mordecai had lived little more than a stone's throw from me, yet I had done nothing for him. I'd met him briefly when my sister was getting married, but for the most part, he hid in his gorgeous historical home and peered at the world through a slit in heavy curtains.

"Don't get the wrong idea. He never invited me into his home, but he always came to the door for his food."

"Natasha has been trying to get inside that building

since the day she saw it. She had the gall to go inside when the rescue squad arrived to check on poor Mordecai. I mean, the guy wasn't even cold yet!" Mars shook his head and slugged down coffee.

*Eww.* That seemed a bit uncaring, even for Natasha. Located on a corner lot, Mordecai's house, the color of soft butter, stood out among all the redbrick Federal-style houses that surrounded it. White pillars on the front porch added to the southern charm.

Mars's jaw tensed in an angry reflex. "I told her last night that if she intends to move into that house, she'll do it without me."

Natasha, with whom I'd had a friendly rivalry when we were growing up, had set up housekeeping with my husband, Mars, after we split up. There were those, notably my family, who insisted Natasha had stolen Mars from me. The truth was far less exotic—Mars and I had grown apart. Nevertheless, in spite of Natasha's considerable efforts to march Mars down the aisle, he'd balked at every opportunity. I wondered if he worried about this exact scenario. He had a lot more leverage over the willful Natasha if he could threaten to walk away from the relationship.

"We dumped a small fortune into our house to renovate it, *even though it didn't need it,* and Natasha still hasn't sold her country home. It's sitting out there, pretty as a picture book, with a huge price tag and no buyers. I'm not taking on another mortgage. I'm just not."

Bernie's eyes met mine, and I suspected Mars's old pal was thinking along the same lines I was. Had the relationship reached its breaking point? Natasha couldn't be easy to live with.

Under his breath, Bernie said, "There's a big meeting going on in the back corner about Mordecai's estate. Seems he left the place to his little dog."

The waitress delivered my sandwich as Natasha strode in. Her dress clung to her thighs, showing off long, slender legs.

She tossed her coat onto a chair. "Beef and bread, Sophie? No wonder you're pudgy." She turned to the waitress. "I'll have an Evian, garden salad, no dressing, and a cup of defatted chicken broth, please."

I ignored her and sank my teeth into the savory meat.

"Great news! Mordecai's house is going to be sold, but it's in such disarray that they're letting me—well, the Design Guild—make it into the spring Show House. Isn't that wonderful?"

"You mean one of those houses where a different decorator fixes up each room, and then the public parades through to see it?" asked Bernie.

"Exactly. I can shoot episodes about decorating, and I have fabulous ideas about remodeling the kitchen. We could shoot shows about how it's done. Some of the leading designers in town are clamoring to take on a room. But can you imagine, that awful Iris Ledbetter told Camille DuPont that Iris and I should co-chair the Show House!"

Bernie listened, his fingers wrapped around a mug of coffee. "Why don't you give Sophie a room to decorate?"

I glimpsed a moment of panic in Natasha's perfectly made-up face. She held a hand to her throat and tilted her head. "Now, Bernie, don't embarrass Sophie. We all know she's not much of a decorator."

"That's not true. Everyone loves Sophie's kitchen. Her house is beautiful."

Natasha's lips pulled into a thin frown. "It wouldn't be fair to Sophie. This has to be done fast. I have people and I'm still hiring a new assistant to help me."

At any other time, I'd have leaped at the opportunity, just to put Natasha in her place, but Rooms and Blooms was a major production. "Thanks, Bernie, but with Rooms and Blooms in full swing, I really don't have the time."

"It will be over in a few days," Bernie persisted. "I'll be Sophie's assistant. I spend far too much time here anyway. It would be good for me to get out and use my hands a bit."

"I will, too," said Mars. "We could get started right away if Sophie tells us what needs doing."

I groaned inwardly. What was Mars thinking? He knew Natasha would be impossibly jealous if he helped me instead of her. But then it dawned on me that Mars knew exactly what he was doing, and after his rant about not buying Mordecai's house, I wondered if he volunteered so he could spy on her.

When I'd walked into the restaurant, I couldn't have cared less about decorating a room in Mordecai's house. Nothing had been further from my mind. But my lengthy rivalry with Natasha always brought out the very worst in me, and I was enjoying her discomfort.

Natasha couldn't control her expression anymore. A storm cloud washed over her face, and then she smiled—a wan, bitter smile that reminded me that Mars was totally useless around the house. He couldn't even hammer a nail to hang a picture.

"Very well. Meet me at Mordecai's at four o'clock to pick up your key."

Bernie high-fived me, looking quite smug about trumping Natasha. I hated to leave the fun and the cozy fire, but I had to get back to work.

"Don't you have a job to go to anymore?" I asked Mars, my tone loaded with sarcasm since he worked for himself as a political consultant.

"I have a meeting two blocks away. C'mon, I'll walk you out."

But as soon as I donned my coat, Adam Swensen, a local attorney, waved me down and took my hand between his. "I'm so sorry for your loss, Sophie."

"My loss?" The only loss I felt at the moment was my cluelessness about what he meant.

"Mordecai spoke so fondly of you. He said he wouldn't trust anyone else with it."

I thought Natasha might choke.

"With what?" I asked. Had he left me his dog?

Swensen looked at his watch. "I've taken care of my part." He smiled at me. "When Mordecai came to me last summer to make arrangements, he said the oddest thing." Adam held up his hand as though no one should speak while he collected his thoughts. "He said—for nearly twenty years he thought he knew the truth, and then his little dog dug up something and he realized that he'd labored under a misconception all that time. Do you know what he meant?"

It sounded like the ramblings of a confused mind to me, but I couldn't say that. "I'm sorry, I haven't a clue."

Adam nodded. "I guess we'll never know. Well, a courier should deliver it to your home any time now. I do apologize for the late notice, but no one can plan these things. Right? Mars, aren't you in my meeting? We're going to be late."

I wanted to follow Adam to ask what he was talking about, but Natasha grabbed me by the arm. "Mordecai left you something? But I'm the one who invited him to dinner last summer. I'm the one who befriended him. Why would he leave *you* anything?"

I didn't have the faintest idea.

Natasha tossed me a withering look as she returned to her broth. I wasn't sure I wanted to be involved in one of her grand schemes. On the other hand, Rooms and Blooms was well in hand, and it might be fun to paint and fix up a room in Mordecai's house.

Bernie winked at me. "I'm off tonight. What say we get started this evening?"

Nothing doing. I was finally going out with Detective Wolf Fleishman. Our schedules made it difficult to get together, but we'd both vowed to make tonight's date. "I'm busy tonight," I said, "but you and Mars could get started. Why don't you meet Natasha and me at Mordecai's just after four, and we can see what needs to be done?"

At a quarter past four, I perched on the steps of the front porch to Mordecai's house and pulled my coat closed against the wind. Working in the springlike atmosphere of Rooms and Blooms had made me forget how dismal it was outside. I checked my watch and hoped Natasha wouldn't be late since I wanted to shower before Wolf picked me up for our date.

"Em-ma-line? Emma-puppy . . ." I bent forward enough to see Nina crouching with a piece of fried chicken in her hand.

I was about to pretend to bark when a soft "woof" came from behind Nina. She glanced up, and promptly fell over in a highly undignified *plop* onto her rear end. From my vantage point, I could only see Nina's tomato-red face and a hand reaching out to her.

# THREE

**From "The Good Life":**

Dear Sophie,

I inherited some money from an elderly aunt and would like to use it to fix up my house. My husband wants to finish the basement as a man cave with a theater. I think we should update our old, not yet vintage, kitchen. We'd appreciate your opinion.

—Spelunking in Springfield

Dear Spelunking,

Updated kitchens and bathrooms bring the most return on a remodeling investment. Maybe you can work on the man cave after the kitchen is done.

—Sophie

I nearly fell off the steps in an effort to see.

The hand belonged to a man with boyish good looks, although I judged him to be in his forties. A swatch of dark hair fell into his eyes, and an endearingly crooked grin topped a square chin.

"Nina Reid." He said her name softly, almost dream-like. "You're about the last person in the world I expected to see." He hoisted her up, and Nina dusted herself off, her face and ears still scarlet.

Her eyes sparkled in a way I had never seen before. In a voice that was low and husky, she managed to choke out "Kurt."

After a long moment of staring into each other's eyes, they broke into self-conscious laughter, hugged, and talked at the same time.

"Gosh, I'm such a mess. Our neighbor died, and I'm looking for his dog."

"You live around here?"

"A few houses down. What are you doing here?"

"I'm meeting Natasha—you know, the TV Diva—about doing a kitchen renovation for her show. Have you been to Rooms and Blooms? You should come by to see my exhibit."

Nina beamed at him. "I hear you're the kitchen designer of choice in Old Town."

Kurt stepped forward. Squinting at the graceful front porch, he said, "Is this Professor Artemus's house?"

"You knew him?" asked Nina.

"I was one of his students. I remember coming here for a party a long time ago. So the old guy finally passed on. That's too bad. He was brilliant, you know, almost a genius. He was one of those cool professors who let his students learn by doing." He grinned and held his fingers in a circle, like he was holding an invisible ball. "We had to build structures to protect a raw egg, then he had us lob them off the roof to see whose egg survived intact."

Natasha's arrival interrupted his memories. She promptly greeted Kurt by name and doled out keys to Kurt and me. She unlocked the front door, and when Nina tagged along inside, Natasha asked, "Are you on Sophie's team, too?"

"Oh, yes!" Nina sidled up to me in the entrance hall and whispered, "What team?"

Natasha flicked a light switch, and a colonial-style brass chandelier shed light in the dark foyer. "The first thing everyone has to do is open curtains. I've never seen a house this dark. Sophie, your room is there to the left. It's the most important room in the house, so I'm expecting miracles. We cannot let Iris show us up." She walked over to me and whispered, "Don't let me down this time. The Guild will take this into consideration when they make their annual award."

Kurt smiled at me, and held out his hand. "We haven't met. Kurt Finkel, Finkel Kitchen and Bath."

I'd seen his dream kitchen display at Rooms and Blooms. He certainly knew how to lure customers with gleaming granite and fancy cabinet finishes. Local people boasted about their Finkel kitchens.

Nina blushed when she said, "We used to date. A long, long time ago."

Their little reunion was interesting, but I was more concerned about something else. Natasha assigned me the most important room in the house? My rat-fink radar was beeping like crazy. The Natasha I knew would reserve the important room for herself. Something didn't smell right.

I walked through the doorway into the oh-so-important room, and wedged behind a sofa to open the drapes. Dust flew from heavy velvet curtains when I pulled them aside. Underneath, blackout curtains blocked the sun. Even parting the blackout curtains didn't help. A thick shade blocked the window. Mordecai had been determined that no one would see inside his home. I pulled on the shade, and it flew up with a sickly rattle, sending dust through the air like lazy snowflakes. Waving my hand in front of my nose, I went through the same procedure with the other window. When waning daylight dappled through the dirty glass, I realized why the room was important, and why Natasha saddled me with it. Every horizontal surface was covered with personal papers, trash, newspapers, magazines, blankets, cutlery, dishes, and clothes. I couldn't tell if the floor was hardwood or carpet because it, too, was covered. Boxes, bottles, and stacks of newspapers rose to my elbows, and a patchwork of clothing and blankets covered the floor in a narrow path through the room. Unless I missed my guess, Mordecai spent his final years almost exclusively in this room. As much as one might want to throw out everything en masse, Natasha had *generously* given me the room because someone had to comb through everything to be sure a stock certificate, cash, or other valuable item wasn't thrown out by accident.

My temper flared, but before I could lash out at her, I recognized the wrappers left by the rescue squad near the middle of the room. "He died in here," I murmured aloud. Guilt weighed on me. Poor Mordecai. He'd lived so close, but I hadn't taken the time to know him. He'd spent his final years closeted in a dark house, hiding from the world. I'd never brought him homemade bread, or a piece of cake, or food he could warm in the microwave for an easy meal. I never checked on him to see if he felt sick. I never shoveled the walk in front of his house, or offered to rake the leaves. I had been a horrible, too-busy-to-be-bothered neighbor. The least I could do was help clean up the house, and look for the dog he loved so very much.

Nina followed me through the room. "What a disaster. I pity the people who have to clean this up."

"Welcome to the team."

"You're joking."

"Look at it as a contribution to the Design Guild."

"Why don't we just write them a check instead?"

Nina's husband, a renowned forensic pathologist, could probably afford to write them a hefty check. Unfortunately, I couldn't. "The Good Life," my advice column, had been picked up by newspapers in Florida, but the income wasn't enough to cover the revenue I'd lost through corporate cutbacks. Besides, I was still paying on the sizable mortgage I took to buy Mars out of his share of our home.

I could hear Natasha talking elsewhere in the house. "So who is this Kurt?" I whispered.

"Talk about a blast from the past! I was madly and deeply in love with him once. Huh, I can't even remember why we broke up."

Kurt ambled into the family room. Smiling seductively at Nina, he said, "We should get together and catch up. Dinner tonight? I wonder if that old Chinese place downtown is still around—the one that used to be open until three in the morning? I'll call and find out."

Mars and Bernie appeared in the doorway. "No wonder Mordecai wouldn't let anyone inside." Mars stared at the mess in dismay. "Holy cow! This is a pigsty."

"But look at this woodwork." Bernie skirted trash and eased a gentle hand over a built-in bookcase that covered an exterior wall of the room. "This is all hand-carved. Do you think Mordecai did it himself?"

Carrying a clipboard, Natasha marched in and said, "I suppose Kurt and Bernie will be engaged in demolition tomorrow? Can you do it in one day, or shall I schedule you for two?"

Kurt held up two fingers. "If you want that brick wall in the kitchen removed, you'd better count on at least two days. It's going to be a mess."

She looked at Bernie. "And how long will you need?"

He glanced at me, his brows furrowed. "What am I tearing out?"

"That horrible built-in that covers the wall." Natasha smiled at him.

"Horrible? That's walnut. And the workmanship is exemplary."

Natasha's head jerked as if he'd lobbed a ball at her. "It's dark and it's dated. No one will ever buy the house with that monstrosity. Sophie, you simply must tear it out."

Leaning against Mordecai's oversized desk, I studied the wall. The built-in housed books, a TV set, and assorted knickknacks, and heaven knew what awaited us behind the doors. The wood *was* dark, but I wasn't altogether sure that it wouldn't brighten up a bit if we cleaned it. "It's very practical. And it's quite ornate. You'd have to pay a fortune at an architectural salvage company to get something a quarter that size."

"Quite right. It's exquisite." Bernie ran his hand over an intricate scroll that had been chiseled out of the wood. "Someone put a lot of effort into this. Look at this owl, it's carved from one piece of wood, not pressed like the junk they sell today. In fact, I'm thinking a window seat in that corner would balance it nicely. What do you think, Sophie? You could run up some feather-stuffed cushions and make a cozy reading nook by that window."

Natasha huffed. "I knew you two would be trouble. I want that thing gone. Cleaned out. Do you understand?" She tromped off to the kitchen.

Kurt grimaced. "She's never like that on her show."

"Meet the real Natasha," said Nina.

Kurt blew air out of his cheeks. "She talked to me about renovating her kitchen a few years ago, and now it's all coming back to me. Aw gee. She's going to be a pain to work with, isn't she?"

"We'll be right here if you need reinforcements." Nina grinned at him coyly.

In the meantime, Bernie had whipped out a measuring tape and was calling out numbers to Mars, who jotted them down. They seemed to be on a roll, and headed off to pick up a pizza and buy wood for the window seat. Nina and I walked home together—I was looking forward to my date, and she wanted to change for a drink with her old flame Kurt.

"This little date wouldn't have anything to do with your husband and the vixen on his cruise, would it?"

"Spoilsport. It's not a date. I'm just catching up with an old friend. Haven't you ever run into one of your old beaus?"

"Only Mars."

"It's just an innocent drink and dinner—like when you have lunch with Mars. And if I should happen to need a name to throw at my husband on his return, well, I'll have a little ammunition of my own."

As I crossed the street to my home, I put Nina and Kurt out of mind. Tonight, Wolf and I would finally get together. No more broken dates. No more dinners with my ex.

I opened the little gate to the service entrance and found a local courier holding a box the size of a large microwave oven. I signed for it and carried the heavy package into the kitchen. Mochie jumped on the table to sniff the box while I retrieved a knife. I double-checked to be sure it was addressed to me before slicing it open. It was from Adam Swensen, Attorney-at-Law.

# FOUR

From *"Ask Natasha"*:

*Dear Natasha,*

*I'm done with cleaning grout. I want to replace my tile countertops with a solid surface, but granite and marble don't appeal to me. Are there any alternatives to stone?*

*—Grout-free in Gretna*

*Dear Grout-free,*

*My favorite material for countertops is stainless steel. It's easy to clean and has a modern, up-to-date look. In fact, if you take a peek in the kitchens of most restaurants, that's what you'll find on their counters. If stainless doesn't appeal to you, then consider the latest thing in seamless countertops—copper or zinc, which simply ooze Old World charm.*

*—Natasha*

A letter lay on top of the contents.

*Dear Sophie,*

*I am very sorry to inform you that your neighbor and friend, Mordecai Artemus, has passed away. Prior to his demise, he came to our firm and left specific instructions, which we herewith carry out on his behalf.*

*Mr. Artemus has chosen to forgo a formal funeral and wake. Instead, it is his wish that you arrange a small soiree to dispense his bequests. He has laid out the details rather precisely in the enclosed envelope. Your standard fee will be paid by his estate.*

*The five individuals involved have been contacted per Mr. Artemus's instructions, and all plan to be present at his home tomorrow afternoon at three p.m. I apologize for the short notice, but given the circumstances, it cannot be helped.*

Tomorrow!

I dug under white tissue paper and found an envelope with my name handwritten across it. Underneath, the box contained five long packages neatly wrapped in white paper and tied with red ribbon. Each bore a name.

Holy moly. The old guy hadn't understood that event planning meant big events. I wasn't in the business of arranging small parties. But I could hardly turn him down now that he was dead. Not to mention that the invitees had already been notified.

While Mochie investigated the box, I sank into a chair by the fireplace and opened the remaining envelope.

*Dear Ms. Winston,*

*Last summer at your sister's wedding, you handled the dinner after the murder of your relative with such aplomb that I knew you were the right person to undertake this function for me. I would like you to provide food and beverages in accordance with the attached menu. No substitutions, please. In the event that someone has moved the furniture in my living room, I have provided a diagram of how the room should look. Please ensure that the furniture is exactly as shown. You will find dishes and necessary accoutrement in the butler's pantry. The vases on the fireplace mantel should be filled with purple lilacs. I realize that it may be difficult to obtain lilacs at certain times of year, but they are crucial to the gathering. The room must smell of lilacs.*

*Please present the bequests to my guests with my very best wishes.*

*Mordecai Artemus*
*Audacior in morte quam in vita*

I knew serving dinner after a murder at my sister's wedding would come back to haunt me. Mordecai's menu wouldn't be much of a problem, though. It was a little dated, but the dishes were probably the height of fashion before he became a recluse.

Strawberry daiquiris

Baked Brie

Savory onion quiche

Crudités with spinach dip
(served in a hollowed-out bread loaf)

Chocolate-chip blondies

Old Mordecai had certainly thought through the details. I was perturbed by the notion that Mordecai and his attorney assumed I would throw everything together on such short notice. On the other hand, the people who catered wakes usually only had a day or two lead time. Post-death functions weren't the sort of thing one could plan in advance.

The only thing that might pose a problem was the lilacs. A quick phone call to my florist took care of that little matter. It was a bit early in the season, but they could be had for a price.

I would have to pick up groceries and cook tonight, maybe stop by Mordecai's early in the morning to dust, and make sure the living room was in order. Why did he have to die during Rooms and Blooms, when I was so busy? I slapped a hand over my mouth. What a horrible person I was. Mordecai had died, and this was all he wanted. No funeral, no wake. This was his last wish, but all I could think of was me, me, me.

Ashamed of myself, I made a quick list of the groceries I would need, and in the middle of writing the word "Gruyère," I remembered Wolf.

Who'd have thought a hand from the grave would interfere with our date? Sighing, I phoned Wolf and explained.

But instead of breaking our date, he offered to help. "I'm not the best cook in the world, but I can slice and dice."

Grinning from ear to ear, I dashed upstairs for a shower. I dressed in a lilac sweater, soft as bunny fur, and a pair of casual trousers. I added dangling amethyst heart earrings, and tried to use mascara without leaving any hateful clumps on my lashes. I finished just as Wolf banged the knocker on the front door.

Our adventure in the grocery store yielded some interesting sides of Wolf. I was used to Mars, who would have said, "Cheese is cheese is cheese." But Wolf sniffed cheeses, and bought a small wedge of artisan cheese with black truffles for us to try. To simplify things, we decided to make two quiches and eat one for dinner. Wolf selected a Riesling to go with the Gruyère I was planning to use in the quiche. I couldn't remember ever smiling so much in a grocery store.

Back at home, while I put groceries away, Wolf lit a fire, and soon the dry wood crackled and warmed the kitchen. Mochie sat in front of it, entranced.

Wolf found the blender, whipped up strawberry daiquiris, and handed me a glass of the icy concoction. In spite of the winter temperatures outside, the bright red drink brought instant festivity to our work. He slathered the expensive truffle cheese on crackers and offered me one. Our eyes met as the rich cheese melted in our mouths. "Heavenly," I murmured with my mouth full.

True to his word, Wolf began slicing cauliflower, red peppers, mushrooms, carrots, and cucumbers for Mordecai's party. "This is a little different, isn't it?" he asked. "Not many people plan a bequest party."

"He obviously gave it a lot of thought." I mixed butter, flour, water, a splash of vinegar, and a little bit of salt and sugar into a dough for the quiche crust.

Wolf started a rasher of bacon in a pan. "It's not a bad idea. I hate funerals and wakes. This way, it's just a very small group of people that he cared about, and nobody has to stand out in the freezing weather."

I lined two quiche pans with the pastry, and had enough left for the Brie and two more pies. The extra dough went into the freezer for future use. "It's a little morbid, though, don't you think? Kind of like a dead person reaching back to the living." I spread piquant grainy mustard around the bottoms of the quiches, and let the pastry stand while I made quick work melting the brown sugar for the blondies. The scent of sizzling bacon perfumed the kitchen, and Wolf waggled a crispy piece under my nose. To my complete surprise, he held it while I bit into the salty meat. He popped the rest into his own mouth, and returned to the bacon to crumble it for the quiche.

"I don't see it as creepy," mused Wolf. "He probably wished he could have done this while he was alive. He wanted to do something nice for the people he loved."

I spread chocolate chips on the blondie mixture and poured the rest of the dough over top of them. While the blondies baked, I whirled sour cream, mayonnaise, spinach, and spices into dip in seconds in a food processor.

Glad to have that done, I gave a stir to the onions Wolf had sliced. They began to caramelize, sending their mouthwatering aroma into the air. I layered translucent onions and nutty Gruyère cheese in the quiche shells, omitting the bacon from the quiche for the party, in case anyone was a vegetarian, poured seasoned and beaten eggs, mixed with cream and milk over the top, then slid them into the hot oven.

Wolf and I had made quick work of Mordecai's menu. It seemed premature to say so to Wolf, but I thought we made a very good team. He sliced a few extra mushrooms and some black olives while I prepared a salad of young mixed greens for our dinner. He didn't ask if he should toss them into the salad, just did it on his own, while I made a sweet red raspberry balsamic vinaigrette.

As Wolf ambled away, I couldn't help sneaking a few glances in his direction. He poked at the fire, threw on another log, and ran his hand over Mochie's fur.

As a homicide detective, Wolf had seen things I didn't even want to imagine, but he didn't have a hardened appearance. I'd seen him under pressure in some dire circumstances, and he always kept his cool. His physique reflected his love of food, but not in a bad way. The extra pounds just softened him a little bit.

Wolf caught me watching and smiled. "Ready to switch to wine?" He poured two glasses, and we settled in front of the fire while our quiche baked.

The flames cast shadows that danced on Wolf's face, and his hand sneaked out to squeeze mine and stayed there. "Poor Mordecai. He lived his life in fear of nothing. He called the police constantly. Always thought someone was breaking into his house."

"I feel terrible for not doing anything for him. He was so alone. It wouldn't have hurt me to invite him for dinner sometimes."

"Don't beat yourself up about it. Mordecai's problems—whatever they were—ran deep."

"Someone said he used to wander the neighborhood at night."

Wolf snorted. "Not likely. He rarely left his home."

"He came to Hannah's wedding last spring. Have you heard the rumors about the body of his wife being in the house?" I wanted to bite my tongue as soon as I said it, since there were ugly rumors of a similar nature about Wolf's wife.

Wolf sat up and leaned toward me. "You don't believe what they say about me, do you?"

I cleared my throat. I'd heard the rumors that he murdered his wife, but I didn't believe them. Still, I did want to know the truth. Everything was going so well that I took a chance. "What really happened to your wife?"

He looked me straight in the eyes. "She left me. She took her things and left. But you know how it is. The husband is always a suspect when the wife disappears. And it doesn't help that I'm a homicide detective. You can imagine what her parents said—*he knows how to hide a body.* But I didn't hide anything."

"She never turned up?"

"Not that I'm aware of. I was surprised that she didn't get in touch with her parents so they wouldn't worry. Maybe she has by now. The first year I tracked everything that could have been a lead. The second year, I searched the Internet, sure she'd turn up somewhere."

"Nothing?"

He released my hand to rub his brow. "In spite of all our modern technology, a person can still disappear and start a new life. Tens of thousands of people vanish each year, and some of them are just living elsewhere, under a new name."

I meant to ask if his wife had a reason to want to vanish, but the timer rang on the oven. We ate by candlelight at the kitchen table, with the fire casting a glow our way. It couldn't have been more romantic. I wasn't about to bring up the missing wife again when we had a savory quiche, a crisp salad, a lovely Riesling, and the perfect atmosphere. Mordecai's request for a party had resulted in a wonderful evening for Wolf and me.

He left around midnight. I wouldn't get much sleep if I cleaned Mordecai's living room in the morning before work, but it was worth it. I could catch up on sleep after Rooms and Blooms closed.

Dog-tired but giddily happy, I went upstairs and nestled in bed with Mochie.

I woke to the sound of banging. Mochie stood on the bed, his tail raised in alarm. Disoriented, I sat up and looked at the clock. One thirty in the morning. Wishing I could ignore the noise and snuggle under my feather comforter, I flung my feet to the floor and blearily walked downstairs, the wood floor cold under my bare feet. The banging continued unabated, and I could hear Nina outside, screaming something incoherent.

I swung the door open, and Nina burst into the foyer. "I've killed Kurt!"

# FIVE

**From "The Good Life":**

Dear Sophie,

I'm not very adventurous when it comes to decorating, so I went with beige walls in my dining room. But now I can't find an area rug in the same color. Who would have thought there could be so many shades of beige?

—Beige Gal in Bayshore Gardens

Dear Beige Gal,

All colors, even beige, have undertones that can make it hard to find an exact match. Look for a complementary shade, perhaps a darker hue in the same family, or be bold and go for a contrast that will make your dining room pop!

—Sophie

Unlike Natasha, Nina wasn't a drama queen, so her words made me uneasy. "Calm down. What happened?"

She paced the floor. "I need a Scotch. No! I have to keep my wits about me. The police will ask me all sorts of questions."

Now she really had me worried. "Where is Kurt?"

Nina seized my arms. "I forgot! You have a key! We have to go *now*. Maybe it's not too late." Her voice droned off in a whine.

I grabbed a coat and shoved my feet into flip-flops. "Where are we going?"

"Mordecai's house. Everything was going so well. We had drinks and a lovely dinner, and we laughed about old times."

I found the key to Mordecai's house, locked my kitchen door, and we jogged out to the street.

"Then he said we should come back to Mordecai's to see if Emmaline came home, what with it being so cold and all. But when we got there—oh, Sophie—I guess he misinterpreted the evening, and he attacked me."

I caught a glimpse of her under the streetlight. I'd never seen her so distressed.

"Honestly, he turned into this octopus and was just horrible, and he wouldn't let me go. I just wanted to catch up with an old friend. I never meant to have an affair. So I pushed him to get away, and he fell and hit his head. I never should have left him, but I was so angry and upset."

We'd reached Mordecai's front door, but I fumbled with the key and the unfamiliar lock in the dark.

"Why did I leave?" she moaned. "I should have stayed to help him, but I ran out and fled for home. I was furious. Then I started to worry that he had been hurt, so I called his cell phone five times—he never answered. Of course, I figured he was pretty upset with me, and wasn't taking my calls, so I went back over to Mordecai's. But he wouldn't come to the door. I tried looking in the windows, but it's nearly impossible to see inside this house. I'm afraid he's sprawled on the living room floor, bleeding to death."

The front door swung open, and I relaxed. "It never occurred to you that he could have just gotten into his car and driven home?"

Nina swallowed hard. "Before I went to your house, his car was still parked where we left it."

We stepped inside, and heard the faint, hollow clank of metal.

Nina placed her hand on my arm. "What was that?"

Assorted lights were already on and nothing appeared amiss. I shrugged. "Kurt?" We headed straight for the living room, but there was no sign of him.

"There"—Nina pointed at the fireplace—"right there is where he fell. He hit his head on those fancy fireplace thingies."

Gilt bronze andirons featuring lyres graced the fireplace and looked like they could be dangerous. Kurt was nowhere to be seen.

"Kurt," I yelled, "it's Sophie." Silence surrounded us. "I think he left. Did he have a lot to drink? Maybe he took a cab home or called a friend to drive him."

"We should search the house. What if he staggered someplace and fell again? It would be terrible if he died because we didn't look around."

It was the prudent thing to do. The two of us took a quick tour of the house, most of which appeared to have been undisturbed for years, if the dust was any indication. He wasn't in any of the five bedrooms or two bathrooms, and he wasn't bleeding to death on the stairs leading up to the third floor. We made a quick round of the first floor again, but he just wasn't there.

"What about the basement?"

"Honestly, Nina, if you had hit your head and you felt woozy, would you go into a basement?"

"No. But . . ."

"You're not going to let me sleep tonight unless we search every corner, are you?"

She had already opened the basement door, and was peering down ancient stairs. I followed her, but there wasn't much to see. Smaller than my basement, it was typical for a historic home. The washer and dryer sat near a wall, and a large furnace took up most of the space.

"*Shh.*" Nina stuck out an arm to stop me.

A distinct scratching sound came from behind the wall. "*Eww,* mice." Nina shuddered and motioned for me to head back up the steps.

"Are you satisfied?" I asked.

"I guess so. But then, what happened to him and what was that noise we heard?"

I had to admit the clank was peculiar. "It's an old house that creaks?" I didn't believe that, and from the look on Nina's face, she didn't, either. "It was probably Kurt sneaking out the back door. He most likely went home. Like we're going to do right now."

"Can we check his car one more time?"

"Sure. Would you feel better if you slept at my place?"

She thought about it. "No. Maybe he'll call me back. He was a total worm, but at least I'd know I didn't kill him."

I switched off lights as we walked toward the foyer. "Will you stop saying that?" Locking the door behind us, I said, "The fact that he's not bleeding to death on the floor ought to clue you in that he's alive. Dead people don't usually walk away."

Unfortunately, Kurt's SUV was still parked where they had left it. "Maybe he walked down to King Street for a drink."

Nina nodded. "I could use one myself right about now."

We parted ways in front of my house. Agitated and wide awake, I made a toasty hot chocolate to warm up, and rubbed my feet, now little more than frozen blocks, in front of the dying embers of the fire while Mochie head-butted me for attention.

Although I thought it obvious that Nina hadn't killed Kurt, I slept uneasily, tossing and turning. Maybe it was guilt for not doing anything for Mordecai while he was alive to appreciate it. Maybe it was worry about Kurt.

I finally gave up on sleep. Since I planned to do some cleaning at Mordecai's, I passed on a shower and pulled on old jeans and a sweatshirt that had belonged to Mars. It hung almost to my knees and made me resemble a gray penguin, but it didn't matter. It was still dark outside when I trotted downstairs. I poured bracing coffee into a thermos, and fed Mochie canned shrimp and crab. I snarfed a dry piece of toast, pleased with myself for not eating any butter or jam. The streetlights were still on when I crossed the road to Mordecai's, armed with dusters and cleaning supplies and towing my vacuum cleaner.

I unlocked the door and was greeted by silence. Not even a clock ticked. Although I'd been in the house the day before, there was something creepy about being there alone. Some people thought they could feel a spirit in my kitchen, and I wondered briefly if Mordecai's spirit still lingered in his house. I paused to listen for a clank like Nina and I had heard the night before, and scolded myself out loud. "Stop it! There's no one here."

Brushing morbid thoughts aside, I left my cleaning supplies in the living room and checked the backyard for poor little Emmaline. Mordecai had carried her everywhere. It seemed as if her sweet little paws never touched the ground.

She must be in shock to be out in the cold, all alone. But there was no sign of her out back.

Just as Mordecai had predicted, china, stemware, and serving pieces waited in the butler's pantry to be used. There was something unsettling about it, as if the plates had been carefully stashed there to wait for his death. I washed them all. Who knew how long they'd been collecting dust in the cabinets?

Somehow the living room felt empty. Unlike the family room, where Mordecai had clearly lived, the living room appeared to be stuck in a time warp—as though it had been abandoned years ago. Thick dust clung to everything, but there wasn't much in the room.

I strode to the middle of the living room and checked it against Mordecai's diagram. The sofa was against the wall, across from the fireplace. Faded blue velvet wingback chairs flanked the sofa, and an antique painting of a landscape filled the wall above it. The biggest Oriental carpet I'd ever seen covered a good bit of the hardwood floor. A table and two graceful chairs with oval backs filled a spot in front of the windows that looked out to the street, and an antique secretary with ball-and-claw feet and latticework doors stood against the wall. Artfully arranged knickknacks were visible through the glass doors, and I wondered if they'd been touched at all since Mordecai's wife passed away. I was willing to do a little dusting, but my generosity had its limits when it came to the sport of cleaning, which I despised.

I left the knickknacks alone. As long as no one opened the doors to the secretary, they probably wouldn't notice anyway.

As I tried to wipe surfaces clean without kicking up the dust of the ages, I was glad the room appeared to match

Mordecai's sketch, and that I wouldn't have to search the house for something that was missing. After dusting, I ran the vacuum and decided I'd had enough cleaning.

Although an enormous Louis XV sideboard filled the wall that led to the dining room, the long coffee table would be ideal for serving Mordecai's menu to a small group. Not exactly a big job for his final request.

Day had dawned outside. I checked the backyard again for any sign of Emmaline, but she wasn't there. When I returned with the food in the afternoon, I could put out a little bit to see if she would show up.

On my way out, I paused for a moment in the family room. Bernie and Mars had shoved aside some of the clutter. I'd been so alarmed late last night when we searched the house that I hadn't even noticed a basic window seat of unstained wood resting on a tarp near the window. It was bigger than I'd expected, nearly sofa size. I had to give Bernie a lot of credit for whipping it up so fast, since I knew Mars couldn't have been much help. Bernie had been right—it would be charming with loads of cushy pillows.

Anyone else would have kept it simple, but I appreciated Bernie's nod to the ever-present need for storage by putting hinges on the top. I lifted the lid . . . and slammed it down.

My heart beat in my chest like it was trying to run away by itself. Swallowing hard, I opened the top again. Kurt lay on his back. All hint of color had drained from his face, but his hair matted in one horrible red spot, and a dried cherry stain marred his forehead.

I closed the lid, gently this time, and my thoughts flew to Nina. She would be devastated. I didn't want to implicate her in anything, but I had no choice. I had to call the police. Amid the jumble of panicked thoughts racing through my head, it dawned on me that Kurt probably wouldn't have crawled into the window seat to die. Someone had put him there. Someone who could still be in the house.

Like a shot, I fled out the front door to the sidewalk. I paused for a second to look up at the windows of Mordecai's house, afraid I would see someone peering out at me. Chills ran through me and spurred me to race home and call 911.

When I hung up, I phoned Nina. She might be hysterical and say the wrong thing to the police, but she had to know that Kurt was dead and that the cops were on their way. Despite the early hour, I got her answering machine. I nearly left a message, but then I wondered if it would look bad. Besides, wasn't this the kind of news best delivered in person?

I hung up and took a deep breath to calm myself and fetched a down jacket in case I had to wait outside. I had no intention of going into the house without a police escort. Willing myself to be calm, I locked my door, crossed the street, and was waiting in front of Mordecai's porch when a squad car pulled up.

I expected to see Wolf, but a woman stepped out of the car and regarded me icily. "You again. You call about finding a dead person?" Her name tag identified her as Tara Borsos. She tossed a long, dyed-blond ponytail over her shoulder, and sized me up with eyes ringed with so much makeup that a raccoon would have been ashamed. Despite the fact that she wore a wool uniform, she appeared to be a size zero, which made me want to suck my stomach in.

"Just inside. Follow me."

I hurried up the steps and opened the door.

She seemed to be taking in everything. "The door wasn't locked?"

"It was this morning when I arrived—at least I think it was—but when I found Kurt's body, I left in a hurry."

She followed me into Mordecai's family room and stopped cold. "Whoa. What happened in here?"

"An old man lived here, and he died a few days ago. We haven't had a chance to do much cleaning up yet."

She sniffed the air. "He died a few days ago? Didn't you say he was dead the night before last when I caught you in his backyard? How did you know he was dead then if you just found him this morning?"

I understood her confusion. "No, no, no. The owner, who died a few days ago, is at the funeral home."

"So there are two dead men?"

"Technically—yes."

"A lot of dying going on in this house. And you knew both of them?"

"I knew my neighbor, but I only met the second dead man, Kurt Finkel, yesterday." Why did I sound like such a goofball? "He's in there." I pointed at the window seat.

"This box?" She lifted the cover.

I averted my eyes. Poor Kurt. Did he have children? His family would be crushed. Except for his attack on Nina, he'd come across as a nice guy.

When I glanced back, Tara was studying me. "Do you see him now?"

What kind of moronic question was that? I peered into the box. It was empty.

# SIX

**From** "THE GOOD LIFE" :

Dear Sophie,

I love fabrics with patterns but I'm scared to death to combine them. I want to make pillows for my sofa but I don't know where to start.

—Bewildered in Bee Ridge

Dear Bewildered,

Choose fabrics with a color in common. If using a periwinkle blue, for instance, be sure it's in all the patterns. But vary the kinds of patterns. Mix a floral with a plaid and a polka dot. And vary the sizes, too. If you use a fabric with tiny bees embroidered on it, combine it with a medium plaid and a large floral.

—Sophie

"That can't be. He was in the window seat. Really he was. There must be . . ." I'd intended to say "blood," but the box didn't even show a pink smear.

Tara pulled out a pen and notepad. "You know, we don't take kindly to this kind of prank. Your name?"

"Sophie Winston."

She snapped her notebook shut. "That explains everything. You have quite the reputation. I'm going to file a report on this incident, and I'm giving you an official warning. The police department does not tolerate false reports. You're going to end up in big trouble inventing dead bodies. Am I clear?"

"But, Kurt looked so—dead." Tara continued to lecture and warn me, but I tuned her out because I knew what I had seen. Was it possible that Kurt wasn't dead after all? Had he leaped from the box when I left Mordecai's house? Had someone intended to play a prank on me? Or on Nina? Had Kurt wanted to punish Nina by giving her a good scare?

"Are you listening? I'm going to tell Wolf about this."

"Good idea. Maybe he can figure it out."

Her head tilted to the side, and a crease formed between her eyes. "You're not very bright, are you? You're in trouble."

She was the one who didn't get it. Something was definitely wrong. I didn't think I should argue with her, though. No matter what I said, she clearly wasn't going to believe me. And why should she? I'd sounded like a blithering idiot, and there wasn't even any blood. "I'm sorry. I'm not making anything up." I did *not* like the way she was scowling at me. "I guess Kurt meant to play a trick on me. Not very funny."

She eyed me critically, and for no good reason, I was suddenly self-conscious about the oversized sweatshirt and my dusty jeans. I turned away from her intrusive scrutiny. Now that a cop was there with me, the house didn't seem so scary. Could Kurt be hiding somewhere, laughing his not-at-all-funny head off? I wanted to take a look around, but I'd already lost a lot of time, and I had to get to work.

I collected my cleaning equipment, but realized we would need it when we tackled the family room and decided to leave everything at Mordecai's.

Tara walked out onto the front porch with me, and made a point of gazing up and down the street, as though looking for something. Apparently satisfied, she bounded down the steps to her car.

I heard rattling, and found Nina shaking dry cat food into a bowl next to the front steps. "Where have you been?"

She looked up at me with the haggard face of a person who hadn't slept all night. "There's this—" She stopped abruptly and watched Tara get into the squad car. Nina's icy fingers gripped my arm. "What happened? Is it Kurt?"

I filled her in while we crossed the street to my house. Her expression fluctuated between horror and anger. "I saw the window seat last night when Kurt and I went back to look for the dog. Kurt joked about it and said if they'd tapered one end, it would look like the old-fashioned pine caskets they used in the wild west."

Nina didn't cook, but I was certain she was capable of boiling water, so I left her in the kitchen to make tea while I dashed upstairs to shower and change for work. She brought a mug of steaming brew to me and sat on my bed while I dressed.

"He really looked dead?" she asked with fear in her voice.

"I'm afraid so." He had. Though I wanted to think he'd used poor judgment and played a very ugly prank, it bothered me that he'd appeared lifeless.

I didn't have time for makeup or curls. Taking the fast and easy road, I pulled my hair back with a big banana clip.

Nina looked out the window, but I didn't think she was seeing the view. "What if he heard me come back last night, thought I had a key, and hid in the box to scare me?"

"I hardly think he would have waited in the box until this morning."

She turned around, her face grim. "What if he suffocated?"

"Now you're reaching."

"He was woozy from hitting his head, passed out or fell asleep, and suffocated. Dear heaven, I bet that's exactly what happened."

I clipped on earrings and said, "There's just one problem with that scenario—if he suffocated, why wasn't he in the box when the cop came?"

"That's right!" Nina followed me downstairs. "That skunk! I bet he was trying to pull a fast one on me. And to think I lost sleep over him last night."

"What were you doing there this morning anyway?"

"An orange and white momma cat who just had kittens has been coming around, and I've been trying to figure out where she has the babies stashed. It's too cold for them to be outside. I've been trailing her through the neighborhood, and I think she might be living under Mordecai's porch. When are you going back over there?" she asked.

"I'm off to Rooms and Blooms." I filled her in on Mordecai's last request. "I'll be back around two to bake the quiche and the Brie for the bequest party."

I arrived at Rooms and Blooms shortly before it opened to exhibitors, and an hour before the public arrived. An escalator deposited me at the entrance, and I was distressed that I was able to stroll in without anyone stopping me.

The exhibitors were displaying expensive items like chandeliers, silver tea sets, paintings, and, in one case, a fancy little bulldozer designed for homeowner use. I didn't want them walking off during the night. The hotel had promised to post a security guard, but it appeared they'd forgotten.

I walked the entire exhibit to be sure everything was in order, pausing to admire a few spectacular booths. Iris Ledbetter's dining room featured an antique table so highly polished that it reflected the lights trained on it. She'd installed a chair rail on the three walls and used a tone-on-tone wallpaper above it—a rich salmon pattern that repeated on a slightly lighter background. She'd picked up the salmon in the background of a fabric with white polka dots on the upholstered dining chairs. A toile window treatment repeated the salmon color on stark white, and a cushy chair in the corner was covered with the same toile. A pillow on the chair matched the polka-dot fabric on the dining room chairs and sported a salmon fringe. Silver pigeons graced a buffet of inlaid wood and a crystal chandelier lit it all from above. The room would surely bring her new design clients.

I strolled on, picking an empty bourbon bottle out of vivid purple irises at the base of a gazebo. I found Natasha's booth, and couldn't imagine why she was upset that Iris would probably win Best of Show. Natasha had covered the walls with black cloth. The center featured a gigantic TV screen, on which she played episodes of her show during the day. Frightening, bigger-than-life head shots of Natasha flanked the TV screen on both sides and repeated on the adjoining walls. In the middle of the floor, a glass table displayed a tool kit. I stepped inside to have a closer look. A hard plastic case of robin's egg blue, embellished with "Natasha" in glittery letters, sat open, displaying household tools. Hammer, measuring tape, screwdrivers—everything in girly robin's egg blue. A larger case displayed a cordless nail gun and a cordless reciprocating saw. Natasha had made sure her name was everywhere—on the tools, the cases, and even the saw blades.

A soft staccato noise drew my attention. I followed the sound, my Keds allowing me to tread the floors without alerting anyone that I might be near. It grew stronger, and I thought it sounded like snoring. I was dead-on.

In Nolan DuPont's Asian-inspired bedroom, smack in the middle of a bed that appeared to float on air, a grown man slept, stretched out comfortably. I suspected I'd found my security guard. I hustled to a kitchen exhibit, borrowed a timer, returned to Sleeping Beauty, and set it off. The jangling alarm reverberated through the silent hall with such force that Sleeping Beauty flipped right off the bed and onto the hard floor.

I peered down at him. "Rise and shine."

He rubbed his head and sat up. "You're not supposed to be here."

He had to be kidding.

He scrambled to his feet. "I'll have to escort you out."

I held up the timer. "If I were sneaking around, do you think I'd have bothered to wake you up?"

He wiped his nose on the back of his sleeve. "*Awww.* This isn't good."

"You'd best go tell your boss. It'll be better if he hears it from you."

"Yeah, yeah." He ambled off and I hoped he wouldn't see another bed because he might decide to take a nap on his way out.

My small staff drifted in and gave me reports about the previous day. All in all, it was going pretty well.

But midmorning, angry voices floated to me. I hustled in

the direction of the sound, and found a short woman with curly black hair making a fuss at Finkel Kitchen and Bath. She wore a low-cut sweater that seemed designed to show off cleavage, and revealed so much that her bust reminded me of old movie stars who wore bras that propped their breasts up like shelves. I wondered if they would hold a cup of coffee, but then her menacing tone jolted me back to reality. "Where is he?"

A freckled redhead, wearing a Finkel Kitchen and Bath T-shirt, stammered, "He left yesterday afternoon, and I haven't seen him since."

"I'll bet you haven't. He's old enough to be your father. Doesn't that just gross you out?"

The redhead, who couldn't have been more than nineteen, seemed puzzled. "No. I always assumed my boss would be older than me."

The irate woman was at a loss for one moment, but then her expression changed to one that was pure evil, and she said in a low, level tone, "Don't you pretend to be stupid. Do you think you're the first pretty girl he ever hired for other purposes?" And then she hissed, "Where is my husband?"

# SEVEN

From *"Ask Natasha"*:

*Dear Natasha,*

*My husband watched your show about building ponds and now he thinks that would be a great summer project. I really don't want a muddy ditch in my backyard, nor do I relish the idea of a mosquito factory. A proper pond looks complicated. Wouldn't you suggest hiring a professional?*

*—Landlubber in Landover Hills*

*Dear Landlubber,*

*A backyard pond is an easy homeowner project. Let hubby at it! Be sure he locates the pond near an electrical outlet so you can install lights and enjoy your new water feature at night.*

*—Natasha*

In some ways, it wasn't really my problem, except that I wanted to calm or remove this woman before she made a bigger stink. On the other hand, there was my overwhelming fear that the husband in question was Kurt. I smiled at her, offered to help, and coaxed her away from the booth.

"What can I do for you?" I asked as sweetly as I could.

She ran nervous fingers through her hair. "My husband never came home last night." The muscles in her neck pulled taut. "I'm sorry, I shouldn't bother a stranger about it. It's not the first time this has happened. I thought I might find him here with his latest bimbette."

I thought I knew the answer, but I had to ask. "Who is your husband?" I held my breath.

"Kurt Finkel, head rat fink of Finkel Kitchen and Bath." She heaved a huge sigh and clutched her throat with one hand. "This is the last time. I've said that before, but this really is the last time he's going to do this to me." Her voice trembled. "I just can't take any more nights of uncertainty. He doesn't care about me. If he did, he wouldn't put me through this. I've had enough."

"I'm very sorry. If it's any consolation, I saw him yesterday evening." What else could I say? I certainly didn't think it was my place to tell her he'd had a drink with his old flame last night, or that I thought I saw his corpse. After all, I didn't know what had happened to him. But my conscience hammered at me. Maybe I *should* spill the beans. But what if the guy really was just playing a prank on us all? "Was he prone to . . ."

In a low growl, she uttered, "What did he do?"

The pressure to tell his wife the whole truth weighed on me like an elephant. "He was"—I cleared my throat—"*is* going to remodel a kitchen for Natasha's TV show. She's renovating a house for the statewide Home and Garden Tour."

"Natasha?" she squealed. "*The* Natasha?"

I nodded.

"Natasha called him once before. That mutton head better not mess it up this time."

Too late for that. I swallowed hard before I continued. "I was at the house in question this morning to clean up, and . . . well, I thought I saw him inside a window seat." Something told me not to mention that I thought he was dead, so I added lamely, "With a head injury."

She recoiled. "What!?"

"Wait, it gets even stranger. I called the police, and when the cop arrived, he wasn't there anymore."

Her mouth dropped open. "Who *are* you? And why would you say such a thing? That's just sick. Sick!" Tilting her head, she glared at me as she backed away and left.

I could understand her reaction. What *had* happened to Kurt last night? I asked the young redhead to let me know when Kurt showed up. Then, since my cell phone didn't work in the convention hall, I took the escalator up to the hotel entrance and called Nina to tell her what had happened.

Afraid of what she might say, I asked, "Any news from Kurt?"

"No."

"Did you know that he's married?"

"Of course. His wife's name is Earl, and she's out of town, visiting her mother."

"Did you say Earl or Pearl?"

"Earl, like Earline." Nina drawled the name in her North Carolina accent.

"Nina, he didn't go home last night, and Earl turned up at the home show looking for him."

"*Eww.* He must have shacked up with someone else. Poor Earl."

"I gather he's had some affairs."

"*Ugh*. He used to be such a great guy. What happened to him? After the way he acted toward me last night, I guess he flops into bed with anything that has a pulse these days."

I hoped she was right, and that he'd found someone else when Nina spurned him. "You're not worried anymore about that fall he took?"

"You're the one who said dead people don't get up and walk away."

I *was* the one who said that, so why was I upset that he hadn't shown up anywhere? It was still early, though. If he'd taken a hotel room to shack up with some floozy, he wouldn't have to check out until eleven, and he could ask for an extension. "Do me a favor and look for his car. I'm curious about whether he ever moved it."

I hung up and tried to put Kurt Finkel out of my mind. He might be the best kitchen designer in the area, but I was beginning to think he was also the biggest Lothario.

And maybe he wasn't the only one who was cheating on his spouse. As I began to descend on the escalator, I caught a glimpse of Camille DuPont stepping out of the elevator that went up to the hotel rooms. She strode with her usual self-assurance, head held high, but she also gave a furtive little glance around, and adjusted the collar of her jacket.

No sooner had I returned to the convention hall than I was snagged by an apologetic Ted Wilcox about a leak in the exhibit that he had installed. Strawberry blond with a sprinkling of freckles, Ted was the owner of Leisure Landscapes. He lacked the paunch that often came with middle age, probably because he spent a good chunk of time outdoors, building and planting.

His exhibit, called Ted's Backyard Escape, was adorable.

Essentially a one-room A-frame building, the peaked roof was built of rustic caramel-colored beams that supported large panels of glass. The bottom featured French doors on all sides that could be opened to let in summer breezes and night air. The few parts that weren't glass were covered with quaint fish-scale shingles of a vivid blue hue. Ted had surrounded the building with purple and pink azaleas, except for the entrance, which was accessed by a walkway over a shallow pond.

Gauzy white curtains danced at the French doors as if set up for a photo shoot. He'd outfitted the interior with shabby chic whitewashed furniture, a fluffy bed that begged to be napped upon, airy blue linens, a cozy wood-burning stove, and sparkling lights that glittered along the roof windows and in the filmy curtains.

It would be an adorable getaway on a large estate, I supposed, but I didn't know many people inclined to build an extra bedroom detached from the house. It could serve as a gorgeous playhouse or studio, though.

I understood why Ted intercepted me when I saw a woman with hair the color of black cherries striding toward us, pointing and jabbing a finger at Ted. Her hair feathered around her face, super short, but she had the bone structure for it. The daring color emphasized her pale skin. But her dark eyes blazed, and I suspected she wasn't someone I would want to tangle with.

"Ted, I swear if that water comes one inch closer to my wall, so help me, I'll tear down your fancy little house—fish scale by fish scale."

Ted introduced her as Posey Powell.

She gave me a distracted nod, then turned to me with new interest, as if she'd just realized who I was. In a sweet drawl that sounded more like Mississippi than Virginia, she said, "Isn't that just like you, Ted. Already kissing up to the woman who organized the show." Flashing a gorgeous toothy smile at me, she added, "Don't let him fool you. If that pond of his leaks any more water, you'll have a major mess on your hands, and I won't be the only angry exhibitor."

"Posey, darlin', Sophie was just coming to help me." Ted looked at me hopefully. I walked toward his exhibit with them while he insisted that the water hadn't done any damage yet. But Ted wasn't helping things by rolling his eyes every time Posey opened her mouth. "Don't mind Posey," he whispered. "We've known each other since college. She likes to play the excited drama queen."

Posey whipped around. "I heard that, Ted. If I were swinging a wrecking ball near your little glass house, you'd be plenty agitated."

When we arrived at Ted's exhibit, I understood Posey's concern. Ted had built a clever water feature. Since he couldn't dig into the convention hall floor, he'd constructed a large frame and lined it with a sheet of thick plastic. He'd cleverly hidden the frame with rocks and plants, tucked lights around the edges underwater, and added golden koi to his pond. But on the side closest to Posey's exhibit, water seeped out. Hardly a flood, but it rolled steadily in the direction of her booth.

Ted asked me to hold the edge of the black plastic liner while he searched for the source of the leak.

While Ted patched the plastic, I held the liner and arched back for a peek at Posey's booth. An accomplished artist, Posey had used trompe l'oeil techniques to transform her area into a wine cellar. I'd noticed her remarkable room during my morning walks through the exhibits. A dark side wall appeared to open to a writing nook with an antique desk lighted by candles. The sun shone through faux open doors on the back wall, which featured a view of a charming vineyard so authentic that I felt I could walk into the image. She'd even painted a cloth that covered the floor. It looked exactly like a stone floor with an Oriental carpet carelessly tossed on top of it with one corner flipped over.

I couldn't see to whom she was speaking, but Posey's irritated voice came through loud and clear. "I don't care if he hears me. In fact, I hope he does. He can't just steamroll through life oblivious to other people. He didn't spend days painting this floor cloth, so he doesn't care if it's ruined. Do you know how many people can build a glass house like that? Besides, who wants a detached bedroom without a bathroom? It's nothing but a ridiculous indulgence."

"Sophie." Someone poked me in the shoulder. The voice came from behind me, soft, almost a whisper. "Sophie, she's here." I turned to find Humphrey, pale as the corpses he handled. Under the harsh lights, his fair hair seemed almost translucent. I tried to appear glad to see him but hoped he wouldn't press me about his mystery woman right now.

His eyebrows met in an endearing wistful expression. "She's perfect. Beautiful and smart. And she's here! You can invite her to dinner."

Oy. Like I didn't have enough on my plate at the moment. "In a couple of weeks?" I said. "After Rooms and Blooms is over."

"It ends tomorrow."

Apparently, he couldn't take a hint. "But I'll still be busy. Two weeks from now would be great." I couldn't evade him the way I usually did—by running off—because I was still holding the liner. I contemplated dropping it, but the fight that would surely ensue between Posey and Ted forced me to stick it out.

"But she's here now."

I nodded toward the liner I held. "I'm a little tied up.

Find her and say something to her about an exhibit. Just strike up a conversation. It doesn't have to be brilliant. Then, when you're comfortable, ask her if she'd like to get a cup of coffee. Take the coffees over to the center, where all the flowers are, and sit on a bench and talk. It's that simple."

He frowned. "I'm afraid she'll turn me down."

I was afraid of that, too. "Humphrey, that's how people meet. How will you ever get to know her better if you don't spend time with her?"

He brightened up. "I have tickets to the Design Guild dinner tomorrow night."

I wondered why a mortician would be interested in the Design Guild dinner, but I didn't really care. "Perfect. That would be a lovely first date. And on Valentine's Day, too. What could be more romantic?"

He flitted off in search of a red rose to give her when he asked her out. Poor woman. Then again, maybe she was as shy as Humphrey, and he'd finally met the right person. I hoped so.

Ted shouted for me to release my hold on the plastic. I let it go and exercised my stiff fingers.

When he came to thank me, I said, "Not the best-quality liner?"

"There's nothing wrong with the liner." Ted held up five sharp nails.

"Finishing nails?"

"Exactly." He held one between his fingers and pretended to aim it like a dart. "Just about perfect for making holes in liners when shot with a nail gun."

"I thought nail guns had safety catches. Don't you have to press them against something to make them fire?"

Ted laughed. "Every guy who has ever used one knows how to hold back that latch and fire in the air."

He didn't appear to be too upset, but I was worried. "Are you saying someone intentionally caused that leak?"

"Don't be so shocked. Designers and decorators aren't beneath a little sabotage. In fact, it wouldn't surprise me if Posey herself flicked these nails into my pond."

# EIGHT

From *"Ask Natasha"*:

*Dear Natasha,*

*We're building a new house and my mother-in-law insists that all proper homes have a butler's pantry. I'm not sure I've ever seen one, but I am sure I will never have a butler. Is she just making fun of me?*

*—No Butlers in Butler Beach*

*Dear No Butlers,*

*Listen to your mother-in-law! Butler's pantries aren't just for butlers anymore. They provide additional storage for fine crystal and china, and for those bulky serving pieces that clutter up kitchen cabinets. Today these little hallways between the kitchen and the dining room even double as bars. They're the perfect place for wine storage, an additional sink, a dishwasher, or a refrigerator. Or build in drawers for storing table linens.*

*–Natasha*

I skipped lunch since I would be taking time off for Mordecai's bequest party. By one o'clock, I'd had enough of scheming designers and gladly walked home. As I strode along King Street, I caught a glimpse of Wolf seated at the front window of Café Ole with Tara, the officer who'd responded to my call about Kurt. They sat side by side, and she leaned toward him with familiarity, her head tilted and her hair swinging loose. Momentarily surprised at seeing them together, I felt a pang of jealousy that quickly swerved to uneasiness. Even though I knew I'd done nothing wrong, the mere fact that she must be telling him about our bizarre encounter early that morning made me uncomfortable. Hoping they hadn't noticed me, I backtracked and cut up a side street.

When I swung open the gate that led to my service alley, someone squealed. I peered behind it and found Nina crouching on the ground. She tugged me inside and held a finger to her lips.

"What's going on?" I whispered.

"Do you see anyone?"

I peeked over the gate. "Who am I looking for?"

"There's no one hanging around, watching?" She rose up just enough to see the street.

"Does this have something to do with Kurt?" I feared the stress of Kurt's disappearance was playing on Nina's nerves. "C'mon"—I motioned to her—"there's no one there."

She followed me into my kitchen. "I'm not so sure. Have you told anyone about Kurt?"

"I haven't mentioned your name."

Mochie head-butted Nina, and she ran a hand over his shiny fur. "I was putting up lost dog notices about Emmaline, and I got the feeling someone was watching me." She carried Mochie to the bay window and looked out while I packed the food for Mordecai's soiree.

"Kurt has you spooked." I eased the crudités and dip into a box with the bread and blondies. "Did you actually see anyone?"

"It's just a feeling. I kept seeing a thin blond looking into store windows, but she might have been shopping."

I smacked her hand when she reached for a blondie. "Could it have been Tara? The cop who came to Mordecai's?"

She frowned at me. "I don't know. She wasn't wearing a uniform. Why would she follow me anyway? If you didn't mention my name, she wouldn't have any reason to tail me."

I loaded a second box with food while Nina fidgeted and looked out the window. "I think it's Kurt," she finally said.

"Nina! Why would he do that? You've been watching too many horror movies."

"It's all coming back to me—why we broke up. He can be a mean, vindictive person. I think he's trying to punish me for dumping him all those years ago. Is it okay if I go over to Mordecai's with you? I want to search that house from top to bottom."

I held out the box with the quiche and the daiquiri ingredients. "As long as you give me a hand." I didn't think Nina would find Kurt hiding in a closet at Mordecai's, but she needed something to keep her busy, and she would probably feel better if she weren't alone.

An hour before the guests were to arrive, the quiche was baking in Mordecai's oven, and Nina was on the third floor, looking through closets.

When I heard footsteps, I thought Nina had given up on her search, but it was Natasha who discovered me in the butler's pantry, whipping up strawberry daiquiris in the blender. She shrugged off her coat. "What do you think you're doing? Are you baking?"

I explained about Mordecai's last request.

Her mouth flapped open angrily, but then a laughing fit overcame her. "That's what he left you? A job?" She cackled with glee. "I couldn't for the life of me understand why he left you something and not me. *I'm* the one who invited him to my home. *I'm* the one who tried to befriend him. I even threw my mother at him, for pity's sake."

Fists on her hips, Natasha continued, "If she'd only listened to me, this house would belong to her today. Not to some yappy little fur ball."

She inspected the assortment of foods that were ready to be served. "Not the most creative menu, Sophie. You should have asked me for suggestions. I mean, really, no one has served quiche in years."

"Fine. Think of it as a cheese tart."

"Well, that's different. But blondies?"

"Mordecai requested this menu."

"*Hmmph.* You'd think he would have asked my advice or asked me to throw his little party. Everyone knows I'm better at these things than you are." She inhaled sharply. "Unless I'm a guest, of course. That would explain everything."

I ignored her slight but pointed out a little too gleefully that all the invitees had already been notified.

When the doorbell rang, Nina yelled, "I'll get it!" and clomped down the stairs. She appeared in the kitchen a moment later, carrying long florist's boxes.

Natasha eyed her with suspicion. "What were you doing upstairs?"

"Just having a look around." Nina flipped the boxes open. "These are gorgeous." She inhaled the fragrance. "Nothing else comes close to the scent of lilacs. No wonder Mordecai wanted them. Who knew he was such a romantic?"

Natasha ignored the flowers and was checking the names on the bequest packages. "I know almost all these people. Why would he leave them something, and not me? Kurt Finkel? Well, well. I wonder what a person had to do to be in Mordecai's good graces. I bet they never invited him to brunch." Her tone, already bitter, changed to furious when she added, "I can't wait until Kurt gets here. I have a few choice words for him for failing to show this morning."

I was walking into the living room, carrying a vase of heavenly lilacs, and stopped short when she said that. "He was supposed to meet you? Did you call his cell phone?"

She followed me to the living room, holding a large bottle of bourbon. "Of course. All I ever get is his voice mail. But he's a contractor, after all, and they're notoriously unreliable. He missed two weeks when he renovated Iris's kitchen. It's so aggravating. You'd think they would understand that everyone is waiting for them, but noooo."

I breathed a little easier on hearing that he had missed engagements before. Maybe this was normal, or almost normal, behavior for Kurt.

Natasha held up the bourbon bottle. "This was full yesterday."

I placed the lilacs on the mantel, wondering why she was telling me about the bourbon. "So?"

"Did you drink it?"

I laughed. "If I had consumed that much bourbon, I would still be flat on my back."

"Not many people had keys to Mordecai's house last

night, but someone emptied it." Natasha eyed me with suspicion, but I ignored her and returned to the kitchen.

I slid the quiche and the baked Brie out of the oven, and everything was ready. The packages of bequests waited in the butler's pantry, the food was on the table, except for the quiche and the Brie, which were cooling, and Mordecai's living room smelled of lilacs.

Nolan DuPont, Camille's husband, was first to arrive. The owner of an outrageously expensive antiques store in Old Town, Nolan generally sported an obnoxiously superior attitude. Tall and fastidious about his appearance, he carried himself with the same self-assured poise as Natasha. He'd always been friendly to me, but I'd seen him intimidate people just through his bearing.

I showed Nolan into the living room.

"Camille informs me that I'm to furnish this room." He surveyed it with distaste. "Basically a box, isn't it? Good molding at the ceiling, but otherwise, it's architectural milk toast."

"The fireplace is attractive."

"*Mmm.* At least the room has a focal point." His gaze drifted down to the golden andirons, and I suspected he was sizing them up for sale.

The door knocker sounded as I set the quiche on the table. I hustled to the front door and found a bearded man waiting on the porch. Ted Wilcox was walking up the stairs behind him.

The bearded one smiled easily and said, "Hi, Mike Osmanski. I was told to be here?"

"Mike?" Ted craned his neck and took a hard look at him. "Ted. Ted Wilcox. I never would have recognized you behind that thicket on your chin."

The two of them shook hands and hugged. I showed

them in and, from the greetings when they saw Nolan, I gathered they all knew each other.

Leaving them to catch up, I poured strawberry daiquiris and served them while we waited for the others to arrive.

Nolan wrinkled his nose at the drink with the umbrella in it. "Perhaps I could have a scotch on the rocks?"

"I'm sorry, Nolan," I said. "There isn't anything else. Mordecai specified no substitutions."

"*Aw*, Nolan, don't be such a stuffed shirt. Have a pink drink." Ted sipped his daiquiri. "It's not bad. Like a fruit slush with rum."

Mike sniffed the air. "What's that smell?"

"Parisian hooker's perfume." Nolan said it with a straight face, but the other two laughed heartily.

"Lilacs." I pointed to the vases. "Per Mordecai's instructions."

I wouldn't have thought it possible for Nolan to be more rigid, but I thought he stiffened.

"Please, help yourselves. We're waiting for two more."

When the knocker sounded, I was certain Kurt had finally turned up. I ripped the door open, ready to lash out at him for having worried us, but Posey waited on the porch.

"I believe I'm expected?"

Before I could ask her in, she stepped inside, saw Ted in the living room doorway, and let out a shriek that could wake the dead.

I skedaddled out of their way, hoped they would manage to behave, and checked the time. Where was Kurt? With each passing minute I became more convinced that he'd been dead when I saw him in the window seat. For no good reason, I returned to the family room and opened the window seat again. He hadn't magically reappeared. I sucked in a deep breath. Maybe he *was* alive. I went back to the kitchen and asked Natasha for his cell phone number.

She gave it to me, and peered into the living room. "Nolan. *Hmmph.* Who's the guy in the black turtleneck?"

"Mike Osmanski."

"Don't know him. I suppose I should introduce myself."

I held the phone to my ear and shot out my other arm to stop her. "Later, please. This is about them."

Her mouth twisted, but she stepped back. "When do they find out what Mordecai left them?"

"As soon as Kurt gets here." I tried to keep my tone casual, but at that moment an annoying recorded voice on the telephone said, *This mailbox is full.* I groaned and clicked the phone closed. "Full mailbox."

"That's contractors for you. You never know when they'll show up. It's like they're oblivious to the schedules of the rest of the world."

I checked the time again. Mordecai hadn't said anything about all the recipients being present simultaneously, so I would just have to give Kurt his bequest when he finally arrived. If he ever did.

I carried the packages into the living room. Mike and Posey had settled on the sofa, and Ted took a chair, but Nolan stood by the fireplace as though he was anxious to leave.

"We're missing Kurt. . . ."

"Kurt?" Mike's bushy eyebrows shot up. "There's a guy I never wanted to see again. Just like him to be late."

"I suppose we should go ahead with the bequests." Each package bore a tag with a name. I handed them out and retreated to the butler's pantry.

One minute later someone called my name. I rushed back into the living room. Each one of them held a bottle of wine.

Posey bent forward, the wrapping from her package spread on the floor. She looked up at me and asked, "Is this some kind of joke?"

Nolan snorted. "That old curmudgeon. It's a wild-goose chase, don't you see that? From the looks of this place, he didn't have anything of value left anyway."

Mike rubbed his face. "I drove down here from Pennsylvania for this?"

"I'm sorry," I said, "the boxes were already wrapped and labeled. I'm afraid I don't know what they contained."

Simultaneously, all four of them held out a key and a piece of a jigsaw puzzle. I looked closer. The jigsaw pieces could have been from the same puzzle, but all of the keys fit different types of locks. I was as surprised as they were. "Surely they must hold some significance for you."

"They do, indeed." Nolan shoved his key into his pocket. "They tell me that Mordecai suffered from some sort of dementia and was a sick old man."

I doubted that. Mordecai hadn't just stuck any old thing in their packages.

Mike rested against the sofa back. " 'Fraid not, Nolan. This was far too well organized. It's not the work of a sick brain, it's the work of the clever old professor. He always loved games. Were there any instructions, Sophie?"

"They were only about the food and flowers. There was nothing about the contents of the packages, if that's what you mean."

Ted snorted. "Are you saying that no one knows what these lead to? Some untold fortune could go unnoticed for decades if we don't find it?"

Mike chuckled. "You think the keys all lead to the same thing? Not a different thing for each of us?"

"What about the sherry?" said Posey. "Maybe it's valuable."

"Amontillado? Hardly. Not even twenty dollars a bottle." Nolan seized the strawberry daiquiri he'd ignored and drank it in one long swig. "I have been volunteered to redecorate this ode to bad taste. I can assure you, though, that I don't intend to waste another minute on this nonsense. Interesting seeing you all again." He nodded curtly and departed.

The second the door shut, Mike said, "Still the same arrogant cur. Well, I don't mind admitting that I got divorced last year—nearly wiped me out. My car's on its last legs, and I've got a kid in college. If Mordecai left me anything of value, I'd sure like to find it."

"Divorced? What ever happened to that old girlfriend of yours? What was her name? Hot Lips?" Posey grinned at him.

"We lost touch. I've tried finding her through the Internet, but no luck so far. To be honest, I was hoping she might be here since she was Mrs. Artemus's niece."

"We could help you find her." Ted stood, tossed his key, and caught it. "Hey, I've got a guest room. I'm sure my wife wouldn't mind if you stayed with us awhile. We can work together. Whatever we find, we split."

"Sounds good to me." Mike wolfed a piece of quiche.

"Count me in." Posey studied her piece of puzzle. "Although I probably ought to search on my own. I always beat you guys in Mordecai's class."

Mike shot her a doubtful look. "You wish! It was Kurt who always figured out stuff first."

Chuckling about getting a head start on Kurt and Nolan, the three discussed a methodical search strategy. I was about to slip away to clean up when the doorbell rang. It had to be Kurt.

# NINE

**From "The Good Life":**

Dear Sophie,

What on earth is a kitchen triangle? My neighbor says mine is all wrong, but I don't have the foggiest idea what she's talking about.

—Lost in Bermuda

Dear Lost,

The three points of the kitchen triangle are your stove, refrigerator, and sink. When we use our kitchens, we constantly move between these three objects. The farther they are from each other, the more steps we have to take. Even if you want a big kitchen, be sure the fridge, sink, and stove are relatively close together, because that's your work triangle.

—Sophie

I rushed to the door. Much to my dismay, Kurt's wife, Earl, waited on the porch.

"You?!" She smacked her open palm to her forehead. "I should have known he was having an affair with you because of the peculiar things you said." She lowered her hand and scrutinized me. "Though you're really not his type. *She's* his type."

I followed the direction of the finger she pointed—to Nina, whose shapely figure made a simple button-down blouse and jeans look sexy. For once, bold Nina looked afraid.

Earl stepped inside, crossed her arms over her chest, and said to me, "Well, what do you have to say for yourself?"

"What's going on?" Natasha wedged herself in front of Nina.

The effect was magical. Earl almost swooned. "You're Natasha. *The* Natasha. I love your show!"

Natasha beamed. "Thank you. Which was your favorite episode?"

"Last year, when you showed how to beam a picture onto the ceiling and paint it, I talked Kurt into making us one. We almost divorced over it"—she giggled—"but it turned out fabulous, and now we have a huge mural on our ceiling that makes it look like it opens to a Roman sky with fabulous columns and statues. Like Caesar's Palace in Las Vegas." She gazed around and held out her empty hands. "I can't believe I don't have anything for you to sign."

"You're Kurt's wife? You're so lucky. I bet you have a fantastic kitchen."

I shifted away to fetch paper from Mordecai's desk for Natasha to autograph, but that must have reminded Earl that I was there. "Do you know this woman?"

Natasha looked around. "Sophie? Of course. We've been friends for years."

"Well, your *friend* is playing around with my husband."

Natasha broke into laughter. "*Sophie*? Are you kidding?"

I smiled, thankful that Natasha would defend my character.

"I admit she's desperate to find a man, but look at her. No makeup, hair pulled up with a plastic clip because she won't take the time to fix it, and today, for some reason, she looks sallow, don't you think? Honestly, she can't even keep her own boyfriend. She's hardly a threat to the rest of us."

I didn't know whether to be glad or to lash out at Natasha. Only a few months ago, she was afraid I had designs on Mars.

Earl seemed puzzled. "It's just that my husband isn't answering his cell phone, and he didn't show for work this morning. I found this address jotted down on his office calendar."

Natasha waved a hand through the air. "Not to worry, honey. He's redoing the kitchen for me."

More likely he'd jotted down the address where he would receive a bequest from Mordecai. But after my outburst earlier, when I'd spilled the beans about seeing Kurt in the window seat, I thought it best to keep quiet about the bequest. Earl struck me as the sort of person who would demand Kurt's bequest, and I didn't know if I was allowed to give it to her.

I took advantage of Earl's starstruck rapture with Natasha and slipped away to begin cleaning up. Ted, Mike, and Posey had migrated to the family room, and I could hear Posey saying, "How are we supposed to find anything in this mess?"

When Earl left, Natasha joined Nina and me in the kitchen. While I washed dishes and Natasha dried them, Nina huddled in a corner, snarfing the leftover Brie and quiche like she hadn't eaten in days.

"I'm inclined to agree with Nolan—Mordecai wasn't operating on all cylinders anymore," said Natasha. "I mean, really, leaving this mansion to his dog?"

"That little dog meant a lot to him, Natasha. He wanted to be sure that Emmaline would be taken care of after his demise."

"Like a dog could tell the difference between a house and the concrete floor of a dog run."

"Of course they can!" When Mars and I split, we agreed to share custody of our dog, Daisy. At the moment, Daisy was staying with Mars and Natasha. "Where is Daisy?" I asked, worried.

"Mars took her for a ridiculously long walk this morning. She's probably asleep in his den."

I sighed with relief. It wasn't easy knowing my sweet Daisy had a wicked stepmother who didn't like her.

I returned the last plate to its proper place in the butler's pantry. "Are you going to be here for a while?" I asked Natasha. "I suppose someone ought to hang around while Mordecai's heirs snoop."

Natasha checked her watch. "I have to stay anyway. Two designers are coming to check out bedrooms."

*Uh-oh.* "What if a designer finds the thing Mordecai's heirs are supposed to receive?"

Natasha made a dubious face. "Look around. It can't be anything valuable or important. He clearly didn't spend a cent in the last twenty years."

I wasn't so sure. I pulled out my cell phone and called Adam Swensen, Mordecai's lawyer. He laughed when he heard what the heirs had received. "I should have known Mordecai was up to tricks." Fortunately, his lawyer also understood the urgency of fixing up the place, and suggested he draft an agreement with the decorators. I passed the phone to Natasha so they could work out the details.

Nina perched on a chair at the kitchen counter, pulling bits of bread off the hollowed-out loaf that had held dip. She nibbled at them mindlessly.

"Are you okay?" I asked.

"Where could he be?" she whispered. "I don't know what else I can do. I felt terrible when Earl came barging in saying you were having an affair with Kurt. Soph, you believe me when I say I didn't sleep with him, don't you? It was completely aboveboard. In fact, if I hadn't rejected him and pushed him away, none of this would have happened."

What she needed was a nap, but I suspected that she was too agitated to sleep. I couldn't leave her like this. "Come with me to Rooms and Blooms. I could use some help." It was a fib, but maybe it would take her mind off of Kurt.

Natasha grabbed me as we put on our coats. "Would you stop by my booth and check on Beth Ford? She's new to the area and doesn't know anyone. I just hired her, and I hate to leave her alone all day but I had no choice." I readily agreed and Nina and I left, with Nina munching on blondies during the short walk to the hotel.

At the convention hall, our first stop was Finkel's Kitchen and Bath. The redhead was slouching in a chair and looking sullen, even though potential customers were opening cabinets and exclaiming over the clever storage inserts. They ran their hands over the rich woods and glossy granites on display, but she ignored the customers entirely.

"No word from Kurt?" I asked.

"I didn't even get a lunch break." She folded her arms over her chest and pouted.

Poor kid. "You have exactly fifteen minutes. Go get some food."

"Are you serious?"

"Go!"

Nina grinned at me. "That was a smooth move. I'll be in the back, nosing around."

I didn't think she would find anything helpful in the booth, but it wouldn't hurt to look. I moseyed toward the back, where Nina opened display cabinets and drawers. The countertops held brochures and samples of tile, but there was nothing that would help us understand where Kurt had gone.

Nina turned toward me and said with resignation, "Nothing personal."

As I thought about Kurt, I wondered the same thing I had wanted to know about Wolf's wife. Did he have a reason to disappear? His business seemed to be booming, but his personal life was clearly a mess. If I could believe his wife—and why not?—Kurt had brought on problems in his marriage. But a lot of people had affairs and worked through them to save their marriages.

A frustrated Nina now slouched in the chair where the redhead had sat. I asked if Nina would mind waiting for her to return.

She brightened up. "Maybe she knows something."

I doubted it, but it would help Nina feel like she was doing something. I took off in search of my staff but made a quick stop at Natasha's booth to check on her new employee, Beth Ford.

With remarkable patience, the blond woman in Natasha's booth explained to an earnest couple that a well-planned kitchen triangle between the stove, sink, and refrigerator would make cooking easier. "You don't want to walk half a mile just to get the milk and eggs from the fridge," she said. "And think how easy it would be if the sink were behind you and the stove were in front of you. To fill a pot with water, you'd only have to turn around. And dirty pans could go straight into the sink, without having to carry them across the kitchen."

I guessed Beth to be in her mid-forties. A plain beige sweater clung to her ample hips. Not the best choice of clothes for her figure. Not that I was in any position to criticize anyone's figure, since I needed to shed weight myself. Besides, her round face and easy smile would make anyone comfortable. She needed to rethink the big, blond perm, though. I'd been down that road myself—not my best look. I couldn't believe that no one had told me I was too short and chubby to pull it off.

I was impressed with Beth's responses about the couple's kitchen problems. It appeared Natasha had made a good selection. As soon as the couple left, I introduced myself.

"You're Sophie Winston? Don't tell Natasha, but I *love* your column. I like hers, too, of course, but I never miss yours. My twins graduated from high school last year, and my dolt of an ex-husband refused to contribute to a graduation party. Your hint to throw an afternoon party at a local lake with hot dogs and burgers saved the day. With college costs looming, I just couldn't see spending a lot on a party, and the kids had more fun swimming and boating than they would have had at a stuffy party in some restaurant."

I thanked her, glad that I had helped someone through a problem. "Looks like you have everything under control."

She handed a brochure of Natasha's new line of tools to a man who perused them. "I thought I'd be doing things behind the scenes at her TV show, but I don't mind filling in here at the convention. It's an easy way to start the job. I like talking to people."

I wanted to get to know Natasha's new assistant a little

bit better, but at that moment Humphrey found me and pulled me away.

"I asked her out."

"That's great, Humphrey." I reminded myself to be patient with him. He didn't know about the problem with Kurt, and this was important to him. I walked in the direction of Ted's glass cottage to be sure the pond wasn't leaking again.

"But we have a problem."

We? I didn't think so. I had enough problems without taking on Humphrey's.

"She already has a date to the Design Guild banquet—Wolf."

# TEN

From "*Ask Natasha*":

*Dear Natasha,*

*My husband thinks our gorgeous tone-on-tone pastel blue living room is boring. He wants to ruin it by mounting an antelope head over the fireplace. Ugh!*

*–Fighting in Fishers Island*

*Dear Fighting,*

*Satisfy hubby's need for the exotic by covering one chair in an animal print and adding a zebra throw rug. Animal prints are classic decorating devices that will give your room pizzazz.*

*–Natasha*

"Wolf? My Wolf?"

"The very same. How do we stop them?"

His news shook me. It wasn't like Wolf and I had a committed relationship, but our date had gone so well that I thought we might be headed in that direction eventually. Apparently not. On the other hand, Wolf might have made his date with Humphrey's heartthrob months ago. I should have asked Wolf to the banquet myself, but I'd learned long ago that dates and work didn't mix. If I spent time with my date, I wasn't paying attention to the event the way I should be. And if I hopped up from the table and worked, I was ignoring my date. And then my heart and hopes plummeted. He'd asked this other woman to the banquet on Valentine's Day. It didn't get more obvious than that. I had planned to bake him a Black Forest cherry cake for Valentine's Day, but now I wasn't sure if I should.

"We're not going to do anything, Humphrey. We're all adults."

"But you belong with Wolf, and I know Tara's the one for me."

"Tara? The policewoman?" That was why she looked so intimate with Wolf when I saw them having coffee.

He smiled dreamily. Oh no! It was worse than I thought. He was really smitten. I couldn't imagine svelte Tara with the raccoon eyes being interested in Humphrey. She had to be at least ten years younger than us. Why couldn't he find someone less flashy? Someone like Natasha's new assistant.

"But we can't just stand idly by and allow their misconceived relationship to flourish."

"Interfering isn't going to make them come running back to us. It could have the opposite effect and bring them closer together."

I could tell he didn't like my advice, but I wasn't going

to do anything sneaky. Besides, I was having a difficult moment myself, trying to cope with the news that Wolf was dating Tara. Why couldn't it have been someone older and less attractive? Was it always going to be like this now that I was over the age of forty? Would younger and more vivacious women appear to continually whisk men away?

Since it was the final evening that the show would be open to the general public, the doors didn't close until eight. Most of the fires had been put out days ago, so the remaining hours dragged by, and I wallowed in my misery, trying to reconcile the charming Wolf who'd helped me cook last night with the man who was chasing after Tara.

Nina found me at the latte stand, swilling coffee to stay alert. "I'm not making any progress here on the Kurt situation. I'm headed out to look for Emmaline, and then"—she closed her eyes and drew a deep breath—"I'm going home to do some yoga to calm my nerves."

When the exhibit hall closed, I trudged home, debating whether to bake a cake for Wolf. I knew I was overly tired because I wasn't even planning to raid the refrigerator.

But as I approached my block, a police car eased into an empty spot in front of Nina's house. The streetlights gleamed on Tara's long ponytail when she stepped out. As she had in the morning, she gazed up and down the street. Her eyes stopped on me briefly, but she didn't acknowledge me. She shut the door to the car and walked up to Nina's front door.

There was no way this could be good. I ran to Nina's, arriving just as she answered the door with Hank on her shoulder.

Tara said, "Are you Nina Reid Norwood?"

I saw fear in Nina's eyes when she nodded.

"Ma'am, I've received a report that a Kurt Finkel has gone missing. May I come in?"

Nina threw me a wide-eyed look and stepped aside.

Puffing, our elderly neighbor Francie ran up to the door with her dog Duke. "What are the cops doing here?"

Nina motioned for us to come inside. She closed the door and showed us all into her living room. The lavish use of sumptuous sky blue fabrics reminded me of Iris's booth at Rooms and Blooms. I made a mental note to ask Nina if Iris had been her interior decorator.

Tara acted like a human camera. She took in everything as though she were snapping mental pictures of details. "Ms. Norwood, are you acquainted with Kurt Finkel?"

Hank the parrot shrieked, "Kurt!"

Nina shuddered. "Yes."

Tara frowned. "When did you see him last?"

"I'm sorry, but I can't answer any questions." Nina spoke softly, almost like she didn't want to offend Tara.

"You can't tell me when you last saw him?"

"Look, my husband testifies at murder trials for a living. I know I'm not supposed to answer any questions. I'm sorry."

Tara licked her lips. "Ma'am, no one said anything about murder."

Nina looked to me, but I didn't know how to help her.

Tara's gaze followed Nina's to me, and then she quickly looked back to Nina. "Ma'am, Mr. Finkel's cell phone records indicate that you phoned him repeatedly after one o'clock last night."

"Kurt! Your cheatin' heart. *Awwk.* Kurt, answer the phone."

Hank's timing couldn't have been worse. Nina closed her eyes slowly, like she figured she'd been caught. Blinking them open, she said, "Excuse me while I put my parrot in his cage."

We waited in painful silence, and even though Nina shut the door, we could hear Hank singing "Your Cheatin' Heart."

Nina appeared to have regained her confidence, though. "If I thought Kurt was dead, why would I bother calling him?"

Francie, who'd been silent, chose that moment to speak up. "Unless you called him so it would look like you thought he was alive."

Nina and I glared at her.

But it was Tara who began to look uneasy. She stared at me like she meant to pierce my thoughts. "That's why you were cleaning that house this morning—you were cleaning up the murder scene." She pointed at Nina. "You killed him, and then your friend came and tried to hide the evidence."

"Then why would I have called the police?" I asked, smug in my ability to poke a hole in her theory.

She paused. "I haven't quite figured that out yet, but I think it probably had something to do with Wolf. Maybe you thought they would send Wolf if you said you'd found a dead man. But then I arrived and messed up your little scheme—whatever it is." Her dark eyes blazed like they would bore a hole right through me. "Maybe . . . maybe you planned to use him as an alibi of some sort."

Francie shook her head like we were idiots. "I don't know what happened, but I think you'd better tell Police Barbie, because it's beginning to sound pretty bad."

Nina opened her mouth, and the torrent of words that followed stunned me. She spewed the entire story, including the fact that Kurt hit his head when he fell.

When Nina finished, Tara turned an accusatory expression toward me. "Why didn't you tell me all this earlier?"

I shrugged. "You didn't believe me when I said I'd seen him in the window seat. You just lectured me about false reports."

Anger and embarrassment stormed across her face. *Great, Sophie—make her mad.*

"I'd like to see his car, please." Tara's words were polite, but delivered in an icy manner.

The four of us and Francie's golden retriever, Duke, walked the three blocks to Kurt's SUV. When we reached the spot where he had parked, Nina froze. A new Cadillac occupied the spot where Kurt's SUV had been parked. His car was gone.

# ELEVEN

From "THE GOOD LIFE" :

Dear Sophie,

If I had a fortune, I could have a gorgeous house. But the prices of furniture are unbelievably high, especially on the antiques I love so much. How can I get the same look for less?

—Antique Lover in Paris

Dear Antique Lover,

Learn from the expensive stores, but take your business to secondhand shops, yard sales, and flea markets. Try to see past fabrics and finishes, because they're easily changed. Look for pieces in good condition with classic lines, then get to work with fresh fabric and paint.

—Sophie

I breathed more easily. "I guess that settles it. Dead people don't drive."

Under the glare of the streetlight, I could see Tara was *not* amused. Her mouth twitching from side to side, she scanned the block. "Nice try, ladies." She focused on Nina. "I don't know why you lied about his car and dragged me out here. It appears that your story is falling apart. It will go easier on you if you come clean."

"I've had about enough of you!" The words burst from my mouth before I could control myself. "Wolf knows all about the reason I was cleaning over at Mordecai's. And I'm sure somebody on this block noticed Kurt's SUV parked here. Maybe if you would do your job, you'd find out that we're telling you the truth."

A gentle wind blew, but I knew my goose bumps came from fear, not the cold.

"Leave Wolf out of this. Maybe you thought you could use him as an alibi while your friend committed murder, but he has his own dark history and doesn't need more black marks against him from being associated with your despicable crime." Tara stepped closer to me and her voice became husky. "Leave Wolf alone."

She'd invaded my personal space, and I took two steps back as it dawned on me that she had a major thing for Wolf. Their date for the banquet wasn't a coincidence. No matter how much I wanted to imagine there was nothing between them, Tara had just proven her dedication to Wolf. Nina and I would be fighting a losing battle if she wanted me out of the picture. I tried anyway. "Maybe you ought to take a closer look at Kurt's wife. She was supposed to be out of town, but she marched into Rooms and Blooms this morning, demanding to know where he was."

"So? That seems logical to me."

Maybe Police Barbie wasn't all that bright. "When the

cat's away?" The blank look on her face indicated that she still didn't get it. "Clearly, Kurt thought his wife was out of town, and he could play around. But either she lied about being gone, or she came back early and caught him carousing."

"I see, and now you're going to tell me that he thinks it's fun to hide in a box, and then disappear."

Well, there was that. It didn't make sense to me, but some people had peculiar ideas about what might be funny.

"All I know is that the three of you are knee-deep in it."

"Not me!" Francie protested.

"Maybe. Maybe not. I do know that I plan to get to the bottom of this."

Nina, Francie, and I left Tara standing on the sidewalk, looking angry. Even though Tara was clearly on the wrong track now, I hoped she would clear up the matter of Kurt's disappearance. We would all feel better if we knew what had happened to him.

When I returned home, I curled up in my kitchen with a mug of decaf English breakfast tea and mulled over my situation with Wolf. Why were men so complicated? I tried to shove away my emotions and think clearly about facts. I'd seen Wolf and Tara being very familiar in the café. They had a date for the banquet on Valentine's Day. Wolf knew I would be at the banquet, didn't he? It didn't seem like him to flaunt another woman in my face. But Tara clearly had a crush on Wolf. I sank to a slouch in the chair.

On the other hand, I knew how attentive and loving he'd been right here in my kitchen only last night. Not many guys would help cook. In the end, I decided to go with my instincts and bake a cake for Wolf anyway. If it turned out that he and Tara were indeed an item, I could always drown my sorrows in chocolate cake, whipped cream, and cherries.

The next morning, I arrived at the hotel bright and early, feeling much better after a decent night's sleep. The fact that it was the last day of Rooms and Blooms also boosted my spirits. All the exhibits would remain in place for the banquet that evening, and then exhibitors would have a day to remove everything. I could hardly wait. I usually enjoyed Rooms and Blooms, but Kurt's disappearance had cast a pall over it this year.

Still, in the light of day, the mystery about Kurt didn't seem so awful. The guy was clearly a creep, and was avoiding his wife. He'd meant to spook Nina when he crawled into the box. I probably gave *him* a scare when I opened it.

A guard waited for me at the entrance to the exhibit hall. "Are you Ms. Winston?"

Even though I assured him that I was, he demanded to see identification. "I have strict instructions not to leave until you're here."

I thanked him for being so conscientious, and was willing to bet that I wouldn't find any empty booze bottles this morning.

As usual, I walked the entire hall. Everything seemed to be in order.

But midmorning, Natasha barreled toward me with a steamed expression. "It's your turn to babysit the fortune hunters at Mordecai's house. That Mike is determined to find something and won't leave. But I have to be here because I can't beat Iris Ledbetter for Best in Show unless my booth is perfect and I talk people into voting for me." She leaned toward me and whispered, "It wouldn't hurt me to kiss up to the other exhibitors—I know Iris has been."

"Wish I could help you"—okay, that was a lie, I wasn't

a bit sorry—"but I have responsibilities here. Besides, I'm not a co-chair of the Show House."

Natasha's nostrils flared and she began to argue, but I interrupted her. "Why don't you send the other co-chair?"

She scowled at me until it sank in. "That's brilliant! I can get rid of the competition by sending Iris over to Mordecai's. What would I do without you, Sophie?"

It was a rhetorical question, and Camille was motioning to me. Natasha would have to deal with Iris, who would surely not be pleased by her demand.

Camille was holding a cell phone to her ear. She lowered it, scowling. "I hate these things."

"They won't work down here. Something about the steel and the way the convention hall is constructed."

She laughed. "Just yesterday I was saying how pleasant it was that people weren't gabbing on their phones. No wonder. Listen, have you seen my husband?"

"Sorry."

"If you do, tell him I've withdrawn his booth from consideration for the prizes. Iris Ledbetter is having a hissy fit about people voting for Nolan's booth just because I'm president of the Design Guild. It's all so ridiculous. Nolan couldn't decorate a hatbox. The only thing he could ever win would be the prize for most expensive furnishings."

I hoped I didn't show my surprise at her acknowledgment that his furniture carried outrageous prices. I must not have concealed it, because she said, "Oh, give me some credit, I'm not blind. *I* wouldn't shop at his store. That place has been nothing but a money pit since the day it opened." She switched gears without missing a beat. "Everything ready for tonight?"

"I think so. I was just on my way to discuss the switchover to tables for the banquet."

"Great. Be sure they understand that the lights are to

go down so they can put spots on the winning booths as they're announced."

Camille bustled off, and I headed for the center of the convention hall. Since the awards for the best booths were being given at the banquet, the Guild had chosen to group the gorgeous garden landscapes in a cluster around a park-like area. During Rooms and Blooms, visitors could rest, relax, and enjoy a cup of coffee among the flowers. When the doors closed behind the last visitor, the hotel staff would move the park benches out of the way and bring in round tables and chairs for the banquet. The man in charge of making the switch waited for me in front of Ted's back-yard cottage. He assured me all systems were go.

At five o'clock, the last of the visitors were shooed out. Like magic, hotel staff appeared and began to transform the park. I watched them for one hour to be sure they had the right idea. When it seemed they had everything under control, I hustled home to change clothes for the banquet.

I'd planned to wear spring colors in keeping with the spirit of Rooms and Blooms, but now that I knew Wolf would be there with a woman a hundred pounds thinner than me and much younger, I felt a pressing need to try to look sophisticated. I couldn't erase the years or the pounds, but I could try to appear pulled together.

Recalling Natasha's words about my ponytail and lack of makeup, I lined my eyes with a smudgy pencil, used mascara, dusted powder on my face, and curled my hair. I slid into a simple black sheath that always made me feel confident and added rhinestone earrings that I usually reserved for only the dressiest occasions. When I looked at myself in a full-length mirror, I wanted to scrub my face, but the image of that slender, raccoon-eyed cop kept popping into my brain. I couldn't compete with her and didn't want to. If Wolf wanted a younger woman, then maybe it was time to forget about him.

I took a few deep breaths to clear my head and emotions, slipped into higher heels than I would normally wear at a function where I might have to walk a lot, and stepped carefully down the stairs. Mochie was curled up in his favorite chair by the kitchen fireplace. I added a little food to his dish, which probably infused me with the delicious scent of eau de stinky tuna, and headed back to the hotel.

When I arrived, the tables and chairs were in place, and were being set with the Valentine red tablecloths and stark white china selected by Camille. Right on schedule, the florist delivered potted azaleas that would be given to the winners along with the Design Guild's crystal Award of Excellence. Lined up across the foot of the podium, the masses of red and white flowers on the azaleas added a festive punch of color. In a nod to living green, Camille had opted for azaleas that could be planted outdoors by the recipients, instead of traditional flower arrangements. She also chose centerpieces of rich red gladioli planted in white pots. The bulbs could be saved and planted outdoors. It was a simple tablescape, but one that reflected Camille's refined taste and sensibility.

I walked up to the podium to test the microphone. It worked fine. From my elevated vantage point, I could see that the lighting crew had already lowered the lights in the recesses of the convention hall. Spots flickered on and off as they made sure they could highlight the winning booths. The aisle from the entrance doors remained lighted, though somewhat dimmer than during the day.

Tara walked that path energetically and appeared to be headed for me. She breathed heavily, as though she'd been running, and she wore her uniform, not a dinner dress.

# TWELVE

From "*Ask Natasha*":

*Dear Natasha,*

*My son and new daughter-in-law are living with us, temporarily I hope, in my son's old room. I knew she would want to make the room less masculine, so I very generously said she could make a few changes. That dreadful child took a glue gun to my expensive designer cushions and headboard, and has attached glittering beads and garish faux diamonds. How do I instill taste in her without seeming the evil mother-in-law?*

*–Apopleptic in Apopka*

*Dear Apoplectic,*

*Enroll dear daughter-in-law in an interior design class so she can learn design basics. And make sure that glue gun of hers mysteriously vanishes.*

*–Natasha*

Tara stopped between the tables being set and looked up at me. "Where's Wolf?"

Oh, I did not want to go there. This was the reason I never invited dates to my events. I should be concentrating on the event, not bickering with another woman. I spoke very calmly, hoping she wouldn't make a scene. "I have no idea."

"He must be here somewhere. I haven't been able to reach him on his cell phone."

I shrugged, and she took off at a jog, headed deeper into the exhibit hall. Somehow, I didn't think he was hiding in one of the booths, but that was her business.

Satisfied that the microphone worked, I rushed to the banquet manager to remind him about the music that should already be playing.

I'd just returned when Camille and Nolan arrived. Nolan nodded in my general direction and wandered off, while Camille expressed her delight with the simple decor she'd chosen.

One by one the exhibitors filtered in and waiters poured wine for them. The classical music Camille had requested played over speakers, but that didn't drown out clinking, hammering, thuds, and the echoes of a nail gun as exhibitors showed off their products to each other. The proud vendor of the backyard bulldozer started it up and gave rides through the hall, much to Camille's chagrin. I noticed, though, that Nolan was one of the first to try it out.

Posey chatted with Nina, Iris, and an older woman I suspected was Iris's grandmother, since I could see a strong family resemblance.

Nina sidled up to me, wineglass in hand. "Iris says that Tara spent hours poking around at Mordecai's house this afternoon."

"Did she find anything?"

"She was very excited when she left. I'm going over to Kurt's booth to snoop again. If Earl shows up, tap the microphone so I can get out of there."

It wasn't a good plan, but I was certain nothing had changed, so it wouldn't hurt for Nina to snoop if it would make her feel better. I was glad to see Ted checking the liner on his pond. The last thing I needed tonight was another leak. His wife and Mike looked on, laughing about something.

Natasha walked in like she owned the place. Wearing a form-fitting dress adorned with bugle beads, she turned on the charm and flitted from one person to another. But she found the time to annoy me. "You must help me convince Camille to stop holding this banquet on Valentine's Day. Valentine's should be a couples' evening, not spent in a crowded room. Mars didn't have to do a thing beyond tell his secretary to order flowers for me. We should be having a romantic interlude right now, not glad-handing everyone."

As the crowd grew, it became difficult to keep track of the guests, but I did notice Earl, in a dress cut so low that everyone was talking about it. I scooted back to the microphone, tapped it a couple of times, and muttered "testing." Hopefully, Nina could hear me back at the Finkel Kitchen booth.

When I stepped off the podium, a hand slipped around my waist and someone nuzzled my ear. I jerked away. As soon as I saw Wolf, dashingly handsome in a dark blue suit and a red tie, I wished I hadn't shifted away. But then I thought it a rather daring move for a man who came with another woman. Did that mean there was nothing between them? I struggled with that question, confused yet pleased at the same time.

"Did Tara find you?" I asked.

Subtly, so that no one would notice unless they were

paying close attention, he wound his fingers into mine. "No. Was she looking for me?"

"Just a little while ago."

"I'll see her when we sit down to eat."

So it *was* a date. And he didn't seem the least bit perturbed by the fact that I knew. How could he have a date with her, yet be so intimate with me? I never imagined Wolf as a two-faced kind of guy. He had always impressed me as being straightforward. I didn't think I cared much for this side of him. I wanted to ask questions, to find out what was going on with him and Tara, but it was neither the time nor the place. As much as I'd have liked to pursue the subject, I had a job to do first. Making an excuse, I wandered away into the crowd.

To my surprise, Humphrey arrived with Francie, who'd dressed for the occasion in a sturdy tweed skirt and jacket more suited to walking the moors. Certainly not the date Humphrey had hoped for, but maybe they would enjoy themselves.

Humphrey made the mistake of leading Francie to the same table where Iris Ledbetter and her guest placed their purses. Francie took one look at Iris's guest, who wore oversized glasses with enormous white frames that covered nearly half her face, and said, "Bedelia. Still dressing like a drag queen, I see."

"Good heavens! Is that you, Francie? What's it been—twenty years? And you still fit into that thrift store outfit."

"Where are my manners?" Francie cooed. "Allow me to introduce Humphrey. While you came with your granddaughter, I'm here with a date. Who, I might add, is thirty years younger than me."

Bedelia looked him over. "How much is she paying you to be her escort?"

Humphrey flushed with embarrassment, and I was sorry

I didn't have time to hang around and listen to the two old ladies go at it.

But I stopped long enough to find out more about what had excited Tara. "Iris, I hear Tara spent the afternoon at Mordecai's house."

"She's an odd duck." Iris shuddered. "I hate to think our safety is in her hands. She found a feather and carried it around with her like it was important."

A feather from Hank I wondered?

"And then she kept dropping it in the family room. She'd throw it down and pick it back up. Throw it down, watch it, and pick it back up. Very odd. I'm just thankful that Kurt wasn't there."

"Oh?" Iris had a problem with Kurt?

Iris's mouth bunched up like she'd eaten something sour. "Is Natasha always so stubborn? I'm furious with her for hiring Kurt without consulting me. We're co-chairs, but she thinks she's running the show."

"Natasha thinks she knows everything," I conceded. I waited for Iris's anger about being forced to babysit the house instead of tending to her exhibit.

"She's met her match this time. Natasha wasn't at Mordecai's this afternoon, so I contracted with Ted and Mike to redo the kitchen. But we're going to be sly, so that Natasha will think it's her idea." Her laugh had a wicked tinge to it, and was so loud that several people turned to look at us. "She may think she's manipulating me, but I'm no dummy."

Beside me, Iris's Nana suddenly screeched, "Teddy, darling!" Ted ambled over, grinning from ear to ear. Bedelia planted a kiss on his cheek and lifted a lock of his hair. "Not as curly as it was when you were little, but you're still so handsome." She turned to Iris. "Do you remember all those curls? The girls loved him, but poor Teddy was so shy."

I excused myself because Nina was motioning to me, panic on her face. "He's here."

"Who?" I asked.

"Kurt. And I saw his wife."

Now she had my attention. "You saw Kurt?"

"No. But he's here. His cell phone and car keys are in a drawer in his booth. They weren't there earlier today."

I sagged with relief, but not for long. "He better run in the opposite direction if I see him. How dare he scare us this way?"

She grinned. "We have to think of a way to get him back. Something he'll remember for a long, long time."

Camille climbed to the podium and welcomed all the guests. In an instant, the chatter ceased and everyone was seated. Waiters served smoked salmon, and asparagus wrapped in savory goat cheese while Camille explained that the awards had been broken into categories this year. There would still be only one Best in Show award, and it would count substantially toward the Design Guild Award given annually to the person who made the most significant contribution to the design community.

When Camille stepped down, she hurried toward me. Speaking quietly, she said, "I don't know what happened to the little Waterford bowls we were going to give with the azaleas. A bellman unloaded them from our car, but they're not here."

As she sat down at the head table, next to an empty chair where Nolan should have been, I went in search of the bellman and the missing bowls. Luckily, I found that when he didn't know what to do with them, he'd held them at the bellman's stand. The only problem was convincing him that he could release them to me.

"I know I'm not the woman who brought them. But she's already eating dinner at the banquet. And she will not be happy if these bowls aren't down there when she finishes her dinner and presents awards."

"Lady, I'm not handing these things over to a total stranger."

He prattled on while I watched Nolan pace in front of the hotel, cell phone to his ear. He snapped it shut, and when he rushed past me, he seemed upset about something.

At long last, I managed to convince the bellman to bring the bowls to the convention hall. I carried them up to the podium, and when they lowered the lights and trained a spot on Camille, the bowls glittered behind her and I relaxed. It wouldn't be long now.

Camille wore her hair pulled back off her face. Very elegant and not at all pretentious. Her dress probably came from a fancy designer—a bluish gray that changed tone ever so slightly when she moved. She announced the various prizes, handing each winner a small Waterford bowl and a live azalea. Iris Ledbetter won for best room design. Nolan applauded halfheartedly, not bothering to hide his disgust. Ted won for best landscape, and Natasha won in a miscellaneous category.

And then Camille heaved a tall Waterford vase to the top of the podium. I glanced at Natasha, who sat so straight her back almost arched. At the next table over, Iris grabbed Bedelia's hand.

After a brief speech about the outstanding quality of the booths, Camille said, "And the winner of the coveted Best in Show award is Ted Wilcox of Leisure Landscapes for his magical glass cottage!"

Soft spotlights highlighted Ted's house as applause broke out. It was positioned perfectly for everyone to admire, the little lights twinkling around the French doors. Ted jogged up to the podium, his arms in the air like

Rocky. Smiling, he accepted the vase and azalea and air-kissed Camille.

But as the applause subsided, a titter spread through the audience. I followed their line of sight and realized that a waif-thin model type in a police uniform had staggered out the front door of the cottage. She paused on the little foot-bridge, swaying as though she was drunk, and for no reason that I could discern, the audience applauded again.

And then she toppled headfirst into the pond.

# THIRTEEN

From "The Good Life":

Dear Sophie,

I've moved into my first apartment and I'm looking for art. I'm not allowed to paint the walls, which means I have to rely on art for color. I feel like I'm past the poster stage but I can't afford original paintings. Any suggestions?

—White Walls in White Hall

Dear White Walls,

Styrofoam. It's the least expensive way to make instant art. Cover large sheets of styrofoam with gorgeous handmade blankets, quilts, fabric (from the sale bin), or even wallpaper. You'll have fabulous original instant art of your own in any size, color, and style you like.

—Sophie

Wolf and I reached the pond at the same time. Tara floated facedown, which couldn't possibly be good. A pink tinge began to color the water.

Wolf plunged in, but I took a second to slip off my heels. The cold water barely came up to my knees. Wolf had already grabbed Tara under her arms and was trying to lift her. I hooked an arm underneath her, but with the weight of the water soaking her uniform, she might as well have been a whale.

"Flip." We said it simultaneously and turned Tara onto her back, which enabled us to tug her to the side of the pond where Ted and Humphrey waited. They pulled her past Ted's decorative rocks and tulips onto the concrete floor and began CPR.

I wished for the best, but held out little hope that they would be able to revive her. Wolf swapped places with Humphrey, and when he stood up, the knees of his suit bore dark splotches. I took a closer look. A puddle of rose-tinged water spread beneath Tara.

Posey, Mike, and a host of people I didn't know took turns at CPR, and managed to keep it up until the rescue squad arrived. I looked on, water dripping from my dress, the concrete floor freezing my panty hose–clad feet.

"Dear Lord, is she dead?" asked Francie.

I looked up and found a very pale Nolan DuPont standing next to Francie. "I think so."

Camille pushed between them. "Who is she?"

"Tara Borsos. She's a cop."

Nina wrapped a hotel blanket around me and held another. "Where's Wolf?"

I blinked at her, feeling dazed. Until that moment, I'd been in overdrive with adrenaline pumping through me. I tugged the blanket close, as if it would make the nightmare go away. How could this have happened? Tara had been so vibrant, so young. How could her life have ended so abruptly and horribly?

Camille pointed. "He's with the other cops."

"Other cops?" I looked for Wolf. He stood with a group of men and women near Tara, all of them dressed for dinner. "They're all cops?"

Camille answered as if she were thinking about something else. "*Mmm-hmm.* They bought a whole table. Some cop's wife exhibited cute stuff she sells in her store. Oh no," she moaned. "I was hoping she'd had some kind of attack or was drunk, but there's blood. This will be another black mark on Rooms and Blooms."

"Really, Camille. Don't you think about anything other than your precious Design Guild?" Nolan strode away, leaving Camille speechless.

Nina leaned so close that I could feel her breath on my ear. "It's Kurt."

Had she drunk too much wine? The body was clearly a woman's. "No, it's definitely Tara."

"I mean Kurt did it," she whispered. "This is spooking me. He's here somewhere, probably lurking in a dark corner. Did you notice that he never sat down to dinner with Earl? And what's worse, the cops won't suspect him because they don't even know he's here."

A shudder ran through me and I gazed around. Between the booths and the dark recesses of the cavernous hall, a killer could sneak about undetected. "Stop that!" I hissed. She was creeping me out. "Why would he want to murder Tara?" On the bright side, if she was right and Kurt was lurking somewhere, that would mean he wasn't dead.

"Sophie!" Ted motioned to me. I skirted the EMTs but shivered when I got closer and realized he was speaking with Detective Kenner. The disagreeable homicide cop hated me.

"Sophie, would you please tell this detective that someone tried to sabotage my exhibit?"

I'd forgotten all about that. "You think there's a connection between Tara's death and the sabotage of your pond?"

"I don't know, but don't you think it's odd that Tara walked out of my cottage?"

Kenner smirked at me, and suddenly I felt exposed and vulnerable. Kenner always reminded me of a hungry vulture ready to pounce. I avoided his cruel eyes and focused on Ted. "Yes. There's no question that someone shot nails into the liner of Ted's pond. I saw the nails when he removed them and patched the liner. Do you still have them, Ted?"

"Long gone, I'm afraid. But I'm glad I showed them to you. Who'd have thought I would need a witness?"

I avoided Kenner's beady eyes. "I can readily confirm the sabotage. Excuse me."

But as I moved away, Kenner stepped with me and caught my arm. In a low voice he said, "I've got you this time."

I was forced to look into his menacing face. "What's that supposed to mean?"

"It means your luck has finally run out. You had motive, opportunity, and, as soon as we know how she died, I expect you'll have had the means, too."

"That's absurd."

"Is it? Don't think I didn't notice you slip away during the dinner. Your doting Wolf won't be able to bail you out of this mess."

Too many thoughts ran through my head, and I was slow to pick up what he meant. "Motive?" I said it too loud, and a few people turned to look at us.

But the slime weasel grinned and turned his attention to

Posey, who was staggering backward, away from the body. She flailed her arms as though she might lose her balance. In the process, she managed to back right into Humphrey. His eyes flicked wide, and he instinctively reached out to steady her. Posey turned around and sobbed into his shoulder. Humphrey tentatively patted her on the back, and I suspected I knew who his next object of desire would be.

In my haste to get away from Kenner, I'd come within feet of the EMTs and could hear their chatter about what had happened to Tara.

"The cops confirm smeared blood on the floor of the glass house," said one.

Another ran his hand over his goatee. "Weird wound. They find any bullet casings?"

"Not yet. But it looks like she was injured inside the house and managed to find the strength to walk out."

I got through the next two hours in a semi-daze. In spite of the heroic CPR efforts, no one was able to revive Tara. In short order Ted's cute cottage had been roped off with yellow police tape. Eventually, the EMTs removed Tara's body. They corralled the guests in the area where they had dined, but it was obvious that the numerous empty seats meant a lot of people had left in the chaos immediately after Tara's death. From what I could tell, Earl, Iris, and Bedelia had departed.

The police wanted a list of everyone in attendance. I managed to find it and turned it over to Wolf, who didn't even look at it. He passed it straight to Kenner, who took the podium and asked everyone to have a seat so the police could come around to question them.

Wolf sidled over to me and whispered in my ear, "Do you have a backup copy of the list?"

I nodded, and he drifted away.

Still wrapped in the blanket, I sat down at a table of my neighbors—Nina, Francie, Natasha, and Mars.

Natasha leaned toward me. In a low voice, she said, "Mars and I have seen Tara in our neighborhood a lot lately."

That didn't surprise me. "She's been looking for a missing person for the last few days."

"She's been hanging around for weeks." Mars loosened his tie. "I take Daisy out late sometimes, and I've seen Tara walking in the neighborhood."

Francie scooted the gladiolus plant out of Natasha's reach, no doubt so she could take it home with her.

Nina raised an eyebrow, and I suspected she was thinking about the night we saw a light in Mordecai's house. Tara had turned up out of nowhere that evening.

Nina leaned back and motioned to Wolf. He strode over to our table, looking worried—not surprising, since the police took the murder of one of their own very seriously.

"How come Tara was on our block so much?" asked Nina.

Wolf's forehead furrowed. "She was a patrol officer assigned to your sector. Tara was relatively new to the force, and I think she usually worked the night shift."

Nina thanked him, and he ambled away.

I rested against the back of the chair. There were probably a lot of people who resented cops and might want her dead. On the few occasions when Wolf and I had gone out together, he'd insisted on sitting with his back to the wall so he could see what was going on and who came into the restaurant.

Of course, it didn't help that Tara had died at the banquet. The people involved in Rooms and Blooms would surely be suspects—even if a total stranger had followed

Tara in to kill her. I wished I'd paid more attention to her when she showed up looking for Wolf prior to the banquet. I hadn't seen her leave, but then again, I wasn't watching for her. She could have slipped out any number of ways without my noticing. But the fact that she still wore her uniform suggested that she'd never left the hotel. Maybe not even the convention hall. Where had she been all that time?

"I hope they'll get to our table soon," said Francie. "If I'd thought it would be this boring, I would have left with Bedelia."

I forced myself to focus and realized that the police were letting guests go. But I sat up straight and paid attention when Wolf left. He should have remained to interview people or search the crime scene. Something wasn't quite right.

Humphrey rushed to our table and took the chair next to Francie. Speaking confidentially, he said, "I just overheard a couple of cops talking. Apparently, Tara had a stalker."

# FOURTEEN

From *"Ask Natasha"*:

*Dear Natasha,*

*I love monochromatic bedrooms because they're so relaxing. I have a blue floral comforter and I painted the walls a coordinating blue, but it doesn't have that tranquil feeling. It's positively little-girlish.*

*—Too Sweet in Sugar Land*

*Dear Too Sweet,*

*Ditch the floral comforter and add texture to your wall. Sew a new comforter out of solid blue silk, and use the same blue silk fabric like wallpaper across the entire wall behind your bed. Add white pillows and you'll achieve that crisp, elegant monochromatic look.*

*—Natasha*

When the police made it to our table, Detective Kenner cut me from the herd and asked pointed questions. I had nothing to feel guilty about, except maybe for Kurt being missing, but that wasn't my fault. Still, the beak-nosed guy sent chills down my back, and I decided to answer truthfully but without offering additional information. There was no telling what he might use against me.

He asked when I last saw Tara, and I told him about her early arrival at the banquet, but some sense of loyalty or prudence prevented me from mentioning that she was looking for Wolf.

His eyes nearly sparkled when he said, "As the coordinator, I assume you are intimately familiar with the various exhibits and their locations."

I nodded but didn't understand where he was going with that line of thought.

"And you could have helped yourself to anything on exhibit."

"Why would I want to?"

"Did you ever have any arguments with Tara?"

"Of course not!"

"But you were upset that Tara was dating Wolf."

He sneaked in that statement so smoothly that it gave me pause. I really didn't think it was any of his business, but from the way he leaned forward a bit, a smile playing on his thin lips, I realized that was the motive he'd mentioned earlier.

He flushed an unhealthy beet red when I laughed. "Believe me, I wouldn't kill anyone over a man. Not even over Wolf."

"You couldn't stand the idea of Wolf with another woman." He almost shouted, drawing attention to us. "You killed Tara because of her relationship with Wolf, and you shoved her under the bed in the glass house. But she fooled you, didn't she? Because she wasn't dead."

"And I did that during the dinner service in full view of the two hundred–plus people in attendance tonight." I said it calmly, but something deep inside me quivered nervously. Had Tara's killer really stuffed her under the bed to hide her body? How did Kenner know that already? Pangs of horror ran through me at the thought of poor Tara's final moments.

Kenner peered at me, his face coming too close for comfort. His skin always seemed too tight, as if it had been stretched across his nose and cheekbones. I pulled back, away from his intimidating glare.

"You're ready to confess?" he asked.

"That was sarcasm." I stood abruptly, nearly hitting his sharp nose with my forehead. But I didn't care. I despised the man, and I hadn't killed Tara. "I suggest you follow other leads, because you're wasting your time on me."

With that, I turned on my heel and strode toward the door. I could hear him calling me and saying he wasn't finished with me yet, but I kept going and didn't look back.

Mars caught up to me. "Are you okay?"

I nodded and continued walking.

"Why don't we drive you home?" Mars offered. "Natasha insisted on bringing the car because she thought she would be taking the big Waterford vase home with her."

Natasha's audacity in presuming she would win Best in Show cracked me up and made me feel a little better. I stopped at the top of the escalator and looked back. The rest of my friends were close behind.

"Thanks, Mars. I'll take you up on that. I usually like to walk home, but it's cold out and my dress is still damp."

Natasha, Francie, Nina, and Humphrey stepped off the escalator precisely as Ted, his wife, and Mike ambled by.

Natasha's eyes widened when she saw the coveted vase in Ted's arms. "I'll simply have to make Mordecai's house so spectacular that the Design Guild will favor me. But now that someone's been murdered in Ted's exhibit, shouldn't he be disqualified?"

"Sometimes I wonder how you can stand her, Mars," said Nina quietly. Taking my arm, she steered me toward the garage.

We all squeezed into Natasha's car and minutes later, driving slowly, we approached Mordecai's home. I looked up at the windows in search of suspicious lights.

Suddenly, Francie, in the front seat, screamed something incoherent. Instinctively, I tensed as though bracing myself for the worst.

Natasha squealed and spun the steering wheel. The car swerved and I banged into Mars, seated to my left. Tires screeched. And then we heard the dreaded crunch of metal slamming metal as we smashed into an oncoming Jeep.

In the seconds of silence that followed, I saw a little ball of fur scamper onto the sidewalk and disappear under Mordecai's front porch, apparently unscathed.

Humphrey rubbed the back of his neck, and Mars yammered at Natasha.

Nina threw open the door and bolted after the dog, calling, "Emmaline! Emma!"

"At least we know she's still alive." I scooted out of the car and crouched next to Nina, but couldn't see anything under the porch. My knees complained, though, and I guessed I must have banged them into someone or something in the fender bender.

Humphrey assisted Francie, who appeared to be fine, and the others piled out of the car. The portly driver of the Jeep launched into a tirade, but when he realized the other driver was Natasha, the TV diva, his demeanor changed.

Shivering in the cold, I told the others I'd be back after I changed clothes.

"I'll go with you," said Mars. "It's not safe with a killer on the loose."

I thought Natasha might lose her cool. "But it's safe for me to stand here on the street?"

"*Aw*, quit your griping," said Francie. "My old dogs are too tired to walk. I'll stay with you."

The look on Natasha's face made it abundantly clear that Francie wasn't the companion she had in mind. "Humphrey, you're a gentleman. I assume you'll remain with us to see Francie safely home?"

Francie pulled a stickpin out of the lapel of her coat. "Not to worry, Nat, I'm armed."

Nina stood guard at Mordecai's porch, lest the little Pomeranian decide to make another dash into traffic, and gave us instructions to return with a flashlight and meat or stinky cheese.

I hurried across the street to my house, unlocked the door, and left Humphrey and Mars to fend for themselves while I changed. Thoroughly chilled, I pulled on a huge fleece sweater, plush and cozy. I pawed through my closet until I found fleece trousers that couldn't have been less becoming but were very warm.

When I returned to the kitchen, the counter looked like a chocolate hurricane had blown through. How could two grown men make such a mess in minutes? Mochie happily noshed on sliced turkey, and Mars and Humphrey proudly offered me a mug of hot chocolate. The microwave pinged and Mars said, "We're making enough for everyone."

Humphrey clutched a mug between his hands and sipped gingerly. He was so pale that he appeared almost ghostly, and I felt ashamed for not realizing sooner that his new love had been killed. The rest of us hardly knew her, but he'd imagined that she was the perfect woman for him, and must be devastated.

I placed a hand on his arm. "Are you okay?"

Mars peered at him. "Why wouldn't he be?"

"Humphrey had a thing for Tara."

Mars started to laugh. I discreetly kicked him in the shin and said, "I'm so sorry, Humphrey."

"Death is a part of life. But hers should never have come so soon. I can tell you this"—Humphrey's tone grew stronger as he spoke—"I will find her stalker, and he will have to contend with me."

"Now, Humphrey, don't go doing anything stupid," cautioned Mars. "Anyone who kills a cop has to be pretty desperate. Leave this to Wolf and his buddies. Trust me, the cops will be on this case like hounds after a fox."

Summoning more chutzpah than I'd thought possible for Humphrey, he said, "I will not allow her death to go unavenged. I won't stand idly by."

Mars stuck another FiestaWare mug in the microwave. "Seven cups of cocoa, that's enough. Talk some sense into him, Sophie."

"Mars is right, Humphrey. We don't know what we're dealing with. Stalkers are often sort of unbalanced, aren't they?"

"My life is nothing without Tara. Finding her killer is the only thing left that I can do for her."

Mars made a can-you-believe-this face behind Humphrey's back, and I retreated to the foyer for a warm vest.

I wedged it on over the fleece pullover, so bundled that my arms stuck out at the sides like a little kid in a snowsuit. Back in the kitchen, I stuck a flashlight into my pocket. Mars shoved two mugs into my hands. Humphrey carried two as well, along with some of the sliced turkey I'd bought for panini sandwiches. Somehow, Mars managed to juggle three mugs.

We returned to the scene of the accident. I gave a mug to Francie, and Humphrey handed the turkey and a drink to Nina. The driver of the Jeep was stunned when Mars offered him hot chocolate. "Do you people make a party out of everything? I've never been in a traffic accident where refreshments were served."

Natasha turned steely eyes on Mars. "You know chocolate makes me bloat."

A young cop had arrived during our absence. Mars offered him Natasha's mug of hot chocolate, which he gratefully accepted.

"Where's the flashlight, Sophie?"

I flicked it on and handed it to Nina as she bent down to look under the porch steps. "Well, that's the strangest thing. Emmaline isn't under here."

"That can't be," said Francie. "We'd have seen her run out."

Humphrey and I knelt next to Nina. She moved the golden orb of light slowly. But she hadn't missed the Pomeranian. Emmaline had managed to escape again.

Nina shoved the food deeper under the porch. "She's probably hungry. I'll leave the bowl here. Maybe if we keep refilling it, she'll come by regularly."

"She must not know she's an heiress," said Mars. "That would bring Natasha running."

We all snickered, but I hoped Natasha hadn't heard. She would find it offensive, and between losing Best in Show and wrecking her car, she wasn't having a good evening.

No such luck. Natasha promptly asked, "Who gets the house if the dog is dead?"

I didn't have the faintest idea, but it made me wonder if some estranged relative of Mordecai's was hunting poor little Emmaline.

On that happy thought, I collected empty mugs. Natasha

and Mars drove their damaged car home, and the rest of us strolled toward our houses.

I unlocked the kitchen door, glad to be out of the cold weather. It was late, and I was too tired to make a real meal for myself, but I hadn't eaten anything at the banquet. I shed the vest and stood in front of the open refrigerator, contemplating scrambled eggs. Mochie wound around my ankles, purring. Probably hoping for more of the sliced turkey.

But then he stopped his friendly dance, listened for a moment, and shot into the foyer. I hoped he hadn't heard a mouse scratching inside the old walls.

A minute later, he yowled. An ear-splitting, woeful cry that prompted me to look for him. I found him in the dark sunroom, looking out at the backyard, where a shadowy figure stole across the lawn.

# FIFTEEN

**From** "The Good Life" :

Dear Sophie,

I know that proper lighting can create a mood, but my family won't cooperate. I bought two lamps for a long console in the family room, but everyone turns them off, claiming they're too bright, which leaves that side of the room dark. Getting a new family is too much trouble. Any suggestions?

—In the Dark in Sunshine Acres

Dear In the Dark,

Buy black lampshades. They prevent the light from beaming outward, leaving a cozy downward glow.

—Sophie

I could only imagine that Mochie had heard the back gate open and click shut. He crouched, watching the person who came far too close for comfort. I scooped Mochie into my arms and rushed to the back door.

My pulse hammering, I made sure it was locked, and raced to the kitchen to turn out lights so they wouldn't give away my whereabouts. Holding Mochie against my shoulder with one hand, I pawed in my purse for my cell phone with the other, and debated running out the front door and over to Nina's.

But it was too late. The midnight visitor rapped lightly on the sunroom door. Mochie purred before springing from my arm and dashing into the sunroom. I sidled along the wall, calling him in a whisper. I inched closer, but I couldn't see outside the door without showing myself.

I could hear the person at the door saying in a hushed voice, "Sophie? Soph!"

"Wolf?"

I finally took the plunge and recognized his earnest face looking in. No wonder Mochie had purred. I unlocked the sunroom door and opened it. "What are you doing here?"

"We need to talk."

I had come to hate that phrase. I braced myself for bad news. He probably came to confess about dating Tara. "You scared me half to death, sneaking around like that. Couldn't you have come to the front door, or at least called first?"

He ignored my complaint and locked the door behind him. That tiny action brought on thoughts that he'd killed his wife, and maybe Tara, too, and that I might have just made a huge mistake by letting him come in. But I shooed those ridiculous notions away. After all, it was Wolf, not some deranged killer.

hat was why she'd shown up when I called about see- Kurt in the window seat. "Would a patrol officer inter- w people about a missing person?"

"Unlikely." He frowned at me. "What are you getting ?"

"You don't know about Kurt, do you?"

"Kurt?"

Oh boy. We had some serious talking to do. "Would you mind if I fetched some wine or made some tea? I think you're going to be here a while."

"Sure. Would it be too much trouble to make coffee? With Kenner salivating at the thought of nailing me, I need to be alert. And while you're in the kitchen, take a look at the street, will you?"

I started the coffee and retrieved a velour bathrobe that my dad had left at my house. It wasn't much, but it was dry. I brought it to Wolf, and slipped away while he changed.

When I returned with a tray of coffee, fresh strawberries, and the Black Forest cherry cake, a small fire blazed in the living room fireplace. Wolf stood with his back to me, peering at the street through a slit in the curtains.

"I didn't see anyone. Did you?" I asked.

"No. But I don't trust Kenner."

We settled in front of the fire. I cut the cake, handed him plate with a slice on it, and said, "Happy Valentine's Day. wish it were under better circumstances."

"You made it for me?" Even though Wolf usually tried keep his emotions in check, I could see that he was ased. He tasted it and raved. "You've been promising to ke this. It's absolutely decadent. Thank you." He glanced und, his brow furrowed. "Did you get my flowers?"

"Flowers? No."

"That stinks. I'm really sorry. I'll go by the florist's orrow. He must have made a mistake of some sort."



"Your lights are off. Have you noticed someone watching your house?"

"Only you!"

He strode from the sunroom to the kitchen. "Don't you have any drapes in here that you can close?"

"No, just valances. When did you get so paranoid?" He hadn't minded the curtain-free windows the other night when we cooked together.

He kept going, through the foyer and into my dining room, where he carefully drew the curtains closed, then peered out.

"Okay, you're scaring me now. What's going on?"

He still didn't answer. He walked through the living room, swung the drapes closed, and sat down on the sofa.

"May I turn on a light?" I asked.

"I'd rather you didn't."

I could make him out in the dark, but the uneasiness I felt kept me from sitting next to him. Was this how Mordecai had lived? Surely he had used lights.

"Would it be all right if I lit a candle?"

"Sure." Wolf grunted in surprise, and I realized that Mochie had jumped into his lap. At least one of us wasn't apprehensive. Didn't they say that animals are great judges of character? I located matches in the dining room and lit a pillar candle on the living room coffee table. The feeble light cast an eerie glow.

"Soph, for right now, we probably shouldn't be seen together. I've been relieved of duty for the time being."

"Suspended?"

"Not exactly. They offered me a desk job while Tara's death is under investigation. I chose to take vacation time instead. I'm not going to find out who killed Tara if I'm sitting behind a desk."

"I'm sorry, Wolf. Is this because you were dating her?"

He stood up abruptly, and Mochie leaped for safety. "Where did you hear that?"

"From Humphrey. She told him you were her date for the banquet. And then I saw you two chatting in the Café Ole on King Street, so I thought . . ."

He walked over to me and cupped my face in his hands. "I would never do that to you." He smelled faintly of sandalwood. When he bent his head close to mine and kissed me, I wanted to believe him. My hands brushed the fabric of his trousers, and I realized he hadn't changed out of his wet clothes.

"You must be half-frozen. I'll call Mars. He'll bring you some dry sweats."

"No! No one can know I'm here."

He straightened up and paced the room, rubbing his face with his hands. "Tara and I never dated. Never discussed dating. I have no idea where she got that idea."

"But I saw you at the coffee bar."

"She was always asking questions about moving to homicide. I agreed to meet with her to help her career-wise. Tara wasn't satisfied being a patrol officer. She had a lot of plans for moving up." He spun on his heel and faced me. "Sophie, what would I ever have wanted with someone that much younger than me?"

"Oh, please, Wolf. Men love going out with younger women."

"Not my style. She didn't interest me in the slightest. But it appears she spread word far and wide that we were an item. Now I'm in a rotten position."

I could understand that, especially considering the rumors about his wife. "But what's with the darkness, the curtains?"



"It's Kenner. I know how he operates.
to implicate both of us."

"I know he hates me, but I thought you
working relationship."

"Hates you?" Wolf let out a bitter laugh.
lusts after you. He was madder than I've ever
when he learned we were going out."

"That can't be right. He's always been horrible t

"He'll be worse than you ever imagined if he ge
chance. He's a devious little worm."

I'd never heard Wolf say anything so disparaging ab
anyone. Was I finally seeing the real Wolf? Or was he ju
reacting to the extreme stress of Tara's murder and the terribl
implication that he might be involved? I didn't care for Kenner myself, but Wolf had always been neutral about him.

"I still don't understand. Even if he's jealous, he already
knows about our relationship, so why can't we be s
together?"

Wolf perched on the sofa and leaned toward me. "D
you see, Sophie? He's going to say that one of us kille
Either that I killed her to hide my relationship with h
that you killed her out of jealousy."

"He might say that, but it's not true. He's rea
We don't have anything to worry about. Besides, th
already know Tara had a stalker. Don't you think h
ably killed her?"

Wolf snorted. "I don't know how you manage to
police information so fast. We can only hope tha
case. Kenner doesn't think so."

Something Wolf had said earlier was both
"What, exactly, is a patrol officer?"

"They're on the street, out in the neighborhoo
the first responders when someone needs help."

I leaned toward him. The firelight cast a romantic glow and I basked in the moment, in spite of the horrible situation. "I'm just glad you're here, and that I know the truth about you and Tara."

And then I spilled the story about Nina and Kurt.

"He still hasn't shown up?"

"It's been two days, and as far as I know, I'm the last person who saw him."

Wolf held out a strawberry for me to bite into. "What could Tara have been thinking? Who knows what other matters she might have been investigating on her own?" He sipped his coffee, then lightly touched my fingers. "Why didn't you tell me this sooner?"

"It just happened yesterday. I've been a little busy. Besides, I thought Tara was telling you about it when I saw you at Café Ole with her. I didn't know she had no business going to Nina's and asking her questions."

"She might have found this Kurt guy, for all we know." Wolf slugged back his coffee and poured himself more.

He fed me another strawberry, and I couldn't help thinking it had been a romantic Valentine's evening after all.

But then Wolf said, "For now, don't call me, okay? Kenner will be checking our phone records. I wouldn't put it past him to get a warrant for a roving bug so he can listen to our cell phone conversations. I'll swing by at night if I think I'm not being followed. Or I'll see you in a public place. Where are you working this week?"

I hadn't given it any thought. "If the convention hall is closed and the exhibitors can't move anything out, I guess I'll be at Mordecai's house. But Kenner already knows about us. I don't see why we have to sneak around."

He slid a gentle finger along the contours of my face. "I'm trying to protect you, Sophie. The closer he thinks we are, the more jealous and irrational he'll be."

Whoa. That was a scary thought. "Are you saying he could be dangerous?"

"I don't think he's that unhinged, but he would be thrilled to be in my shoes, the one who rescues the fair damsel from her distress."

"You mean he covets what you have? Like Natasha, who wants everything I have?"

Wolf grinned. "I, for one, am glad she managed to steal Mars from you."

That led to a passionate kiss. But shortly thereafter, Wolf donned his damp clothes, checked the street for signs of Kenner, and crept into the dark of night.

I slept in late the next morning. There was no point in rising early to rush to the hotel. Yellow tape probably sealed the entire exhibit hall by now, and no exhibitors would be allowed to move anything.

In spite of the horror of Tara's death, Wolf's nighttime visit left me with a warm glow. No matter what Detective Kenner did or said, I had a feeling that he wouldn't be keeping Wolf and me apart. In fact, his behavior might just throw us closer together.

I decided I might as well take advantage of my unexpected vacation to get started on the piles of papers in Mordecai's family room. I ate blueberry yogurt for breakfast, patting myself on the back for my restraint—I would surely weigh pounds less tomorrow. After feeding Mochie, I filled a carafe with coffee to take with me.

I pulled on jeans that were tight in spite of my yogurt breakfast. Mindful that Wolf might stop by, I added a fancy long-sleeved T-shirt that would be easy to wash. Armed with trash bags, I headed to Mordecai's.

The elegant front porch of Mordecai's house teemed with people moving furniture. Natasha's camera crew dodged around them, shooting the beehive of activity.

Beth, Natasha's new assistant, stood on the sidewalk, watching with a terrified expression. I stopped next to her. "Guess all the designers chose today to get to work."

"It's a madhouse all right." She glanced at me with a worried expression. "I don't think I can work here."

"But you were doing great at Rooms and Blooms."

She nodded. "Oh, I liked that. I just thought I would be working at a TV studio. I thought the job would be totally different. I need the money, but I don't think I can do this. Tell Natasha I'm sorry, but I can't handle this job." She mashed her eyes closed briefly, as though she were in pain, opened them, turned, and walked away.

# SIXTEEN

**From "THE GOOD LIFE" :**

Dear Sophie,

We moved into our home a few months ago and I've had a ball fixing it up. My in-laws are coming for a visit to see it, so I've been after my dear husband to paint the garage doors. They're peeling and look just horrible. He says he can't paint them until it warms up. I suspect this is a convenient dodge on his part so he won't have to turn off the TV and get off the couch.

—Impatient Wife in Painted Post

Dear Impatient,

This time hubby is right. It's not advisable to paint if the temperature will drop below fifty degrees. While there are some specialty paints for cold applications, most paints won't adhere properly in the cold. They bubble, blister, and peel if it's too cold or too humid. Wait for warmer weather to do your outdoor painting.

—Sophie

But Beth was a split second too late. Natasha appeared on the porch and spied us. She rushed down the steps and took Beth's arm. "Thank goodness you're here. There's so much to do."

As Natasha tugged her up the stairs, Beth turned to look at me with frightened eyes, and I smiled encouragingly. Though she hadn't had the moxie to pull away from Natasha's clutches, she seemed the sort who would be sensible enough to handle most things Natasha might throw her way.

I followed them up the steps and into the swarm of workers. In the family room, Bernie was applying stain to his window seat.

He jumped up when he saw me and gently removed a carved owl from a box. "What do you think?"

I took the bird to examine it. "Did you carve this by hand?"

He beamed. "I like woodworking. Don't get much of a chance these days. I spent a season working with wood after university. Always found it very pleasing."

"It's remarkable." I held it next to one of the three owls on Mordecai's ornate built-in shelving. If I hadn't known better, I would have thought they were carved by the same person.

"They'll help unify the window seat with Mordecai's woodwork." Bernie gazed around. "When do you think we'll start painting?"

"Not until we get some of this junk out of here."

"As soon as I'm done with the stain, I'll call Mars. Maybe he and I can lug out some of this rubbish. Hey, have you seen my hammer?"

I shook my head.

"*Argh*," he grumbled. "Somebody probably borrowed it and forgot to return it. I swear I'm tempted to buy some of Natasha's robin's egg blue tools. At least they'd be easy to identify. Maybe they wouldn't disappear as quickly."

I left the coffee carafe in the family room and ventured into the kitchen for mugs. Mordecai's kitchen must have been the height of fashion once. Double ovens with rust-colored doors occupied the brick corner. The cooktop resided in a center island that featured a table-height countertop on three sides. Gold wallpaper matched the laminate countertops and busy linoleum flooring. The cabinets were clearly solid wood, but extremely dark and dingy. A copper exhaust hood hung in the center of the room. Now a mottled verdigris and drab bronze, it featured a bold black eagle.

Natasha already had Beth hard at work, emptying kitchen cabinets. "What's going to happen to all this stuff?" I asked.

Natasha stopped throwing canned goods into the trash. "I wanted to have a yard sale, but Mordecai's attorney insists that it all go to auction. A truck will be here later today to pick up the first load." She lowered her voice. "Yesterday, I overheard Nolan trying to buy some pieces for his shop."

Passing Ted and Mike, who thumped cabinets in the butler's pantry, no doubt in search of their bequest, I peeked into the living room. Little remained of Mordecai's furniture. Nolan rested in a chair, his shoulders slumped and his head bowed forward. I wondered if Camille had put her foot down about their shop. I borrowed two mugs from the butler's pantry and returned to the family room, where I poured coffee for Bernie and me.

For the next hour, I plowed through papers. Most of them were easy to throw out. Mordecai had saved unimportant flyers for local businesses as well as stacks of catalogs on woodworking, and building with straw bales.

Ted ambled in from the kitchen and scooted around Bernie, who was stuffing a bulging trash bag. Ted sniffed the air. "Do I smell coffee?"

He waved a mug, sat down next to me, poured coffee, and took a deep drag. "Find anything interesting?"

"Just junk."

"Poor old Mordecai."

"Was he a tough professor?" I asked.

"Are you kidding? He was the best. Always won those favorite-professor-type awards. Made the rest of the architecture department nuts. Instead of lecturing, he taught by making his students do things. Oh my gosh, look at this." Ted held up a magazine about building straw houses. "Mordecai was obsessed with the idea of building with straw. He even arranged a grant so we could build a little straw cottage to exhibit at the predecessor of Rooms and Blooms. It was tiny, but I learned more from that experience than any other class I ever took."

"Straw?" I pitched a stack of magazines into the trash. "How can you build a house with straw?"

Ted swallowed a sip of coffee. "It's a time-honored building method. They used it in Europe and here in the States when the settlers went out west. You stack bales of straw and cover them with adobe or plaster."

"Sounds like an invitation for fire."

"You'd think so, but straw in bales is compacted, so it doesn't burn well—not enough oxygen. Plus, the bales act as insulation, and the structures are surprisingly wind- and earthquake-resistant. Mordecai was a nut about it. He thought straw was the answer to providing low-cost housing. He was something of an authority on the subject and was gaining a lot of notoriety, which really irritated other members of the department, who felt straw houses weren't a legitimate architectural endeavor."

"So you and the other students were studying architecture?" asked Bernie.

Ted shook his head. "We were design students. Mordecai taught a basic class to introduce us to a variety of architectural concepts, but it was really his fun class. He was always challenging us to come up with creative ideas."

I tied the top of a trash bag and was handing it to Bernie when Mike wandered in. "I'm beginning to think Nolan was right about Mordecai losing his mind."

"No luck upstairs?" asked Ted.

Mike perched on the enormous desk. "If he wasn't completely crazy, then he would have hidden our bequest in something that isn't what it seems. Like a window seat with a locked compartment that's only accessible from the inside, so when you look at it from the outside, you'd never know it was in there unless you opened the seat.

Bernie paused, the trash bag in his hand. "That's not a bad idea. Like a safe hidden in plain sight."

"Have you looked behind paintings and wall hangings?" I asked.

Mike and Ted cracked up.

"You didn't know Mordecai well. That's entirely too pedestrian. Not his style at all," said Mike.

I dumped a stack of newspapers into a big box for recycling, and Mike offered to carry it outside, but Natasha blocked his way.

Planting her fists on her hips, she said, "I could strangle that Kurt Finkle. We're three days into this already, and I don't know if he plans to show up and do the kitchen or if I have to find someone else. I've already advertised it on my show, so it's not like I can back out now. What am I going to do?"

"Let Mike do it. He might get some business out of it. Wouldn't you like to leave that stifling job running a home improvement store?" Ted yawned and stretched his arms above his head.

"I *need* a professional." Natasha's tone couldn't have been more rude.

Mike looked down into the box he carried, as though he was embarrassed, and for a second I thought we were going to have one of those painful silences when no one knows what to say.

But Ted spoke up. "He *is* a professional. Well, he was once. He and Kurt started out together building kitchens. They were partners."

"That was a long time ago," Mike muttered. The skin above his dark beard flushed purple, and he seemed embarrassed.

"Mike was the one with the creative kitchen ideas." When Mike didn't respond, Ted continued. "*Aw*, don't be so humble. I'll help you. If we don't change the floor plan, then we won't have to do any major plumbing or electrical work. We'll swap out the cabinets and countertops, and it'll look brand-new."

Mike's gaze drifted to Natasha. "Would this be out of my pocket?"

"You're certain you're capable of a kitchen remodel? An *elegant* kitchen remodel?"

A smile crossed Mike's face. "You know, it would be fun to do a kitchen again."

Ted and Mike followed Natasha into the kitchen to discuss her vision. I went back to sorting garbage—until I found a cardboard box under a stack of newspapers. I opened it gingerly, afraid it might contain moldy food. But when I looked inside, I giggled at Mordecai's audacity. Inside the box were thousands of jigsaw puzzle pieces. I scooped up a handful. They had to be from dozens of different puzzles. It would be a nightmare to sort through them.

I carried the box into the kitchen and set it on the counter. "I believe I've found a clue to your bequest."

They all peered in the box, and the kitchen filled with their groans.

"You know what's going to happen, don't you?" said Mike. "We're going to sort those stupid things and find the locks that match our keys and when we open them, the big bequest will be a note that says 'Well done!' "

Even if Nolan wasn't on the hunt for his bequest, I felt we should let him know what I'd found. While they laughed and studied the puzzle pieces, I peered into the living room. Nolan wasn't there, but Beth stood rigidly just inside the doorway.

She turned around slowly and gasped when she saw me watching her.

# SEVENTEEN

**From "The Good Life":**

Dear Sophie,

Our dining room is on the north side of the house, always cold, and a gorgeous tree prevents sunlight from coming through the window. Against my husband's wishes, I insisted we paint it a bright yellow to cheer it up, but now it feels like we're dining inside a lemon. Help!

—No Lemons in Citrus Springs

Dear No Lemons,

Sometimes it's easier to embrace a negative and work with it. Instead of brightening the room, consider painting it a warm, dark color, like cranberry or curry. Most of us tend to use our dining rooms in the evening, when it's dark outside anyway. And if you're not sure which way to go, you might consider the fact that red walls stimulate the appetite.

—Sophie

In a whisper Beth said, "Do you think Natasha would be upset if I grabbed a cigarette outside?"

Now, I can be blind to the obvious, but Beth wasn't any good at lying. "As long as you don't blow smoke in the windows."

With a wan smile, she headed for the door like an express train, leaving me to wonder why she really wanted to escape.

I returned to the family room but stopped short in the doorway. I hadn't realized just how much Bernie and I had already managed to clear out. Except for one stack of papers in the corner, only the enormous desk and the window seat remained. I still had to look through the desk drawers and the numerous cabinets, drawers, and cubbyholes in the wall unit, but we'd made remarkable progress.

The room featured two windows to the west, but I doubted that it ever got much sun. The built-ins that Bernie liked so much weighed the room down. They were enormously practical, though, even if the ornate carvings weren't to everyone's taste. Maybe once the walls were painted, the woodwork wouldn't be so overpowering.

I was thinking about a gingery yellow, in an earthy Tuscan vein, when Bernie said, "I've been imagining something cozy, like a rich butterscotch. A color with just a hint of an orange hue that will blend nicely with the wood. We'll have to wash the walls first, though."

Years of dust and grime had built up on them, and I

had a hard time imagining what color they had been. The current dirty gray certainly did nothing for the room.

"Would you have time to help me take down the curtains after lunch?" I asked.

"Sure." Bernie smiled at someone in the foyer. "Could I be of assistance?" he called out.

An elderly woman in bright colors wandered in. Five chunky necklaces hung on her purple tunic, and vivid pink lipstick had been carefully applied beyond the edges of her lips. I recognized her as Iris's grandmother from her signature piece—enormous white-framed glasses. "I'm just having a look around." She held out a gnarled hand to Bernie. "Bedelia Ledbetter, sweetheart, and who might you be?"

I assumed that Bernie possessed a high tolerance for quirky ladies, since his mother had married seven or eight times. So it came as no surprise when he made a show of kissing her hand.

"Oh, you are a love! Single? Have you met my granddaughter? She's never been married—no baggage, if you know what I mean. I'm going to be helping her decorate the dining room."

If Bedelia had acted that way toward Mars or Humphrey, I would have to come to the rescue. But Bernie took it all in stride and didn't even blush.

"My, but everything looks so different now. That's what twenty years will do." She pulled her head back in surprise and flicked a hand in the air toward the bookcases. "I don't remember that monstrosity at all."

"You knew Mordecai and his wife." It was more of a question than a statement, although I knew the answer.

"Our husbands taught in the same department. As faculty wives, we were often thrown together." She studied

Mordecai's built-in bookcases. "I didn't care for Jean, though. Never understood why people made such a fuss about that woman."

"She won the Guild Award two years in a row," I pointed out.

"Stole it. Just like it was stolen from my Iris last night. I adore Teddy, and if Iris couldn't win, then he would be my next choice, but honestly, now—did you think Teddy's glass house was better than Iris's sumptuous dining room? In my book there wasn't any comparison."

"Nana? Where did you go?" Iris popped in and took her grandmother's arm. "You won't believe this. Nolan's painters are here. Apparently he can't be bothered with anything so mundane as painting. And get this"—she nudged me—"they snickered about how he leaves the store to see his honey every day at noon—and I don't think they meant Camille. Anyway, Nolan is doing the living room in a completely hideous Caribbean turquoise that I cannot work with in an adjoining room. It's garish. Simply the worst possible taste. I can't imagine what he's thinking. So I've trumped Natasha's plans and arranged for us to do the master bedroom. Posey will froth at the mouth when she finds out she's now going to be stuck with the dining room, but at least our room will have a shot at getting me the Guild Award."

They left to have a look at their new assignment, and I could hear them gabbing as they walked upstairs.

"What a pistol!" laughed Bernie. "C'mon, I'll buy you lunch, and we can pick up painting supplies while we're out."

We were almost through the front door when I heard Natasha's trill. "Sophie! Sophie!" I recognized the fake sweetness and was tempted to run.

Under his breath, Bernie muttered, "She wants something."

Before we could flee, Natasha descended upon us. "Soph, sweetie, we have a problem." She smiled her phony beauty pageant smile, and I knew whatever she planned to say meant trouble for me.

"No." I said it firmly.

"No, what?"

"No to whatever you cooked up. You've already stuck me with the most cluttered room in the house. I'm not switching rooms now that we've gotten rid of the garbage."

She clapped a hand to her chest like she was appalled by the thought. "Would I do something like that?"

*Yes*. I stared her down.

"Adam Swensen called. The auction people came by this morning, and they've told him they're not interested in anything but a few pieces of the better furniture and those gaudy andirons. Oddly enough, the same pieces Nolan offered to buy. Anyway, it looks like we'll have to have a yard sale."

I knew where this was going. "Oh no. That is *really* not my problem." I turned to leave. "C'mon, Bernie."

"I offered to take care of it," Natasha said behind me, "but for reasons I cannot fathom, Adam insists you do it."

My shoulders sagged. Adam probably didn't have a clue how much work a yard sale involved.

"He'll pay you," Natasha trilled.

Bernie nudged me. "We'll enlist the help of the entire neighborhood. Francie and Mars and Nina. Maybe the fortune hunters will pitch in, too. I . . . well, I think we ought to do it for old Mordecai."

"When did you become such a do-gooder?" I quipped.

"It's for the dog, Sophie. Emmaline gets the money."

That was low, but Natasha knew which button to push to make me reconsider.

I shook my head. "Bernie, I have no idea when the cops will release the Rooms and Blooms exhibits. I'll be tied up with that any day now. And it's February, for heaven's sake. It will probably rain—or snow! This isn't yard sale weather."

With my luck, the police would release the exhibit hall on the day of the yard sale, and a snowstorm would hit. "Call Adam back, Natasha, and tell him it's not yard sale season. I'll try to find a company that will take Mordecai's possessions to sell. But the decorators have to carry everything to the porch. I'm not doing all the heavy lifting. And you," I said clearly, so she wouldn't misunderstand, "are responsible for making sure it's all out here so it can be picked up."

Her eyes almost sparkled. But I still felt terrible. Bernie's generosity reminded me what a lousy neighbor I'd been to Mordecai. It was time I stepped up to the plate and did the neighborly thing.

Bernie chatted amiably on the way to pick up sandwiches. But I still suffered from bad friend syndrome. I'd known Bernie for years. In fact, he'd been the best man at my wedding. But I knew so little about him. From what I gathered, he'd lived on a number of grand English estates as his mother churned through husbands. I'd always thought him a bit irresponsible and too carefree. His yellowish hair always appeared tousled, giving him a boyish look, and there was little doubt in my mind that the kink in his nose meant it had been broken once, if not twice. Yet he ran one of the most popular restaurants in Old Town for an absentee owner. And I'd had no idea that he could carve wood.

We stopped by Bernie's restaurant for sandwiches. He

disappeared to the kitchen for two smoked turkey, Boursin, and mixed greens sandwiches on round cracked wheat rolls. I settled into a cushy armchair and made some phone calls to auction houses that regularly sold box lots from estates.

From my vantage point, I could see the host's desk at the entrance to the restaurant, and the first person to walk in was none other than Detective Kenner. He spoke to the seating host, who pointed in my direction. Kenner's head swiveled toward me, and I realized that Wolf had been dead-on. Kenner was watching us. I lifted my right hand and wiggled my fingers in greeting with a smile that I couldn't hold back.

I had to guess Kenner found himself in an uncomfortable position. If he waited outside, he wouldn't know who I met in the restaurant. If he came in and sat down in the bar area, it would be obvious that he was watching me. I tried not to show my glee.

He glared at me, spun on his heel, and left so fast that he bumped into Camille. I thought he muttered an apology, but she seemed a bit miffed. She paused at the host's desk, patted her hair into place, and smiled when Adam Swensen, Mordecai's attorney, came through the door. They disappeared from my line of sight when the host showed them to a table.

I was almost sorry to see Bernie return with our food. His restaurant appeared to be a good place to observe people. I spotted Kenner waiting outside as soon as we left the restaurant. He must have been sorely disappointed by my boring behavior.

As we strolled back to Mordecai's, Bernie nodded toward the window of a kitchen store. Ted and Mike were examining an upscale kitchen display of cream-colored cabinets with a honey glaze and loads of glass doors. The island in the middle featured country baskets on shelves underneath the counter. It contrasted with the other cabinets and stood out by virtue of its forest green color.

I'd walked by the place a hundred times but hadn't paid much attention. Glancing up at the sign, I realized that it wasn't Finkel Kitchen and Bath. Mike rapped on the window and motioned us inside.

"What do you think?" he asked.

"Very nice European styling. Reminds me of a kitchen in an English manor. Needs different handles, though." Bernie trotted off and returned in a moment, carrying a burnished bronze handle that he held up to a cabinet. It would make the entire setup look like it had been in a house for ages.

"Good eye," said Mike. "We can get this for a song. They're switching out their display, and if we feature a sign with their name saying where the cabinets can be bought, they'll knock off even more. Best of all, we wouldn't have to special order it. They'll deliver it as soon as we're ready. All we have to do is make it fit the existing space."

I'd seen Natasha's ultramodern kitchen and knew it wasn't her style. Carefully, I asked, "Is this what Natasha had in mind?"

Ted guffawed. "Natasha lives in a dream world. If she wants a kitchen fast, she doesn't have a lot of choices."

"Have you seen her sketch?" Mike held it out to me and pinched his nose as though it smelled bad.

An island appeared to float in the middle of the kitchen, and the stark cabinets along the walls hung midair with a two-foot space underneath them. Reminiscent of Nolan's bedroom at Rooms and Blooms, I thought. Must be the latest trend.

"It's like a spaceship kitchen. A little too stark for me." Mike rubbed his beard. "She thinks all the cabinets should be stainless steel and she wants copper countertops. Do you know what copper costs?"

I preferred a warmer kitchen myself. I lowered my voice so the owner wouldn't hear me. "Have you heard from Kurt? I thought you might go there for cabinets."

"Ted insisted on going to Kurt's store. Against my better judgment, I should add," said Mike. "There's a handwritten sign that says 'Closed Due to Illness.' "

# EIGHTEEN

**From "The Good Life" :**
**Sophie's Painting Tip**

The new latex paints are much easier to use than oil-based paints. If you're painting indoors, look for a semi-gloss latex paint because they're washable. Flat paints don't clean up as well once they're on the walls. Use oil-based paints for painting outdoor items exposed to weather because they will hold up better under tough conditions.

For best coverage, paint walls in an X or zigzag pattern.

"Illness?" Did that mean Kurt had turned up? I had to know. But I couldn't very well call Earl Finkel to ask if her husband was alive. Maybe I could talk Natasha into calling.

Bernie and I left Ted and Mike to work out details with the owner of the kitchen store, and we headed for the paint store.

I'd expected to return to Mordecai's with color swatches, but Bernie and I both pointed directly to a shade called Tuscan Umber. Warmer than beige, but not quite gold, it contained just enough orange-red to seem like the afternoon sun shone on it. The paint store owner agreed to deliver it, and soon we were on our way back.

As we approached the house, I could see that Natasha had been busy aggravating designers. Like Empress of the World, she stood on the porch and directed everyone who carried out a load of Mordecai's belongings. I couldn't help wondering if the secret bequest had landed in a box and rested somewhere on the porch.

Bernie and I paused on the steps. "Makes me want to go home and pitch everything I don't need into the dustbin," said Bernie.

I shuddered at the thought of strangers emptying my drawers and going through my closets. It didn't bother some people, though. A few nosy neighbors were already rummaging through the boxes on the porch.

"Scavengers. Every last one of them." Francie came up behind us. "They're not doing that to me when I go," she muttered. As we scooted by Natasha and walked inside, Francie growled, "So don't hold your breath. You're not getting your mitts on my stuff."

Unfortunately, Bedelia happened to be in the foyer, and she immediately cackled, "No one would want any of your dime-store treasures."

"What are you doing here?" demanded Francie.

Bedelia lifted her chin as though she thought she was lording something over Francie. "I'm assisting Iris in redecorating the master bedroom. I would have won the

Design Guild Award, you know, if Jean hadn't cheated me out of it."

Francie sputtered, "That was more than twenty years ago. Get over it already." She shot me a pleading look and I said, "Okay, fine. You're officially on team Sophie."

Francie flashed a beat-that grin at Bedelia.

While Bernie and I ate lunch, Francie puttered around the house, no doubt annoying Bedelia. The paint arrived exactly as Mars hauled a ladder into the family room.

Mars and Bernie took down the curtains, full of decades of dust, while Francie and I searched for old sheets to cover the beautiful oversized desk.

Natasha sent us to the third floor, where she'd discovered a trunk full of old linens.

As we neared the top of the stairs, Francie sniffed. "Stinks like old house up here."

I thought I heard footsteps. "*Shh.*"

We quietly snuck along the hallway to the bedroom on the right and discovered Nolan trying to slide his bequest key into the trunk lock. Francie sneezed, giving away our presence.

Nolan jerked upright, and hid the key in his pocket.

"I don't think it's locked." I walked over to the trunk and lifted the lid.

"Just what I was looking for." Nolan helped himself to an old bedspread. "Thank you." Holding his head high, he swept past us.

Francie laughed out loud. "What a phony."

So much for his lack of interest in the bequest. He was clearly snooping around just like his former classmates.

I collected a few old sheets, hoping they wouldn't be moldy or stinky, and we returned to the family room, where Bernie had managed to coax Mars into helping him wash the walls. I could hardly believe my eyes when I saw

Mars at work, since he was virtually useless around the house when we were married. Natasha spied him from the doorway to the kitchen, and I could see the ire in her expression.

She pulled me aside. "Did you see what Mike and Ted have planned for the kitchen? I was counting on it to impress the Guild judges, but I can't put my name on this kitchen. It's not at all what I requested or envisioned."

I felt a little bit guilty for even thinking it, but this was my chance to get her to call Earl and find out if Kurt had turned up. "Why don't you phone Earl one last time to see if Kurt is doing the kitchen? You wouldn't want a conflict if he showed up tomorrow."

She pulled out her cell phone and dialed. Her assistant, Beth, worked diligently emptying drawers of cutlery, her hair shielding her face from view.

Although it was wrong, I intended to eavesdrop and drifted toward the butler's pantry. A shout of laughter came from the dining room, and I couldn't help sticking my head in to see what was going on.

Posey, Mike, and Ted noshed on pizza around the grand dining room table. The gleaming, polished top had all but vanished under a pile of puzzle pieces. A mound of pieces rested in the center of the table, and all around it they had begun to group similar pieces. Frankly, it surprised me that they took on the daunting task with such enthusiasm. "Looks like you're making progress."

Ted chuckled. "It's like being in Mordecai's class again."

"I'd forgotten so many of the wacky things we did." Mike helped himself to another slice of pizza. "I never thought I would have so much fun coming down here for Mordecai's bequest." He stopped grinning. "Sorry, Posey. I know Tara was your friend and that you're hurting."

Posey moved two pieces of the puzzle to another section of the table. "It's okay, Mike. You didn't know Tara."

"But you did?" I asked.

Posey focused on the puzzle. "I run an after-school art class for underprivileged kids once a week. Tara used to come by to help." Posey's voice trembled. "She'd just made some major changes in her life and finally had everything on track."

Posey collapsed into a chair and rubbed her forehead, while Ted and Mike shared a look. I wanted to find out more, but Posey seemed too fragile to question, and at that moment Natasha burst into the dining room.

"You won't believe this! Earl has officially filed a missing person report with the police for Kurt." Natasha clasped her hands under her chin. "What on earth could have happened to him?"

Official report? I couldn't help thinking of what Wolf had said last night. A police officer in Tara's position wouldn't normally be pursuing a missing person. So how did she know about Kurt if a report had only just been filed?

Mike blew a mini raspberry. "Kurt missing? Give me a break."

"I thought all of you were friends," said Natasha.

"Once. But I learned the truth about Kurt the hard way," said Mike. "He's a conniving thief who robbed me of my share of the business we built together. Trust me, if he's missing—it's because he wants to be missing. He probably killed somebody and is hiding out." He bit into his pizza with a vengeance.

Posey threw him a dark look. "That's not funny."

Mouth full, Mike held a hand over it and said, "Sorry. I was just speaking hypothetically. . . ."

Natasha launched into a dull discussion of their kitchen

demolition schedule, so I headed back to the family room. Bernie had pried the lids off a couple of paint cans and it looked as though we were finally ready to paint.

Francie took on the tedious task of painting around trim work with a brush. Her dexterity surprised me, and I said so.

"It's not like I've never painted a wall before." She concentrated and produced an immaculate line of paint along a window frame. "They used to call this street 'Decorators' Row' because of Bedelia and Mordecai's wife, Jean. I wasn't really a decorator, of course, but back in those days, none of us had much money, and we helped everyone paint their houses. I painted walls in your house, Sophie."

I rolled paint onto the wall near Francie. "So you knew Mordecai before he retreated from society."

"He was one miserable human being. He was so sour, I'm surprised he made it as long as he did. Most people recover from their problems, but he just never did get over losing Jean."

"Was she ill?" asked Bernie.

I painted in an X, pleased by how well the paint covered the dingy walls.

"Jean? She was strong as an ox. Ran off with another professor. One of Mordecai's colleagues. It was quite the scandal back then. The talk of the neighborhood."

"You'd think he'd have gotten over it eventually," said Bernie.

"He took it hard. He won some kind of fancy prize for excellence in teaching, and we all thought that would bring him around, but it didn't. He withdrew. Didn't want to come to our parties anymore. Just kept to himself."

"*Awwk.*" Hank flew across the room and settled on a high shelf in Mordecai's bookcase. "Your cheatin' heart."

Nina stood in the doorway.

"He better not poop up there," I warned. "Or get in the paint."

And then, to my complete surprise, Mochie scampered in.

"What's he doing here?"

Nina ditched her jacket. "I had to bring Hank. I've been out all day, and he was so agitated when I got home that I didn't have the heart to leave him alone again. And I brought Mochie over because Ted's wife wants an Ocicat. We were talking about them at the banquet, and I thought if he saw what a cool cat Mochie is—he might be persuaded to get one."

She scooped him up and paraded into the kitchen to show him off to Ted.

Bernie and Francie paused to admire Hank, who thrilled them by calling, "Pick up the phone!"

On her return, Nina sidled over to me. "I've been following Earl."

"Did you find out anything?"

"Well," she murmured, picking up a paint roller, "if my husband were missing, I don't think I'd be at the mall shopping."

# NINETEEN

From *"Ask Natasha"*:

*Dear Natasha,*

*I'm an avid watcher of your show, and I know better than to forget the sixth wall—the ceiling. White paint is boring, but I'm positive I can't talk hubby into doing a mural. Are there any other clever options?*

*—No Michelangelo in St. Michaels*

*Dear No Michelangelo,*

*Use wallpaper. Bribe hubby to help you wallpaper the ceiling one weekend. You can use a mural-type wallpaper or a simple pattern, whatever suits you. The results will be fabulous.*

*—Natasha*

"What do you think that means?" I asked Nina.

"What are you two gabbing about?" demanded Francie.

"Kurt is still missing. His wife put a sign on the door of his business that says it's closed due to illness, but she's been out shopping."

"I don't think I know his wife." Francie continued her precise edging with the paintbrush.

"Sure you do. She was at the dinner last night, wearing the, uh, revealing dress." Mars grinned.

"You know her?" I asked.

Bernie, hard at work, laughed. "Even I heard about her. She made quite an impression on a number of chaps in attendance last night."

"Oh, the one who needed a bib to cover up the saline Boobsey Twins." Francie continued painting. "I wondered who she was. The Guild doesn't attract many women like that."

"It attracted you."

I looked over my shoulder to see Bedelia assessing the family room.

"Did you buy all the necklaces they had at the second-hand shop?" asked Francie.

Bedelia fingered one of the many bulky beads hanging around her neck. "You never developed a sense of style, Francie. Pity."

"I hope you don't think that getup is haute couture."

"You wouldn't know haute couture if it sat on you."

Fortunately, Hank flapped his wings and landed, rather elegantly, on Bedelia's shoulder. "Hank couture. Hank couture."

"Now that's a smart bird." Francie snickered.

Bedelia seemed quite agreeable to Hank sitting on her shoulder until he tweaked her giant glasses with his beak.

Bedelia shrieked and batted at Hank.

Nina ran to the rescue. Devilish Hank screamed, extended his wings, and tried to grab Bedelia's glasses again. This time Bedelia wisely protected her face with her hands, and before Nina could grab Hank, he flew back to his spot in the wall unit. Bedelia adjusted her glasses and appeared to take it all in stride. I noticed, though, that she kept a wary eye on Hank as she skirted the paint trays on the floor to get a closer look at Mordecai's woodwork.

Bulky rings adorned the hand she ran over a carved scroll. "This is so ornate. I never would have expected it of Mordecai. Then again, he and Jean had exquisite taste." She paused and stared around the room. "I wonder what Mordecai did with all those wonderful things they had? So many beautiful paintings and architectural pieces from their travels. Do you remember those, Francie?"

"Yeah. Did you find any masks or pottery, Sophie?" asked Francie.

Bedelia opened a drawer and peeked inside. "Even the artwork in the house seems wrong. Didn't they have a bunch of Russian icons?"

"Maybe Jean had the eye for the good stuff and demanded it in the divorce," said Francie.

"Divorce?" Iris loomed in the doorway. "What a dreadful choice of paint," she said, gazing around. "Nana, I thought you said Mordecai killed his wife and hid her in the house."

"That was the rumor at the time." Bedelia slid the drawer shut.

"That's baloney, and you know it, Bedelia." Francie sounded angry. "There was never any such rumor. Mordecai adored Jean."

With an odd glance at Francie, Bedelia steered Iris toward the door. "We'd better hurry if we're going to that fabric store you mentioned."

Bedelia escorted Iris out rather quickly with Francie watching them. "That old coot. Still lying about everything."

"I gather Bedelia didn't care for Jean." I rested my paint roller, and stepped back to check out the transformation.

"Actually, everyone loved Jean. She had such style and class. The kind of person who would never slight anyone—unlike Bedelia. She saw the best in everything. Small wonder that Mordecai was so crazy about her."

Nina applied one last stroke of paint to the wall. "So how come Bedelia didn't like her?"

"Most wives don't think much of the women who steal their husbands." Everyone in the room focused on Francie. "What?" she said. "It happens."

"You're saying that Bedelia's husband left her for Mordecai's wife?" asked Bernie. "And that's what sent Mordecai into such a tailspin that he never recovered?"

"That's the way it happened." Francie appeared unaware that she'd handed them a bombshell.

We hadn't known Jean or Bedelia's husband, but their infidelity years before somehow came as a shock. "That's why Bedelia moved to Florida?" I asked.

"Yes. They sold the house up here. It's across the street a few doors down, the off-white one with the pale blue trim on the windows and the gate. I imagine she couldn't afford to keep it when he left her."

Nina checked her watch. "Four a.m. in Hong Kong. I believe I'll go home and place a call to my husband."

"He'll be asleep," said Bernie.

"Precisely." Nina collected Hank from his perch in the bookcase. "If anyone else happens to be sleeping in his cabin, I might catch her unaware."

As Nina left, without Mochie, I noted, Natasha poked

her head in. "Mars, you're still here. And with the ladder, too. Good. I've decided to take on the foyer because it will be the first and last room all the visitors see. I've bought the most gorgeous wallpaper in hues of gold that would go nicely with these walls, actually, and touches of teal that should brace everyone for Nolan's living room. But I need help putting it up, dear."

It was an enormous request of anyone, but asking Mars to wallpaper was like asking me to sing opera. I envisioned a broken leg in his future.

He must have, too, because he said, "No way."

Natasha fixed a pout on her face that was so fake, I wanted to retch. "But I really want this wallpaper on the foyer ceiling of my new house."

I guessed Natasha had overused the pouty face, because Mars snorted and said, "No paper, no new house."

Natasha's nostrils flared. "You'll help Sophie but not me? I bet Ted would do it for me."

Mars fixed her with a calm stare. "I hope he pays for the house, too, because I'm not moving." Mars fled for the door without waiting for a response.

Natasha eyed Bernie, who would have been my top choice for the job. But Bernie prided himself on not being suckered into Natasha's schemes. He smiled at her politely and bent to place lids on the remaining paint cans.

That left Francie, who flicked a hand at Natasha. "Sorry, I'm on team Sophie. I don't cross to the dark side."

"Honestly, you're all a bunch of cowards." Natasha hoisted the ladder and carried it into the foyer.

Amused that she would think the ladder could be tall enough, I trailed after her, followed by Bernie and Francie. Thanks to the staircase, the ceiling was two stories up. At the very least, Natasha would need scaffolding.

She set up the ladder and gazed at the ceiling. Her mouth twitched to the side, and she turned to glare at those of us who watched her.

The front door opened, nearly hitting her, and she lashed out at poor Humphrey. "Watch where you're going! What do *you* want anyway? Oh no. Don't tell me. You're on team Sophie, too."

He looked so bewildered that I had no choice but to rescue him from Natasha's misplaced wrath. "Of course he is. Come on in and tell me what you think of the color." That sounded totally bogus, but it was all that came to me at that second.

I ushered him into the family room, where he blurted, "I just came from the medical examiner's office. The killer shot Tara in the back of the head with a nail gun."

Just like the person who sabotaged Ted's pond.

Francie listened from the doorway. "I thought you had to have an air compressor to use one of those things. Wouldn't that have been a little bit obvious? They're incredibly noisy."

Bernie shook his head. "They make cordless ones, too. That's what I used in making the window seat."

Humphrey whirled around to face him, his fists clenched.

"Hold it, Columbo," I said. "Dozens of people at Rooms and Blooms probably used one of those things. And the killer could have borrowed or stolen it from someone, too. Natasha even had one on display. I don't think Bernie's your man."

Natasha flew into the family room. "Do you think it's too much to ask my assistant to get up on a ladder and install the wallpaper on the ceiling?"

We answered as one. "Yes."

"Remind me not to hire any of you. I think it's part of the job."

"And what will you do while she's putting up the wallpaper?" I asked.

"Sophie, you're so innocent. I will be supervising, of course. That's what an employer does."

Poor Beth. She hadn't wanted to stay, and now Natasha was badgering her. But the thought of Beth reminded me of Humphrey.

Taking him by the arm, I towed him into the kitchen. "Beth? I'd like you to meet someone."

I swear I saw abject terror in her eyes when she turned around.

# TWENTY

From *"Ask Natasha"*:

*Dear Natasha,*

*My foyer is a dingy nightmare. I can't afford what I really want—an artist to paint a mural that will make the walls appear taller. Any suggestions?*

*—Low Ceilings in Lower Keys*

*Dear Low Ceilings,*

*Trompe l'oeil means "to deceive the eye," but you don't have to be a talented painter to do that. Try painting stripes on your wall one to two feet wide, from floor to ceiling. Alternate similar colors, like light and dark yellows. They'll automatically make your foyer feel taller.*

*—Natasha*

"Beth, I'd like you to meet my friend Humphrey." There. I'd finally introduced him to someone.

They nodded shyly and said hello. And then we all looked at each other in awkward silence. Maybe this was why opposites attract. Someone had to be assertive enough to get the ball rolling.

I was about to say that Humphrey was an undertaker, then reconsidered. That might not be the most appealing way to present him. "Humphrey and I grew up together—Natasha, too."

"That's nice," said Beth.

Maybe this had been a totally stupid idea. I didn't know anything about Beth or what might appeal to her. "Where are you from?" I asked.

"Nevada." She answered with one word and stopped. Not much of a conversationalist.

Humphrey finally came to life. "Nevada has the highest rate of cremation in the country."

Not exactly what I'd hoped for. Beth cringed, and I could see her pull back physically. I forced a chuckle. "Humphrey's a mortician."

"I see. If you'll excuse me, I need to finish up. Natasha's crew will be here to shoot the demolition in the morning."

It looked like I would have to host a dinner after all, to throw them together in a more congenial atmosphere. "Beth, I'm having some friends over for dinner the day after tomorrow. Nothing fancy. I hope you'll be able to join us."

Unless I misread her expression, she was surprised. "That would be nice. Thanks."

I couldn't quite get a handle on Beth. She seemed to run hot and cold. "You *are* coming back to work tomorrow, aren't you?"

She swallowed hard. "I need the job. As long as Natasha doesn't make me break my neck papering that foyer ceiling, I guess I'll be here."

I tried to give her a reassuring smile. "We'll be around as reinforcements if she gets pushy about it."

When I turned back to Humphrey, I realized he'd wandered through the kitchen to the butler's pantry and was observing Posey as she painted on the dining room wall. She'd already completed enough for me to see that her trompe l'oeil involved arched double doors that looked as if they'd just been opened. Mike and Ted were still working on the puzzle.

I wedged past Humphrey, who murmured, as if in a trance. "Posey . . ."

"Looks great already, Posey," I said.

She didn't stop working. "These two morons suggested I paint it to look like the dining table is inside an aquarium."

Mike chortled but concentrated on the puzzle pieces. "The inside of an aquarium would match Nolan's living room. She could even add little fishies."

Ted laughed. He'd tilted his chair back so that it rested on two legs, and he looked rather leisurely.

I peeked into the living room and understood what had upset Iris and driven her to insist on decorating the master bedroom instead of the dining room. Nolan's painters had covered the walls with a shockingly bright turquoise. The window trim and molding shone sparkling white in stark contrast. Maybe he was planning to hide a lot of it with curtain fabric? I tried to reserve judgment, but I didn't have high hopes for Nolan's living room.

"It's dreadful, isn't it?" called Posey. "I think Iris was an idiot to give up the dining room, because anything would look great after that."

Humphrey watched Posey with adoration, making me

glad I'd planned to throw him together with Beth at a dinner party. Posey was as wrong for him as Tara would have been.

Posey turned around, paintbrush still in hand, and exclaimed, "Mike! You did it!"

"Huh?" He frowned and studied the table.

She pointed as she said, "That section goes with the one I was working on down there."

Mike tried to lift as many of the joined pieces as he could, but some tumbled to the table. He ran them down to the end. "Where? Which one? Oh, I see. You're right." He fit the pieces in and retrieved the rest.

"It's an owl. An owl!" screamed Posey. "Like on the wall unit Mordecai built."

We rushed into the family room, each of us breathless in spite of the short distance we'd run. Posey's eyes sparkled with anticipation. She grabbed the owl on the left and tried to move it. Nothing happened.

I glanced around for Bernie. A woodworker might be able to figure it out. But it appeared he and Francie had called it a day.

Mochie pawed at the base of the wall unit, stopping every few seconds to lower his head and sniff.

"There must be some kind of latch," said Mike. He examined the owl on the right, carefully running his fingers over the wood like he was reading braille.

Ted stared at the key in his hand, then looked at the unit that covered the wall as though he was trying to figure out the mechanics of how it might work.

"Here! I've got it." Mike waved with one hand while holding the other in place, "There's a groove. It's ever so subtle—just the size of a fingertip."

We watched as he exerted gentle pressure on the wood and swung the owl to the side, revealing a keyhole.

It took them all of four seconds to realize that Posey's key fit into the lock. She tried to turn it, but it didn't budge.

She pointed to the other two owls. "We have more keys. Let's try those."

In short order, we located similar finger depressions and swung the owls to the side. Mike's key fit into one lock, but Ted's key didn't fit into the other one.

"Kurt's key," I blurted. I dashed out the door and across the street to my house. I seized Kurt's bequest package and ripped it open as I returned to Mordecai's. I entered the family room, triumphantly holding a key that slid perfectly into the remaining keyhole.

"Okay," said Mike, "everyone turn on three. One . . . two . . . three."

I twisted Kurt's key and felt a small shift, as though something could move but was jammed.

"Still nothing," whined Posey. She backed up and looked at the wall unit. "There are five keys," she mused.

Mike's expression changed to hopeful. "Of course. He's forcing us all to work together. There we were, stupid fools, thinking he had something special for each of us, but the old man was teaching us another lesson. We all have to be present to open the thing."

Posey moved closer again. "Are there other owls? Smaller ones, maybe, that we overlooked? This darned thing is so ornate."

And huge. I stepped back and tried to focus on the detail, one section at a time. Posey, Ted, and Mike used a more tactile method, feeling the wood.

A small, lightly gilded swirl caught my eye, and I moved closer to inspect it. Close up, it appeared to be a snake, but Mordecai hadn't gilded the head. The snake coiled on a disk with a tapered edge that made it appear to be part of the unit, but when I tried to move it, I could feel a bit of give. "Is there a snake like this on the other side?" I asked.

"A snake?" Posey peered over my shoulder. "I just saw it!" She shuffled to the other side.

"A snake and an owl?" Mike laughed. "Mordecai had quite an imagination."

"The snake is a guardian of freshness," I muttered.

"How would you happen to know something like that?" asked Posey. "Are you an archaeologist or something?"

I could feel my face flush at her question. "A German cookie company came up with packaging that prevents cookies and crackers from getting soggy from the moisture in the air, and because of that, they use the snake as part of their logo. It symbolizes preservation, protection from danger."

"Cookies?" sputtered Ted. "That's absurd."

"I'm going to call Nolan." Posey pulled out her cell phone. "If we can move the snakes and there are more keyholes, we're going to need his key."

She drifted into the kitchen and I could hear her talking excitedly.

"I was beginning to think this would never happen." Mike couldn't hide his grin. "Mordecai was a sly old fox."

"You must have been his favorite class for him to go to all this trouble setting up a puzzle for you," I said.

Posey marched back, her expression sour. "That stupid Nolan." She lifted her chin and mimicked his superior tone, " 'I've no interest in Mordecai's garbage.' "

Mike laughed. "He's full of baloney. Haven't you noticed him snooping around here? He's every bit as curious about the bequest as we are."

"I'm not beneath swiping the key from him," said Posey. "What say we go get it?"

# TWENTY-ONE

From "*Ask Natasha*":

*Dear Natasha,*

*I am the kiss of death to orchids. I adore them, but I can't keep them alive. Is it too tacky for words to use fake ones?*

*—Orchid Killer in Kill Devil Hills*

*Dear Orchid Killer,*

*You don't have to resort to faux flowers. Frame gorgeous pictures of orchids and hang them in groups. Or stencil orchids on curtains and pillow covers to carry out your decorating theme.*

*—Natasha*

It seemed to me that Mike thought it over for a moment before agreeing. "I'll just get my jacket." He disappeared in the direction of the kitchen.

Although Humphrey had been with us for the past half hour, Posey stared at him and demanded, "Who are *you*?"

Humphrey didn't appear to be taken aback. He held out his hand and introduced himself.

"You met at the Rooms and Blooms banquet." I threw her a lifeline so she could save face.

Although Posey came across as brusque and self-possessed, a shadow crossed her face at the mention of Rooms and Blooms. "I'm sorry. I don't remember you." She turned abruptly and dashed out, Humphrey on her heels.

I ran after him, and Ted followed me. I managed to catch Humphrey's arm in the foyer. "This isn't the time." I wanted to add, *and she'd chew you up and spit you out like a meat grinder*. But I refrained.

Ted cast his eyes toward the ceiling. "Always the drama queen. What would you want with Posey anyway? She's a nightmare. Trust me, I've known her for years. It's not a coincidence that she's still single. She's devoured every man who ever looked at her crossways, like a black widow."

"I believe you're quite mistaken. Posey has a gentle soul," said Humphrey.

"Watch your back," advised Ted, as Posey and Mike joined him. The three of them sauntered down the porch steps, still joking around. The sound of rustling leaves drew my attention, and for a panicked moment, I feared Mochie had gotten out. I leaned over the railing just in time to see Emmaline emerge from beneath the porch. Dried leaves and twigs clung to her matted fur.

"Posey, quick!" I shouted, "Grab her."

Posey was anything but quick. Instead of going for the dog, she glanced back at me, confused.

But Ted and Mike caught on. They leaped toward Emmaline, who sprang into the street and the path of oncoming traffic.

I flew down the steps and darted between slow-moving cars, holding up my arms to make them stop. Emmaline made it safely across and ran down the brick sidewalk like she was running for her very survival.

We dashed after her. She cut to the left and wiggled under a light blue gate.

Ted reached over the top and unlatched it from the inside. "Posey, stay here and block her from running out. Unless the gate in the back is open, she'll be contained."

Ted led the way and Mike, Humphrey, and I followed him into a gorgeous backyard. Winter jasmine bloomed in bright yellow masses around a brick terrace.

Emmaline snarfed food from a bowl near the back door while a long-haired orange cat lazily looked on but didn't budge from its position on a blue bench in the sun.

I crept up behind Emmaline, who focused on the cat food. My hands hovered over her back and, by some miracle, I was able to grab her. She wriggled, but there was no way I was letting go.

The others raised a little cheer, and I hoped the owner of the house wasn't home, because anyone would think we'd lost our minds running into the backyard the way we had.

We snuck out the front gate again. Posey, Mike, Ted, and Humphrey headed downtown. I watched them walk away before turning in the other direction. Only then did it dawn on me that Mike wasn't wearing a jacket.

Though Emmaline would surely have been more comfortable in her own home, I feared we would lose her again with so many people coming and going. Not to mention that she would be underfoot the next morning during the demolition.

I walked straight to Nina's house and rang the doorbell without loosening my grip on Emmaline. I could hear rustling inside, but it wasn't until I said, "Nina, for heaven's sake, I have Emmaline," that the door opened a crack.

Nina squealed when she saw Emmaline. But I held tight until we were inside and the door was safely closed. "She's an escape artist."

Nina bolted the door behind me and held out her hands for the little dog, even though she was clutching an open bag of Reese's Pieces. She hugged Emmaline to her, buried her face in the dog's fur, and burst into tears.

I knew she loved animals, but crying over Emmaline seemed excessive. Placing a hand on her arm, I asked, "Are you okay?"

Nina shook imperceptibly, almost like a shiver. "He's taunting me, Sophie. He killed Tara, and I'm next."

She'd lost me. I'd never seen Nina like this before. "Who?"

Hank flew into the foyer, singing "Kurt! Kurt!" which sent Nina into a frenzy. Holding Emmaline with one hand, she gripped my wrist and tugged me into her living room. I couldn't help noticing that she'd drawn all the drapes.

"Does this have something to do with Detective Kenner?"

Her cell phone rang. It lay on the coffee table, and she edged away from it like it was a coiled snake. I picked it up and saw what had upset her. The call was coming from Kurt Finkel. I pressed a button and said hello.

No one replied. I listened for background noises but couldn't pick out anything distinctive. The caller hung up. On a hunch, I scrolled back through her recent calls. All from Kurt Finkel. "Anyone could have his cell phone and be making these calls."

Nina wiped her eyes and dragged her hand down her face, exaggerating her haunted appearance. "If it's anyone, then why is that person calling me? Why would anyone except Kurt call over and over to frighten me?"

"It could be the cops."

That thought sent her into hiccups. "Call Wolf and find out."

Not a bad idea. In fact, it made me wonder if Nina and I should swap cell phones for a bit. That way I could call Wolf without it showing on my account. But he didn't answer his phone. "I bet he's in the convention hall."

"Let's go. I can't take it anymore. And I don't want to be alone."

I didn't think I was much protection, but something very strange was going on with Kurt. Whether he was dead or alive, the person placing those phone calls to Nina meant to upset her. I didn't blame her for being afraid.

Nina took a moment to feed Emmaline, *tsk*ing over the matted state of her fur, and then the two of us retrieved Mochie from Mordecai's house. He had curled up for a nap on the desk in the family room. I tucked him under my jacket to protect him from the cold air, and he was so exhausted from his outing that he didn't even wriggle in protest. I carried him home and deposited him in the chair next to the fireplace in my kitchen. He yawned before stretching out and closing his eyes.

When Nina and I stepped outside to walk to the hotel, she scanned the street like she was on alert.

"Do you think Kurt would wear a ski mask or be dressed incognito?" she asked.

"You've been watching too many sinister movies."

"And I always know how they're going to end, don't I?"

That happened to be true. Nina could always predict the ending. "But this isn't a movie."

"Soph, this is revenge. Kurt's still resentful about our breakup all those years ago."

I stopped in front of the blue gate where we'd captured Emmaline, and realized that it matched the description of the property Bedelia had owned. "I see," I said sarcastically. "In order to get revenge, Kurt has disappeared, worrying his wife and ignoring his business. Perhaps you can explain why he killed Tara?"

"Because they were having an affair."

"That's ridiculous."

"Is it? How do you think Tara found out about me so fast? Why would she show up at my house like she did?" Nina's cheeks flushed pink, and she shook a finger at me. "And who else would have stalked her? Her lover. Kurt had to get rid of her so his wife wouldn't find out." She took a deep breath. "And now he's after me."

We set off again at a fast walk. I churned through Nina's theories, but the more I thought about them, the fewer loopholes I could see. "Kurt thought his wife was out of town."

"Exactly. But his mistress wasn't. Tara must have seen us together."

"She threatened to tell Earl about their affair," I mused.

"So he killed her."

"Then why would he be after you? Did you threaten him?"

"No. But when I spurned him and shoved him away and he fell, it brought back all the old resentment from being dumped by me years ago."

I didn't want to think that Kurt lurked in the shadows somewhere, waiting to attack Nina. On the other hand, her theory wasn't entirely implausible.

We entered the hotel, and when we took the escalator down to the convention hall, it was teeming with cops.

Kenner saw us coming and blocked us at the door. "If you're looking for Wolf, you just missed him."

"Why does everyone think I'm dating Wolf?" I snarled.

My question hit home. Kenner couldn't hide his surprise. I was sorry I hadn't told Nina, though, since her astonished expression didn't do much to help me be believable.

I hurried to fill in the silence before she said anything. "We didn't attend the banquet as a couple last night, did we? Have you seen us in a restaurant together? Noooo. Honestly! I don't know why everyone thinks we're in a relationship."

"You're trying to pull one over on me," Kenner said haltingly.

"Oh, please!" I flapped a hand at him. "You're too sharp for that."

"Then why are you here?" he asked.

I wished I could think on my feet faster. I needed a reason pronto.

"We knew Tara, Detective," said Nina. "It's not like the police are the only ones upset by this tragedy. Are you making any progress?"

I expected him to rebuff Nina and tell her he couldn't divulge police information. But he puffed out his chest, and boasted, "We have a tape that may show her stalker. It's being examined now."

Well! Who knew that a little sugar could go such a long way with a sourpuss like Kenner? "That was fast work."

"When I'm in charge, we get results. I don't waste any time." He gazed right at me. "And I never sleep."

He looked like he hadn't had any sleep. His attentiveness sent goose bumps to my arms. I tried not to show my discomfort. "It's good to have a man like you on the case." I wanted to gag as soon as the words were out of my mouth. But if kissing up to him would get him off Wolf's back, not to mention my own, maybe it would be worth it.

"We shouldn't keep you any longer. Thanks for taking a minute to speak with us." How could Nina be so calm and collected when she'd been hysterical half an hour ago?

I thanked Kenner and we left. Nina stood in front of me on the escalator, turned around and said, "You're such a lousy liar. I really don't know why you bother."

"Thanks for covering for me. You think he knew we were lying?"

"The man's a dolt. But then, a woman can turn the head of the smartest man. It's all in how well you bat your eyelashes, Sophie." She raised her arm and waved at him.

Frankly, I didn't care to bat my eyelashes, and if I were going to, I certainly wouldn't bat them at revolting Kenner.

"Now what's up with Wolf?" she demanded as we left the hotel.

I explained about his middle-of-the-night visit. "I'll be your go-between," she said. "How romantic. Midnight assignations! And speaking of the handsome devil . . ." Wolf emerged from a bakery, noshing on a chocolate croissant. "I'll go talk to him about Kurt calling me. Be right back."

While I waited, I caught a glimpse of Posey browsing in a fancy florist shop. A bell rang when I stepped inside. Posey was admiring a set of white orchids in an aqua dish.

"They're gorgeous," I said.

"I'd have to win the lottery to afford them."

"Posey, I'm just wondering . . . you knew Tara well. Is there any possibility that she was having an affair with a married man?"

# TWENTY-TWO

**From** "THE GOOD LIFE" :

Dear Sophie,

Our home is red and black brick, and could be so much prettier. We're thinking about painting the brick, but my father says painting brick is always a mistake because when it's not painted, brick requires practically no maintenance.

—On the Fence in Greenacres

Dear On the Fence,

You're both right. Painting ugly brick can transform a home. But be sure you want the upkeep of paint. Removing paint from brick is an enormous undertaking and best done by grit blasting.

—Sophie

Pain invaded Posey's eyes. "You have no idea how much I wish I had pushed her about his identity."

So Nina was right! "Did she say anything about him? Any little tidbit that might help us figure out who he was?"

Tears welled in her eyes. "You sound like Wolf." She winced, and wiped her face with her fingers. "For the longest time he strung her along, and she was certain he would leave his wife. You know how unrealistic young women can be when it comes to a man. Apparently he was good to her." Posey wandered through the store as she talked, but I got the feeling that she wasn't really seeing anything. "Then one day she announced that she'd met someone else. Someone with whom she could make a life, and that she wasn't going to wait for her married man anymore. She seemed so happy."

Posey fingered a huge daisy head on a lush plant. "And now I can't imagine why I didn't butt into her life. Why didn't I ask questions? Why didn't I insist she tell me who those men were?" She accidentally snapped the daisy head off the stem.

"You couldn't have known."

"I was her friend. I should have made it my business."

"Is there any possibility," I asked gently, "that the married man could have been Kurt Finkel?"

"Of course not." But then she lifted her chin and I could see her jaw twitching. "Kurt is at least fifteen years older than Tara," said Posey. "But he *is* a randy sort, chasing anything in a skirt. And just the type a naive young woman might fall for—the way he dishes out flattery."

Posey cast an appraising look at me. "You must know something about Kurt and Tara, or you wouldn't have asked."

"It's just a theory. You go way back with Kurt. Back to your college days?"

"We all hung together then. Kurt, Mike, Nolan, Ted, and me. I guess you could call us Mordecai's gang."

It finally dawned on me that she was the only girl in the group. "Did you date one of the guys?"

She laughed. "Oh, to be young and carefree. Kurt and I were an item for a while. Ted was shy around women, Nolan was only interested in money, and Mike, on whom I should have set my sights since he's the nicest of the bunch, had Hot Lips."

Kurt had been a busy devil. He'd chased Posey, Nina, Earl, and maybe Tara, too. I was beginning to think Nina had been right, and Kurt had been the one who strung Tara along. "But you broke off your relationship with Kurt."

She ran her hands through her dark cerise hair. "After the sabotage of the cottage we built for Mordecai's class, nothing was ever the same again between us. We were a motley group in some ways, but we were friends for the longest time. I was the artist, of course. Mike was the practical one. He could build anything. Ted's family didn't have a lot of money. He was actually in landscape design, and the rest of us studied interior design. He was always doing lawn work for spending money. Nolan was already arrogant and impossible. I'm surprised we tolerated him. And then, Kurt—he was a ladies' man from the get-go. I guess Mordecai was fond of us because we were different from his architecture students. We had fun with his little games and puzzles."

I tried to get her back on track. "But then something happened to the cottage you built."

"We all blamed each other, though I always suspected Nolan. The rest of us worked hard and had invested too much of ourselves to ruin our creation."

"Speaking of Nolan, I thought you were going to get his key."

"*Hah*! He stepped out of the store. I think he knew we were coming. Mike said Nolan probably went to see if he could figure it out for himself, but we're not worried—he can't get in without our keys."

Through the store window, I could see Nina looking for me. I left Posey perusing floral displays and returned to the sidewalk.

Nina launched herself at me. "Don't leave me like that!"

"You were with Wolf."

"He was very interested in my theory about Kurt. And he said to tell you he would try to swing by tonight."

I told her what I'd learned from Posey and that her theory about Tara seeing a married man was dead-on.

"Soph, do you mind if I stay with you?"

"Of course not. It'll be fun. Let's find a funny chick flick and try to forget about Kurt."

"Don't expect me to be good company."

I could see the terror in her expression. "We'll be fine." At least I hoped we would be.

"Could we stop by the market? I have to buy dog food for Emmaline."

"Sure." We needed something comforting for dinner anyway. Even though dusk was settling on Old Town, as we walked along the bustling streets it was hard to imagine that Kurt could be lurking somewhere, or that he could be planning anything malicious toward Nina.

I trusted she would be safe at the tiny market. While she picked out dog food, I asked the butcher for pork chops, buying extra in case Wolf appeared around dinnertime.

As we walked home, someone called my name and I turned to find Camille.

"Sophie, I know you have an in with the cops. Has Wolf given you any indication when they'll release the conference hall? Some idiot actually bought that mini bulldozer, but the cops won't let the owner remove it."

"No one has told me a thing."

"I have half a mind to tell them to contact that Detective Kenner directly. Let him deal with the irate vendors."

"I'm glad to see you," I said. "Everyone's looking for Nolan. We need his key."

"Key?" Camille asked, clearly clueless.

"The key from Mordecai's bequest."

Camille's eyes narrowed. "Bequest? That sneaky scamp. He didn't say a word about a bequest."

"I got the impression he wasn't very interested in it."

Her nostrils flared like a bull's. "He wouldn't be, of course. He thinks money rains from the sky. But I care. What does this key look like?"

She promised to bring it over if she found it. And from the excitement on her face, I had a feeling she was headed straight home to look for it.

Nina and I walked back to our neighborhood without incident. No sign of Kurt or anyone else who might pose a danger. We stopped at Nina's so she could pick up Hank, Emmaline, and a change of clothes. Mochie would have an interesting night with his company.

By eight o'clock, we'd settled into cozy nightwear. Me in flannel pajamas with a sleeping dog print, and Nina in a Carolina blue silk nightgown, with matching quilted bathrobe.

I lit a fire, which warmed the kitchen and went a long way toward dispelling any creepiness. Mochie, who had never feared dogs, didn't seem to mind when Emmaline wanted to play. But he kept a watchful eye on Hank, especially when he sang "Your Cheatin' Heart."

I wished I could stop the bird from screaming Kurt's

name because it only served as a reminder, and I could see the tension in Nina ratchet up each time.

I sprinkled paprika, rosemary, salt, and other spices into a plastic bag, added olive oil, and slid in the pork chops to marinate. In the meantime, I peeled and quartered beets and preheated the oven to roast them. Each time Hank said "Kurt," I said "Nina."

Nina caught on to the game and coached Hank to say "Mochie" and "Sophie." During the time it took to cook sweet onions and crimini mushrooms in butter for a creamy mushroom risotto, Hank learned to squawk all our names.

Just for Nina, I melted dark chocolate with butter, mixed in eggs, sugar, a breeze of flour, a dash of salt, and generous splashes of liqueurs for sinfully delicious and ever-so-comforting Mudslide lava cakes.

And then, in the peaceful quiet of my kitchen, Hank squawked, "*Awwwk*! Kurt! Kurt!"

Nina was pouring wine into tulip-shaped glasses and promptly knocked one over, spilling white wine onto the counter and the floor. "Dear heaven," she said, pointing at the kitchen door. "I nearly had a heart attack."

I recognized Francie's fishing hat through the window in the door. When I opened it, Francie bounded in almost as fast as her golden retriever, Duke. He skidded to a halt in front of Mochie and Emmaline, and polite sniffing ensued. Francie unhooked his leash, and Duke collapsed to a crouch.

Francie tossed her hat and coat onto a chair and shivered. "It's freezing outside. Doesn't seem right to have snow flurries. I've never liked February. It's cold and muddy, and Valentine's Day is always a disappointment." She looked at Nina. "Your husband remember to send you anything?"

Nina held out her right hand, displaying a stunning ruby and diamond ring.

"You don't look very happy about it," commented Francie.

"He bought it before he left for his trip and arranged to have it delivered to me on Valentine's Day. But he was so busy with that evil woman on his cruise that he didn't bother to call me. All things considered, I'd have preferred a phone call to the ring."

"Nina, you've been out a lot. Maybe he just couldn't reach you," I said.

"Caller ID, Soph. You can't get away with that baloney about trying to call anymore."

"Smells good," interjected Francie. "What's for dinner?"

"Pork chops."

"That's a relief." She stuck out her tongue. "Chicken is all they serve at the old folks' home. White bread and chicken and Jell-O. No wonder they all have digestive problems. I've been visiting a friend a lot lately, but I can't stomach their food."

Nina dabbed at the wine she'd spilled. "Knock next time."

"I can't help it if you're a nervous wreck because you murdered someone." Francie stood before the fire, rubbing her hands. "I hope you have plenty of pork chops, because Humphrey just cruised the street in his hearse. I bet he'll be here as soon as he can find a place to park."

Nina muttered, "Like I needed this."

"Safety in numbers," I replied softly, though I was a little disappointed because the presence of Humphrey and Francie probably meant Wolf wouldn't stop by.

At least when Hank screamed "Kurt! Kurt!" again, Nina was prepared. But Duke wasn't. He danced in circles, barking nonstop at Hank, who watched him with a superior attitude from the top of a kitchen cabinet. That set Emmaline to yelping, and Mochie leaped to the safety of the window seat. Nina opened the door to Humphrey.

"I'm so sorry. I'm intruding on your dinner," he said. But he didn't hesitate to remove his coat and make himself comfortable.

Nina poured more wine and set the table for four while the pork chops simmered on the stove and I finished the risotto.

I set bowls and platters loaded with food on the table, family style. Duke waited patiently for a morsel from Francie, but little Emmaline, at a loss without Mordecai, pranced nervously, as though she wasn't sure who might feed her.

Humphrey helped himself to roasted beets. "Adam Swensen came by the mortuary today. He's getting a lot of calls from people who think they'll get to live in Mordecai's house if they take the dog." He cast a glance at Francie. "Including Iris Ledbetter."

Francie's fork clanked to the floor. "That's not possible, is it? It's bad enough having to deal with Natasha at one end of the street, but a Ledbetter? Say it can't be!"

I handed Francie a fresh fork. "Isn't it her grandmother you don't care for?"

"They're exactly alike. They even look alike. It's just a matter of time before she wears ridiculous oversized glasses like Bedelia. She already overaccessorizes."

Nina cut into a juicy pork chop. "Mordecai's lawyer asked me to find someone to take care of Emmaline. How does this work? What if Emmaline doesn't want to sell the house?"

I sat back and relaxed, sipping my wine. "I thought the lawyer had to sell Mordecai's house and that was the whole reason for redecorating it."

Humphrey helped himself to more risotto. "As I understand it, the house was left to the dog in trust, so it's probably the lawyer who's making the financial decisions. I think he'd rather sell the house. If the person who takes the dog lives there, the lawyer would have to manage it like a rental until the dog dies. The person who takes Emmaline will probably get some kind of compensation and money for her needs."

Waving her knife in the air, Francie declared, "That's why they want it. I bet you anything that Bedelia wants to move back up here from Florida to live with Iris. They can't afford to buy the place, so they think the dog will get them that mansion. Shoot, I'll take the little fur ball before I let that happen."

Very softly, as though she was afraid of the answer, Nina asked, "Any word about Tara's killer?"

Humphrey spoke confidentially. "They collected a few dozen of those cordless nailing machines from the vendors. Including the ones Natasha was promoting."

# TWENTY-THREE

From "THE GOOD LIFE" :

Dear Sophie,

I love and need the storage provided by the built-in wall unit in my bedroom. But it looks just awful. I would rip it out and replace it if the cost weren't prohibitive. Any suggestions?

—Despairing in Destin

Dear Despairing,

Paint the wall unit and install a soft fabric or wallpaper that matches your decor on the rear wall of all the openings to unify it. If you have a modern decor, consider painting the back a bright contrasting color to show off your belongings.

—Sophie

"And," said Humphrey, "Posey was caught trying to sneak a cordless nailer out of the convention hall late this afternoon."

"Posey!" That surprised me. "I thought she was close to Tara." Or had she put on an act for me? "That must have been quite a scene." I could imagine feisty Posey protesting.

"She had no choice but to turn it over to them."

"How soon will they know if they have the murder weapon?" I asked.

Humphrey savored a forkful of risotto. "They're all in a complete tizzy because the cops are used to working with ballistics tests for guns, and there are technical issues about whether the same tests will work on nail guns."

"Seems like they would," opined Francie. "There must be marks on the nails like there would be on bullets, so that they can be matched up to the machine that shot them."

Nina and Humphrey stared at Francie, who looked at them with an innocent expression. "I watch the news. I read mysteries. You don't get to be my age without learning a few things."

Nervous Nina ate like a lumberjack. I swiftly steered the conversation to Humphrey's love life and invited Francie and Nina to join us for dinner the next evening, when Beth would be present. Humphrey's face flamed at the mention of it.

Dessert proved to be a huge success, and even Nina loosened up when she dipped the outer cake part of the lava cake into the liquid chocolate that oozed from the middle. Or maybe the wine began to relax her.

In spite of the fact that Nina probably outweighed Humphrey and undoubtedly could pack more of a punch, she talked him into sleeping on the family room sofa overnight, buying my safety in numbers argument. While

Nina and I tackled the dishes, Humphrey walked Francie home. On his return, Nina insisted on a quick nightcap, no doubt to quell her fear of the killer, but we all turned in early.

We woke to the annoying *beep . . . beep . . . beep* of an enormous truck backing near Mordecai's detached garage to deliver a Dumpster. It was barely light outside. Construction people started early. Snow was blowing, and after spending days in the spring atmosphere of Rooms and Blooms, I felt as though winter had returned. I threw on a cozy purple turtleneck and a pair of jeans with an elastic waist that were tight anyway. I knew I shouldn't have indulged in the chocolate lava cake last night. Even worse, the cold, dreary day had me thinking French toast for breakfast.

I hurried downstairs, Mochie scampering ahead of me, and found Humphrey in the kitchen, a blanket wrapped around his shoulders.

"How does this coffee machine work?" he asked.

I shooed him away, and coffee brewed in minutes. Humphrey soon clutched a mug, and I whisked eggs for French toast even though I knew I had gained three pounds just thinking about it.

Nina, Hank, and Emmaline joined us as I tossed frozen blueberries into a pot, added a little water and a splash of orange liqueur, and let it come to a boil.

"That truck was annoying enough to wake the dead," Nina grumbled. "I hope we won't have too many more mornings like this."

The blustery weather turned into a mini blizzard. Since I was already dressed, I clasped a leash on Emmaline and took her out to do her business. Wind whipped my hair, but

I didn't dare let the little escape artist loose in my backyard. Even though it was fenced, if there was a tiny chink, I felt certain she would find it and wriggle through.

Emmaline didn't care for the weather much, and we returned to the house in minutes. After dredging thick slices of bread through beaten eggs spiced with cinnamon, I placed them on the griddle, turned the berries to a simmer, and looked forward to a hot breakfast.

Mochie and Emmaline feasted on leftover pork chops, and in spite of the weather, Hank sang at the top of his little lungs.

While we ate, Nina talked Humphrey into accompanying her to her house while she changed clothes. I felt sorry for her and scrounged around until I located the Taser that Mars had given me months ago. She clung to it like I'd handed her a life preserver.

I filled a huge carafe with coffee, packed some cups, and headed for Mordecai's house. I dodged Natasha's TV crew in the foyer and peeked at the chaos in the kitchen from the family room doorway.

Ted and Mike calmly removed kitchen counters, but Natasha scurried around like a dizzy rodent. On the other hand, Beth, who'd seemed so uncomfortable the day before, watched quietly behind the cameramen, handing everyone what they needed before they asked for it, like she had a special radar.

Behind me someone sniffed the air. "Do you smell smoke?" asked Bernie.

"Maybe it's coming from the kitchen?"

He poured coffee for us from the carafe I had brought. "Smells like someone built a fire last night."

"It's probably coming in from outside. I imagine a lot of people have fires going in this weather."

He sniffed again. "So what's next, boss?"

I forced myself to pay attention to the room I had to decorate. "A sofa, I suppose. A big cushy one, with matching ottomans, so two or more people could comfortably lounge while watching a movie on TV."

"Works for me," said Bernie. "And where do we obtain such a lovely sofa?"

I puffed air into my cheeks and exhaled slowly because I didn't have an answer.

"On loan, darling." Bedelia had paused at the door for dramatic effect. She waltzed into the room and held her hand out to Bernie for kisses. "Surely you don't think designers can afford all those marvelous antiques they use? They borrow everything from dealers—like on consignment, but it's really a loan. You stick a little card on it saying where it can be bought and return it in perfect condition."

"Only one problem, I'm not a designer."

She chuckled. "Sweetheart, we read your column every day in Florida. There's not a dealer around who wouldn't lend you whatever you want."

I wasn't so sure about that, but it was worth a shot.

Speaking in a husky voice, like Mae West, Bedelia said to Bernie, "Come upstairs and see me sometime, big boy."

Bernie just laughed, but I was beginning to see what Francie found so annoying about her. I was immediately ashamed for that thought since she'd told me how to furnish the room at no cost.

Posey barged into the family room, fingering her key. "Are they all here?" She looked into the kitchen. "Where's Nolan?"

"I haven't seen him yet."

"I suppose the unbelievably wealthy get to sleep late." She whipped out her cell phone and dialed. "Oh, and now they're not answering their phone, either." She tucked her cell into her pocket. "I knew this would happen. He has no consideration for anyone."

She stomped into the foyer, and I could hear her demanding, "*Where* is Nolan?"

I explained to Bernie about the keys and why she needed Nolan, but before I could finish, I heard Posey shriek, "No!"

Her dark eyes huge, she dragged a hapless man into the family room. "You won't believe this. Tell her about Nolan!"

He wore a work shirt that bore the DuPont Fine Antiques logo, and held up his hands in protest.

I thought Posey probably intimidated him. "What's going on?"

The man looked at Posey as though he didn't dare take his eyes off her lest she attack him. "Mr. DuPont was mugged last night. He's in the hospital. Mrs. DuPont called this morning and told us what to bring over here for the living room."

"Mugged? In Old Town?" I asked. No one was ever mugged in Old Town.

"In his own backyard. They have a detached garage, and someone hit him over the head when he was walking to the house. Mrs. DuPont found him."

"Will he be okay?" asked Bernie.

The man shrugged. "I hope so. Mrs. DuPont wants to shut down the antiques shop, and if she does, I'll be out of a job."

Posey turned to me, holding out her hands. "Now what? What if he dies and no one can find the key? The rest of us spend our lives wondering what Mordecai left us?"

I didn't have any answers for her. But I did note that she cared so little about Nolan's well-being that she wasn't a bit concerned about his condition. All Posey could think about was opening the wall unit.

Bernie looked from Posey to the wall unit. "Show me the locks."

Posey pursed her mouth in displeasure. "It won't help." Nevertheless, she flipped them open.

"Don't you suppose Mordecai built in a back door?" asked Bernie.

Posey's eyebrows shot up. "You mean another access?"

"He had to," said Bernie. "One person couldn't turn all five keys simultaneously by himself."

I felt a complete fool. Bernie was right. Unless Mordecai had help or never tested his wall, there must be another way to open it.

Bernie walked back and forth, examining the wall unit. "There has to be a main latch, something that will release all the locks at once." Beginning on one end, he opened each drawer and cabinet, and worked his way to the other end until they were all open. He ran his fingers over his chin as if deep in thought.

Bernie released a cry and lunged at a cabinet. He placed his head and one arm inside and reached up.

A *clunk* resounded through the room and an unpleasant odor tinged the air.

Bernie stepped back. "Did anything move?"

I shook my head.

"The mechanics are behind those bookshelves. See how it's shallower than the rest?"

Now that he'd pointed it out, it seemed so obvious. "But how does it open?"

Bernie grasped the middle section and rolled it effortlessly straight into the room, exposing a dark doorway. Only a few feet back, a gilded icon gleamed as though it hung midair.

Posey applauded. “A Russian icon. That’s the treasure!”

Bernie ventured forward first. “We need a flashlight.”

He stepped through the doorway. “Forget the light,” he called. “Old Mordecai thought of everything.” He flicked on a weak overhead light and said, “Sophie, you’d better call Wolf.”

Naturally, I did the illogical thing and stepped through the doorway into what was really only a stair landing. Freezing air accosted me, and I shivered. To my left, a narrow staircase led downward. Near the bottom of the stairs, no doubt the source of the unpleasant odor, lay Kurt.

# TWENTY-FOUR

From "*Ask Natasha*":

*Dear Natasha,*

*While other husbands are at sporting events, mine goes to auctions and collects paintings. I was thrilled at first, but now the house is overflowing. I can't stand being in our living room anymore because it's so full of artwork I don't know where to look. Though most pieces are gorgeous, it's such a clutter that none stand out.*

*—Embarrassment of Riches in Goldsboro*

*Dear Embarrassment,*

*Consider yourself lucky to have such a discerning spouse. Select the longest corridor in your house and install track lighting on the ceiling. Hang paintings in a straight horizontal line at eye level on both sides and train a spotlight on each painting to highlight it.*

*–Natasha*

Wolf had said not to call him, but somehow I didn't think he'd anticipated a situation like this one. Nevertheless, I gave Wolf's number to Bernie and asked him to make the call. Meanwhile, I peered down the stairwell with Posey crowding in behind me.

Kurt looked very much as he had when I saw him in the window seat. I could make out a blotch of dried blood on his head.

"I don't think we need to check for a pulse." Posey clutched my shoulder with a clawlike grip. "Who'd have thought Kurt would come to an end like this?"

Her hand grew heavy, and I realized that her legs couldn't hold her. I swung around to support Posey, and together we shuffled into the family room, where I released her onto Bernie's window seat.

The loud banging of demolition still issued from the kitchen unabated. No one else in the house knew about our discovery yet. Maybe it was better that way. I'd rather have Wolf manage crowd control.

As sick as it was, one person would be somewhat relieved to hear that Kurt was dead. I dialed Nina's number to tell her she didn't have to worry about Kurt's vengefulness anymore. But as her phone rang, a flurry of activity erupted in the foyer. Emmaline's claws scratched against the hardwood floor as she raced in, Hank flew to Mordecai's enormous desk, and Nina and Humphrey trailed after them.

"You have *got* to be kidding!" cried Nina when she saw the open wall unit.

Exactly as she said that, little Emmaline sped to investigate the opening. I rushed to grab her, but only arrived in time to see her scamper down the stairs. Hank flew at me and landed a few steps lower.

I eased down so I wouldn't scare him. No such luck. He hopped farther down the stairs, pausing briefly to inspect Kurt.

Nina scurried down the first few steps and stopped behind me. "Is that Kurt? Oh no! I did kill him." She pressed her hands over her mouth and moaned. "Dear heaven, Sophie, I really killed him." She collapsed onto the stairs. "My life is over. I never should have pushed him. I never should have gone out to dinner with him. This is it. I'm going to prison."

"Nina!" I shook her shoulders. "Stop that. If you had killed him, we would have found him in the living room where he fell."

"What if he died later? What if he had one of those head injuries that seems so innocuous but causes blood clots or hemorrhaging?"

It was a possibility, of course. But it didn't really make sense. "So he hid in the window seat, crawled out, figured out how to open this hatch, closed it behind himself, fell down the stairs, and died? I don't think so."

Emmaline barked from somewhere, and Hank shrieked, "Nina! Kurt!"

Her face tear-stained, Nina scrambled to her feet, pushed past me, and approached Kurt's body. She hesitated only a second before jumping over it, calling, "Emmaline, here Emmaline!" At the bottom of the steps, she turned left and disappeared.

So much for not disturbing the scene of the crime.

"Sophie!" Her voice wavered back to me. "I need help. Quick!"

Had she fallen? I sprang over Kurt. At the bottom of the stairs, I turned the corner and made my way, somewhat hesitantly, along a corridor set up like an art gallery. Fabulous paintings and icons lined both sides of the walls with special lighting that glowed upon them. At the end of the hallway, a door stood ajar, and the concrete floor gave way to dirt. I shivered as a blast of frigid air coursed through, and I hesitantly stepped into a crawl space under the house.

Nina appeared to be trying to keep Hank away from something. "I'm going to grab Hank. You seize Emmaline, or she'll shoot out through that hole again."

Nina pointed behind her at a torn screen in an air vent that led under the front porch. No wonder Emmaline had managed to disappear when she was under the porch. She must have been using the little gap to come and go, hiding under the house at night.

Bent over, I calmly treaded behind Nina, so I wouldn't alarm Emmaline. Luckily, she was digging furiously and didn't notice me sneak up behind her. I picked up the little dog and saw why her tail was wagging. She'd befriended the momma cat Nina had been following. Four orange and white kittens cuddled close to their mother.

It would have been a sweet scene, except for one grisly thing.

# TWENTY-FIVE

From "The Good Life":

Dear Sophie,

I feel like I live in a zoo—one husband, two kids, three dogs, four cats, a gerbil, and eighteen fish. The white rooms in magazines always call to me but I know that's wishful thinking. Any suggestions for colors that hide fur?

—Zookeeper in Tiger

Dear Zookeeper,

Unless all your pets have matching fur, I can't recommend a fur-concealing color. But there are some things you can do. Buy furniture that's easy to wipe clean, like leather. Keep inexpensive throws on your furniture that can be easily swapped out and washed. And instead of carpeting, consider hardwood floors or tile, which make it easier to clean up fur and messes.

—Sophie

Behind the mother cat, dirt was heaped in a long, firm mound the size of a body. Someone, presumably Mordecai, had planted a cross at one end. The whole thing looked like a grave. But could that be? If so it would be the second grisly discovery of the night.

Nina shrieked at me, and Emmaline tried to spring from my arms. "Grab a kitten! We have to get them out of here before the police arrive."

The sound of footsteps on the stairs clued me in that it was probably too late. I clutched Emmaline in one arm, and two squirming kittens in the other as I headed for the stairs.

Nina came behind me with the mother cat and the rest of her babies. But when she caught sight of Wolf she promptly dumped them in his arms, saying "Wolf, would you bring those babies and the mom upstairs, please?" Then she caught Hank and led the way back to Kurt's body. Wolf followed, never noticing the mound of dirt with the cross, and I brought up the rear, thinking what a lucky break it was that Wolf loved animals. I couldn't imagine Kenner collecting kittens and carrying them to safety.

But once we were upstairs, Wolf turned the cat and kittens over to Bernie and Humphrey. "Get them all out of here."

I handed the kittens to Posey so I could hold onto Emmaline more firmly, and we all marched straight to Nina's house. Once inside, I asked, "Are you okay being alone now?"

Nina threw me a doubtful look. "Well, I don't think Kurt is hiding in my home anymore."

The rest of us left Nina to get the animals settled and returned to Mordecai's house.

Wolf immediately asked questions about the wall unit and how we came to open it. Someone from Natasha's camera crew finally noticed when the police arrived in full force. Natasha, Beth, Ted, and Mike crowded into the family room, only to be shooed away by the police.

Kenner tromped in, none too pleased to discover that Wolf beat him to the scene of the crime. Which made me all the more glad that I'd heeded Wolf's advice and asked Bernie to make the call to him. Even if Kenner checked the phone records, it wouldn't look like I had phoned Wolf.

After assessing the situation, Kenner asked me to step into the living room. Crisp white curtains hung at the windows, and huge white pieces of artwork tamed the loud turquoise walls. A white sofa and chairs had appeared, and assorted throw rugs in white with a hint of an aqua border decorated the floor. Even the lamps were silver and white. To break the overuse of white, Nolan had injected a few pillows and decorative items of orange and navy. Much to my surprise, I found it an appealing room—bright and lively.

Kenner stared at me, his eyes half open over his bony nose.

Nina had scored points by being super friendly with him, but I just didn't have it in me to flirt with Kenner. The mere thought of it made me gag. I had to be a little friendly, though, and tried to smile. "What a mess, huh?"

"You found Kurt's body?"

"Actually, I think Bernie saw him first." Though I hated to be too forthcoming, now that Kurt was definitely dead, I thought Kenner should know about Mordecai's bequest and how we came to open the wall, so I told him the story.

Kenner frowned at me. "So what was the bequest?"

"The paintings in the basement, I suppose."

He paced the living room. "Mordecai was a weird old guy. Very paranoid. I guess it wouldn't be too unlikely that he would hide something he thought valuable. But if someone tossed Kurt down there, it meant one other person knew Mordecai's secret and how to get in."

It was the first sensible thing I'd ever heard issue from Kenner's lips. For once he wasn't trying to pin something on me. And he was right. Clearly, someone else knew how to open the wall unit. But who?

"Someone," said Kenner, "whom Mordecai trusted enough to dispense the keys to his heirs. Someone who knew how to get the paintings out in case his heirs weren't smart enough to figure it out for themselves."

My moment of generosity toward Kenner fizzled. I had a bad feeling he didn't mean Mordecai's lawyer. "I had no prior knowledge about any of this. How could I know anything was behind the wall unit? I was as clueless as everyone else."

A young police officer appeared in the doorway and coughed to get Kenner's attention. "Sir? There's something else down there."

Kenner's eyebrows twitched, and he looked at me in astonishment.

I nodded, probably not the best thing to do, but that mound in the basement had looked a lot like a grave to me.

Kenner wasted no time bounding through the crowd of cops. I followed, unsure if I would be thrown out, but no one paid me any attention. Outside the window, I could see a crowd gathering on the sidewalk, and it looked to me like Natasha and Iris were spatting.

I couldn't make it back down the stairs into the basement, though. The narrow entrance teemed like a beehive with police. Since there wasn't anything I could do, and no one had told me to stick around, I sidled toward the front door and stepped out. Yellow police tape already draped across the porch. I ducked under it, and before I reached the sidewalk, Natasha latched onto me.

"They're saying Kurt's been killed. Is that true? Did you see him?"

"I'm sorry, Natasha. I'm afraid the rumors are correct this time. It looked like someone tossed his body down hidden stairs."

"Hallelujah." said Iris. "There's one man who got what he had coming. At least I won't have to be afraid to come to work here anymore."

I was about to ask why she'd been afraid when Natasha turned on Iris. "The man is dead. Show a little compassion. Have you no feelings?"

Iris's left eye narrowed. "Now we'll never finish the house on time for the tour. We were working against the clock as it was. It's your fault, Natasha. You're the one who hired Kurt without asking me. You're the one who brought him into that house. Believe me, I'm going to make sure that Camille is painfully aware of that fact. You can kiss the Guild Award good-bye."

Iris ambled off in a huff, and Natasha buried her face in her hands. She dabbed at tears with a dainty robin's egg blue handkerchief. "Am I smudged, Sophie?"

"Not too badly." It was a lie, but who cared?

"That vile woman. She's going to ruin the Guild Award for me. How barbarically rude to be so pleased about someone's death! She should lose the Guild Award for that reason alone. I don't know why Camille stuck me with her."

Beth wandered up. "Excuse me, Natasha. Will you need me the rest of the day?"

Natasha looked at her as though she were confused. "Given the circumstances, I suppose you can take the rest of the day off."

Beth thanked her. "I'm a little shaken. Besides, I have a dinner party to go to tonight, and I wanted to do some shopping." She smiled at me and left in a hurry, but not before I noticed her hands trembling.

I was glad to hear that she was getting out. Then it dawned on me that she meant *my* dinner party—and I hadn't done a thing to prepare for it. Unless I hustled, there would only be a few of us present. "Care to come to dinner tonight, Natasha?"

Her mouth twisted. "I suppose you need help?" In a bored tone she asked, "What's the theme?"

Theme? Who needed a theme for a dinner party? "It's just friends getting together."

"That's not a theme." She covered her eyes with her hands for a moment. "How can you think about a party when Kurt is dead?"

Good question. If I hadn't promised to get Beth and Humphrey together, I wouldn't be thinking about it at all. "It will be very small."

"As long as Iris isn't on the guest list."

I assured her that wasn't the case and headed for home to call a few friends. When Nina didn't answer her phone, I peered from my kitchen window and saw her marching toward Mordecai's house.

I flew out the door after her, but she was way ahead of me. She marched up the stairs and ducked under the police tape. I arrived in time to hear her say to Detective Kenner, "I can't live with this on my conscience anymore. I killed Kurt Finkel."

# TWENTY-SIX

From "THE GOOD LIFE" :

Dear Sophie,

I love to entertain but everyone ends up in my kitchen, which is far past its prime. I can't afford to remodel it. How can I spruce it up without emptying my bank account?

—Broke in Beverly Hills

Dear Broke,

Paint is always the quickest fix. A bold red shade on the walls will add instant drama, and a pastel can provide the background for a romantic look. Take the doors off your cabinets and display your dishes on the shelves. Collect colorful dishes at yard sales and hang them together in a display. Add a dried wreath, or vintage trays, and don't be afraid to use your favorite serving pieces as decoration.

—Sophie

"Nina! Stop. He'll believe you," I protested.

"He has to know the truth. I can't go on this way." Her back straight and her chin up, she faced Kenner. "It was an accident. A terrible nightmare of an accident."

Kenner's thin lips pulled into a lizardlike grin. "How did you open the wall unit to push him down the stairs?"

"I didn't. The last time I saw him, he was lying on the living room floor. He came on to me, and I pushed him away, and he fell. I didn't know anything about the wall unit or the stairs behind it." Nina spoke in a matter-of-fact tone, as though she were confident.

Kenner's gaze drifted to me. "Nice try, Ms. Norwood. But whoever killed him knew how to open that wall and had the strength to pull dead weight inside. Maybe Wolf helped Sophie with that part."

"No!" Nina cried. "You have it all wrong. How can you be such a dolt when I'm standing here confessing to you? I'm telling you the truth, and it had nothing to do with Sophie or Wolf."

At the word "dolt" a shadow crossed Kenner's face. His beady eyes became black with anger. "Somebody threw him down those stairs. Unless you had help, I don't think you have the strength."

"Hey! I play tennis. I'm in great shape."

"Get out of here," he snarled. "I have work to do."

Nina walked out with me. "I'm so sorry, Soph. I never expected him to turn on you. I had to clear my conscience and tell the cops the truth. You understand, don't you?"

Of course I did, though I thought she ought to have consulted a lawyer first. "Do you feel better?"

"Not a bit. That Kenner is just odious." She paused and turned to me. "We're going to have to figure out what happened. We can't leave it to Kenner. There's no telling what kind of cockamamie story he'll invent."

"How are we going to do that? We've been looking for Kurt for days. There are only two choices. Either he died when you pushed him and he fell, which means someone popped him into the window seat and then hid him behind the bookcase when I left the house—or he was alive when you left him, in which case anything could have happened. Though if he was alive, it seems like someone would have seen him somewhere before he was murdered and shoved down those stairs."

"He had to be alive, Soph. He moved his car and made those phone calls to me."

"Unless the killer did those things."

Nina's eyes flicked open wide, and I was sorry I'd suggested the killer had called her.

"Someone knows I killed him and is after me now."

"Nina!"

"Seriously, Sophie, what if someone else was in the house that night and saw me push him? Ohhh, this is very, very bad. No one has tried to blackmail me, but why else would someone make those frightening phone calls to me?"

I stopped walking and focused on Nina. "Are you saying that someone was hiding in the house, happened to see you push Kurt and leave, then took the opportunity to kill Kurt, and for some reason has been calling you from Kurt's phone?"

Nina's face had gone completely white. "That's exactly what I'm saying."

I found a hole in her theory. "Then why plant him in the window seat? Why not just throw him down the stairs right away?"

"To scare me."

I wasn't sure I believed that. "Why would this mysterious killer think you would be the first to open the window seat? By all rights, it should have been Bernie who found him there."

Nina glanced up and down our block, reminding me of the way Tara had scanned the street. "It's blowing snow again, and I have to get vitamins and food for Mom Cat."

Nina's abrupt non sequitur made me wonder if she was flipping out, but I figured I'd play along. "I have to pick up something for dinner. We can go together."

She nodded. "Good. I'm not going anywhere by myself."

An hour later we were in the grocery store, looking at vegetables, when Nina announced, "It's Earl."

"Where?"

"Not here. Earl is the murderer. Don't you see? Earl suspected that Kurt was having an affair with Tara. She must have been the one who was tailing Tara. Then, to trap Kurt, she told him she was going out of town, but that night, instead of seeing Tara, he went out with me. Earl killed Kurt and Tara, moved his car, phoned me—and I'm next on her list."

"On whose list?" We turned to find Camille listening in. Several of the store's take-out containers rested in her cart, including two tall cups of chicken soup.

"How's Nolan?" I asked.

"He's home from the hospital and conscious." She wearily shoved hair out of her face. "The mugger attacked from behind and took his wallet. Thank goodness he only got a few hundred dollars and credit cards. The police have already all but dropped the case, as far as I can tell. There's just nothing to go on, and a mugging pales in comparison to the murder of a cop."

"But Nolan will be okay?" asked Nina.

Camille waved a hand. "His ego is more bruised than anything else. He's supposed to rest a few days, but he'll be fine."

"I gather you've heard about Kurt?" I asked.

She hadn't, so Nina filled her in. Camille gripped the handle of her grocery cart so hard that her knuckles shone white.

"What's happening to us? It's as though the Guild were cursed. Of course, some woman probably killed Kurt"—Camille lowered her voice—"if not his wife. He was such a womanizer. You know Iris refused to work with him. She even brought charges against him once."

Nina seemed appalled, but I wanted to know more. "What happened?"

Camille shot me a knowing look. "She claimed he groped her, but honestly, I always wondered if it wasn't the other way around—she groped him and he rebuffed her. After all, she did drop the charges, so I always suspected they might have been trumped up."

That explained a lot about Iris's behavior. But it also made me wonder if she could have had anything to do with Kurt's death.

"Good heavens," said Camille, "look at the time. I'd better get back before the nurse wonders what happened to me. She suggested I make chicken soup for Nolan from scratch. Can you imagine?" Chortling to herself, she hurried toward the checkout counter.

Nina and I moved on. I selected a lovely leg of lamb

for dinner, red-skinned new potatoes, and fresh springtime asparagus. The avocados looked so gorgeous, I decided to make a salad with red onions, strawberries, and avocados, topped with a balsamic vinaigrette. I didn't want to spend a lot of time on dessert and hoped I could locate my recipe for Grand Marnier pound cake.

We checked out, and after a quick stop to buy pet food, we wound our way through Old Town and back to our neighborhood just in time to see a covered body, Kurt's body I assumed, being removed from Mordecai's house and placed into an ambulance. Snow flurries blew around Wolf, who watched the process with a group of cops.

I longed to invite him to dinner, but knew he would only say no. Too bad. He would have enjoyed a roast leg of lamb.

In spite of all the police vehicles cluttering the street, I lucked into a parking space in front of Francie's house. Nina refused to go home alone, and when she spotted Francie watching the activities at Mordecai's, she recruited her as a bodyguard. I was shaking my head over her paranoia when Posey showed up unexpectedly and grabbed my arm with such vigor that I nearly dropped the bag of groceries I carried.

Her eyes flaming, Posey growled, "Tell me everything, or I'll go to the police."

# TWENTY-SEVEN

**From "The Good Life":**

Dear Sophie,

I hate cluttered kitchen counters. Between the mixer, food processor, coffeemaker, toaster, and bread machine (and that's only the beginning), I feel like I live in an appliance store. My kitchen designer suggested appliance garages, but the mixer and food processor are too big and I'll lose counter space. Any suggestions?

—Too Many Appliances in Apalachicola

Dear Too Many Appliances,

I'm very fond of under-counter pop-up storage. Sometimes called mixer cabinets, they're the perfect solution for large appliances. The appliance rests on a shelf that pulls out and raises to countertop level. A huge benefit is that they leave the countertop clear for ingredients, even while you're using the appliance. When you're done, the shelf and appliance lower back into the cabinet, out of sight.

—Sophie

I tried to wrest away from Posey. "What on earth are you talking about?"

She followed me to my gate. "You're at the root of this, Sophie. You're the only one who knows what's going on."

That was an exaggeration. I didn't even understand what she was talking about, and I told her so as I unlocked the door to my kitchen.

"There were five of us in the beginning."

"Five?" I asked, setting the groceries on the counter.

"Five of Mordecai's students were invited to the bequest party. Kurt was knocked off first. Then someone went after Nolan but didn't succeed in killing him. That means Mike, Ted, or I will be the next victim."

I slid the leg of lamb into the refrigerator, thinking there must be something in the water that was causing everyone to be so paranoid. "Oh, that! Before his death, Mordecai and I had a long talk about murdering everyone invited to his bequest party." I felt guilty for being sarcastic when I turned around and saw the frightened expression on her face. "Posey! I didn't know anything about the bequests or that you five were Mordecai's students once."

"Are you sure Mordecai is dead?"

"That's my understanding."

"Did you see his corpse with your own eyes?"

"Why would I? I didn't even know Mordecai very well. All of you knew him much better than I did."

"Why would he bring us together and kill us one by one? Why would he strike that kind of terror in us? Either he's alive, or he contracted with someone to kill us on his death."

"I think that's unlikely. Isn't it possible that Kurt's death and Nolan's mugging had nothing to do with Mordecai?"

She winced. "Please, Sophie. You seem like a nice person. Isn't there anything you can tell me?"

"I don't know anything," I insisted. "Maybe you can tell me something. Why the five of you? And why would you even imagine that Mordecai would want to harm you?"

Posey sagged into one of the chairs by the fireplace. "I always thought Mordecai liked us. Maybe he came to hate us because of the cottage we built." Posey rubbed her face with both hands. "We got so much publicity. It was tiny, of course, but we left it in stages so people could see how it was constructed. One wall didn't have any plaster on it, so the straw showed. I painted my first trompe l'oeil wall there, and Mordecai's wife, Jean, helped me enormously. I learned so much from her. TV crews came to interview us while we worked, but the attention we got was nothing compared to Mordecai. He was the envy of his entire department. We thought we were golden—the toast of the town. What a great item on our résumés."

Posey stopped talking and stared at her hands. "And then it all came tumbling down."

"You mean the cottage collapsed?"

"Not exactly. Mordecai and his wife invited us and a bunch of people from his department to their home for a party to celebrate. And that was when someone set the straw on fire." Posey held a palm to her forehead and closed her eyes as she spoke.

"Ted said that straw bales don't burn well."

"They don't. But loose straw burns like crazy. Somebody

kicked straw loose from the wall that wasn't plastered and set it ablaze. We were at the party when we learned that the cottage was burning. Thank goodness no one died. It was in the parking lot of a community center not too far from here. I'll never forget walking down there. We could see black smoke in the air from Mordecai's place. There were a few injuries, though, and the school was sued. That was the last time I ever saw or spoke to Mordecai."

"He didn't come to class anymore?"

"Classes were nearly over. He had a grad student finish up for him, and then we graduated and went our separate ways." Posey groaned. "Maybe Mordecai didn't believe it was sabotage. Maybe he blamed us for being inept and now, in some sick twist, he's taking revenge."

I sat down in the other chair and faced her. "Now listen to me, Posey. If Mordecai were alive, I hardly think we'd be selling all his possessions and redecorating his house. And the house wouldn't be up for sale. Besides, as far as I can tell, the paintings are your bequest. Surely he wouldn't have arranged for you to receive his prized artwork unless he really was dead."

She ran nervous hands through her dark burgundy hair, and it stuck up in odd spikes. "I would feel better if I knew someone who had seen him dead." She gasped. "I don't believe I said that! Don't misunderstand, it's not that I wish Mordecai ill, but who throws a bequest party? What kind of demented mind thinks so much about death that he would set up clues and keys? That kind of person might just fake his death to have the last laugh on all the rest of us."

"Why would he wait this long? If he harbored that kind of resentment, why didn't he kill all of you years ago?" Posey still appeared uneasy. "Why don't you talk to Humphrey? Maybe he can put your mind at ease."

"Humphrey? Who's that?"

"You met him at Rooms and Blooms and at Mordecai's house. He's a mortician, and he probably saw Mordecai's body."

"Or he was paid to play along." Posey stood up, her face haggard and old. "Two down, three to go. If I only understood why." She opened the door to leave and looked back at me. "I don't even know who to be afraid of."

The door never closed behind her. Francie and Nina appeared, hauling Nina's entire menagerie into my kitchen.

"For a person who doesn't even have a pet, you've managed to collect a zoo," I said.

"I thought we'd put Hank in the sunroom. Emmaline can run around, she won't be underfoot, but don't let her out. She's a digger. The ground is like a slab of ice and she almost managed to dig a hole under my back fence. Mom Cat probably wants some peace and quiet. Can I put her in the little bedroom on the third floor?" asked Nina.

"She needs a name," protested Francie. "You can't just keep calling her Mom Cat."

Their voices faded as they trooped up the stairs to settle the cats. I took butter and eggs from the fridge to let them come to room temperature, preheated the oven, and then launched into a frenzy, pawing through recipe boxes for my Grand Marnier pound cake recipe.

I found it, and before long, butter creamed with sugar in my KitchenAid mixer. I was pouring the glossy batter into a pan when Francie returned.

"What's for dinner?"

I reminded her about trying to set Humphrey up with Beth.

"Wish you'd set me up with somebody."

I slid the batter into the warm oven. "Why, Francie . . . you're welcome to invite a guest if you like."

"Thanks, but John Wayne is dead, just like all the other men my age."

"There must be someone." Thinking of Nina and Kurt, I said, "What about old boyfriends?"

"That's the right word for them—they'd be older than dirt by now. *Aw,* nobody's interested in an ancient artifact like me."

I would set her up with someone if I knew a gentleman her age.

Nina must have overheard Francie, because she had a sly look on her face when she returned to the kitchen. "Put yourself in my hands, Francie. I'll match you up."

"I don't know why the two of you bother to play matchmaker." Francie pointed at Nina. "Your husband is on the love boat on the other side of the world with a woman who has the hots for him." She swung toward me. "And you have Wolf right under your nose, and you still can't manage to be a couple." Francie laughed at us. "Not exactly adept at love yourselves. What can I bring to dinner, Sophie?"

I didn't want her to go to any trouble, but I knew she wanted to make a contribution. "Do you still have those napkin rings with hearts cut out? How about lending me those?"

"You got it." She let herself out the kitchen door but returned in a flash. "Quick, something's up at Mordecai's house."

Nina and I joined Francie outside. Traffic had come to a standstill, and people crowded the sidewalk. We dashed between news vans. I spotted Mike on the sidewalk and asked what was going on.

With sad eyes, he said, "They've found something else. There's a mound of dirt in the basement—with a human skeleton in it. Looks like good ole Mordecai murdered someone."

# TWENTY-EIGHT

From *"Ask Natasha"*:

*Dear Natasha,*

*I love your show and want to paint all my walls robin's egg blue. My husband thinks we should paint each room a different color. How do we resolve this?*

*—Singing the Blues in Coral Hills*

*Dear Singing the Blues,*

*I like the tranquil feel of one color throughout a house, too. But should hubby prevail, you must insist on a whole house color palette, limited to three complementary colors, to keep your home harmonious. Be sure to consider how adjacent rooms look when viewed through doorways. You wouldn't want the colors to clash!*

*—Natasha*

Even though I'd seen the mound in the basement and suspected there might be a body buried there, I'd been so focused on Kurt that it never occurred to me that Mordecai might be a killer. Someone had buried that body, and if it really was a skeleton, then Mordecai was the most likely person to have done it. Posey's questions about whether Mordecai might still be alive pummeled me. I'd been so quick to dismiss her idea as nonsense, but if he killed once, he might do it again. Was he a deranged old man, as Nolan had suggested? Even worse, what if he really had brought together his former students, intending to knock them off one by one? I shook my head, as though I could clear away such bizarre notions. Mordecai was dead.

"Do they know who it is?" asked Nina.

"They had to bring in a special forensic team," said Mike. "The second body has been there so long it's just bones. They're digging it up now."

Nina blurted, "So those stories about a corpse in his house are true after all."

"Hogwash!" Francie frowned at us. "It'll turn out to be the bones of a pig or something. Mordecai wasn't a killer. He didn't have it in him to kill anyone."

"I hope you're right," said Mike. "I really liked the old guy. I'd hate to think he had a dark side."

I hurried home since the pound cake was still baking in the oven. But while I set my banquet size dining table with a cheerful red tablecloth adorned with white hearts on the border, and added white earthenware plates, I couldn't help fearing the worst.

Something had prompted Mordecai to retreat from the world and become a recluse. Francie blamed his frame of mind on the fact that his wife, Jean, had run off with Iris's grandfather. But if the body in Mordecai's basement was really human, then it seemed rather likely that it might be Jean.

The buzzer on the stove went off, interrupting my thoughts. I pulled the pound cake from the oven, poked holes in the top, and drizzled a Grand Marnier sugar syrup over it. I set it on a rack to cool, and turned the heat to 425 degrees for the lamb.

Emmaline pranced at my feet. I suspected that she wanted a piece of cake, but I hooked a leash on her and took her out back instead.

She behaved well on the leash, rather remarkable for a dog who'd been carried around most of her life. I crouched to snap an errant twig, and she reached up to lick my cheek. How could a person have killed his wife, yet doted on a dog the way Mordecai had? It didn't make sense.

As we approached the door, Hank screamed, "Kurt, Kurt!" Now that Kurt was officially dead, Nina would have to teach him more words. Cute words, so someone would adopt him.

I selected unmatched candlesticks of varying heights and arranged them in the center of the table with red and white candles.

Checking the time, I returned to the kitchen, sprinkled my favorite lamb seasoning, a mixture of oregano, cumin, pepper, paprika, and rosemary, over the meat and slid it into the oven.

With everything well in hand, I dashed upstairs to shower and change. When I stepped from the shower, Emmaline and Mochie accompanied me to peruse my closet. Natasha would look gorgeous, as always, and make me feel dowdy. On the other hand, I didn't want Beth to feel underdressed. The blustery weather we'd been having made me want to snuggle up in something soft and warm.

In the end, I opted for casual twill slacks with an elastic waistline that wouldn't cut into me all evening, and a lilac sweater set with just a hint of bugle beads for a touch of bling. I peered from my bedroom window. Nina and Francie still waited on the sidewalk outside of Mordecai's home.

I knew that Francie and Mordecai's wife, Jean, had been friends twenty or more years ago. It must be torture for her to imagine Jean might have been murdered by Mordecai. It would tear me up to imagine such a horrible fate for Nina.

Back in the kitchen, I washed tiny red potatoes and placed them in a pot of salted water to boil. I chopped crisp parsley, slid it into a large mixing bowl, and added kosher salt and a generous knob of butter. When the potatoes were done, I would toss them in the bowl and their heat would coat them with lovely buttered parsley.

I took a minute to sprinkle the cake liberally with more of the Grand Marnier syrup.

Hank, safely confined to his cage in the sunroom, alerted me to Bernie's arrival by screeching "Kurt!"

Bernie rapped on the door out of politeness, but opened it himself and held it for Nina, Francie, and Francie's dog, Duke, who shot off to romp with Emmaline. Francie handed me the cute napkin rings.

Bernie carried a dish that he stashed in the refrigerator. "Mango oyster ceviche as an appetizer for the lovebirds." He winked at me. "I like to serve it in martini glasses, if that's okay with you."

While I cooked, he retrieved the glasses and Nina checked on the kittens. She returned with Hank, who appeared perfectly content to ride on her shoulder. Mochie, on the other hand, was a little bit too enthralled at seeing a bird on the loose in his own house, and his gaze never wavered.

I took a moment to slide the napkin rings over pristine white napkins, and the table came together nicely—and almost had a Valentine theme to please Natasha.

"Shall I light a fire?" Bernie asked when I returned to the kitchen.

"We'll be eating in the dining room."

"But we'll all be gathering in the kitchen beforehand." Bernie tossed some kindling into the fireplace and heaved a huge sigh.

"Is everything okay?" I asked.

He lit the kindling, stood, and rubbed the back of his head, mussing his hair more than usual. "I'm having some difficulty wrapping my mind around this business of Mordecai as a ruthless killer."

Nina nodded. "I never expected those rumors to be true."

"You knew him, Francie," said Bernie. "What do you think? Did you ever see a side of Mordecai that would lead you to believe he could kill someone?"

"I've been denying those rumors for more than twenty years. No one is more shocked than me. But I'll tell you this—every time I think I've seen it all, someone surprises me." She seemed tired when she said, "Under the right circumstances, I guess anyone can be pushed to the limit."

It was a scary thought, especially since I couldn't imagine any of us being propelled to that extreme. Fortunately, Hank piped up with a shrill, "Kurt! Your cheatin' heart!" And I knew someone else was nearby.

Mars and Natasha arrived at the front door, and for a moment, I thought they'd brought a guest of their own. Natasha shoved an elaborate arrangement at me. "I brought you a centerpiece for your table, since you always have such plain tablescapes." But I was so focused on the woman with them that I barely noticed it.

Heavy, uneven bangs covered her face in a trendy style. The sides and back were layered, and when she swept a strand of hair out of her eyes, I realized it was Beth. The frizzy, fried yellow hair was gone, toned down to a shiny dark blond. She wore trousers with a blouse and matching jacket that, unless I missed my guess, were brand-new.

"Thank you for inviting me." Beth seemed genuinely happy, almost confident, the way she'd been the day I met her at Rooms and Blooms.

I ushered everyone in, and while Mars hung their coats, I realized that I held a complex project that must have taken Natasha hours to make. Moss covered a wide, shallow bowl. Somehow, she'd managed to coax a branch full of twigs to stand up in it. The twigs bore miniature faux birds and nests filled with candy eggs.

Natasha supervised as I carried it into the dining room. I made it the centerpiece of the buffet.

"Sophie, dear, it's meant for the table. So much more interesting than plain candles."

"Aren't you afraid someone will tip it or break a branch when we're passing food?"

Clearly horrified by the thought, she quickly agreed to show it off on the buffet.

We returned to the kitchen, where I checked the temperature of the roast with an instant thermometer. Right on target. I pulled it from the oven and left it on the counter to rest while I finished making the gravy.

Natasha scowled and whispered to me, "Must Humphrey drive that hearse everywhere? Honestly, it gives people the wrong impression."

I glanced out the window. Sure enough, he'd driven the long funereal vehicle. "I guess it's just another car to him."

He carried a white box as he strode to the door. As soon

as Hank screamed "Kurt," I asked Bernie to open the door for Humphrey.

He set the box on the table and greeted everyone, doing a double take when he saw Beth. I hoped that was a good sign.

"What's in the box?" asked Mars.

"It's for Natasha."

# TWENTY-NINE

From "THE GOOD LIFE" :

Dear Sophie,

I love the Swedish country look but I'm at a loss about where to start. I have white curtains and white linens in my bedroom, but it just looks—white.

—Swedish Lover in Sweetwater

Dear Swedish Lover,

Start with the floors. Bleach or paint your hardwood floors to obtain that milky white effect that sets the scene for the Swedish look.

—Sophie

"For me?" Natasha appeared genuinely surprised and delighted. "Humphrey, you shouldn't have." She flashed him a beauty queen smile and said, "But I'm so glad you did!"

"It's not from me. Mordecai's instructions . . ."

She interrupted him. "I knew he left me something! You see"—she looked around at us and gloated—"when you take the time to be nice to someone, they do appreciate it. I was certain he wouldn't forget me." She tore into the box with everyone looking on. "What . . . Humphrey, what is this?" All friendliness had vanished from her tone and her mouth turned down in distaste.

"I was trying to tell you. It's Mordecai."

Natasha withdrew her hands faster than if she'd discovered a copperhead in the box. "I sincerely hope you're joking."

"I never joke about death. Well, rarely. *Hmm,*" he mused, "actually, since it's my line of business, I guess I laugh in the face of death all the time. But this isn't a joke. Mordecai left you his ashes."

Natasha gripped the arm of a chair and eased herself into it. I didn't particularly want to see the contents of the box, but I had a strong feeling her face had taken on the color of those contents.

"Mars, please remove the box." Natasha's chest heaved, and I wondered if she was hyperventilating.

"Do you need anything?" I asked, setting a glass of ice water in front of her.

Mars picked up the box and turned to me, biting his upper lip, no doubt to keep from laughing. Clipping his words in a pitch an octave too high, he said, "Where shall I put this?"

"Out of reach of the dogs. Seems disrespectful to put it—him—in a closet. How about on the console in the foyer? That way you won't forget it when you leave."

Mars couldn't contain himself anymore. His face bright red, he left the kitchen with me on his heels. He deposited the box on the console, and the two of us stepped outside and guffawed until we could control ourselves. I admit I felt a twinge of guilt, but that didn't stop me from laughing anew every time I saw Mars's face. Making a point of not looking at each other, we returned to the kitchen, where someone had deftly changed the subject to Hank and his singing talent. Natasha, still pale, sat primly and didn't appear to be paying any attention.

Humphrey offered to take the ceviche into the dining room and motioned for me to follow him. When we set the martini glasses on serving plates, he said, "The police have been questioning me like crazy because I sent Tara flowers for Valentine's Day. I sent them anonymously, but they tracked me down through the florist and my credit card." His head dropped, as if he were about to break into tears.

"Humphrey, no one who knows you thinks you killed Tara. We just have to find the real killer."

"Thank you, Sophie. I knew I could count on you to stand by me."

Whoa. I hoped that didn't mean he wanted to switch his affections to me. Where was Beth? I turned to call her, but he stopped me.

"There's something you should know. Wolf sent Tara flowers, too."

I felt my breath drop out of me, right down to my toes, like I'd been punched in the gut. "Are you sure?"

"I'm sorry, Sophie, but you needed to know."

I had no choice but to collect myself and put Wolf out of my mind. I wasn't very successful at the latter, though. When I told the others that dinner was served, I could only think of Wolf and his lies. Was I aiding and abetting him by pretending we weren't seeing each other? Was he using me? It didn't make sense. The Wolf I thought I knew was a straight shooter.

We moved into the dining room, where Bernie's elegant ceviche awaited us. When I told everyone Bernie brought it, Natasha recovered from her malaise long enough to utter, "Oh . . . restaurant food."

I had to do my best not to look in Mars's direction, lest we break into gales of giggles again. But I needn't have worried. When Bernie carved the lamb, the subject quickly changed to Kurt's murder.

"What I find interesting," said Bernie, "is that the person who hid Kurt's body must have known the trick to opening the bookcase."

Humphrey sat up straighter. "So Kurt's killer would have been very close to Mordecai to have known his secret."

"Might even have helped Mordecai build the wall unit." Nina swirled the wine in her glass.

"Or at least have had a familiarity with woodworking." Mars accepted two slices of juicy rare lamb and frowned at Bernie. "I don't think you should go around promoting this theory. You seem to fit the bill."

Bernie chuckled as though he had no worries.

Francie helped herself to asparagus. "Unless Kurt opened the wall unit. He was familiar with building and woodworking."

"I don't think so, Francie." I passed the creamy whipped potatoes. "I'm almost positive he was dead the morning I saw him in Bernie's window seat." Clearly the wrong thing to say, since everyone seated at the table immediately looked at Bernie.

He simply smiled and said, "I can assure you I had nothing to do with Kurt's demise. I barely knew the man."

"But you did know him?" asked Humphrey.

Bernie rested the knife on the carving board and sat

down. "I run a popular restaurant. I don't know all the patrons well, but I've met a lot of local people in passing."

"Posey thinks Mordecai is still alive, and that he gathered his old students for some kind of revenge," I said, to get Bernie off the hot seat.

Humphrey sputtered, and for a moment, I thought he might spew wine. "That's impossible."

"You actually saw his corpse?" asked Nina.

It finally occurred to me that Beth hadn't said a thing and was looking a little pale around the gills. Corpses and murder weren't exactly typical friendly dinner conversation. But Emmaline, who'd restlessly looked to each of us in hopes of a morsel of lamb, had come to a halt beside Beth and watched her with adoring eyes. "Beth, what brought you to Virginia?" I asked.

"My parents. They're getting up in years. It seemed like the right time to make things a little easier on them."

"I think that's lovely," said Francie. "Families should stick together and help each other."

"Have you ever been married?" asked Nina.

Beth seemed a bit flustered to be the center of attention, but Natasha finally broke out of her Mordecai-induced stupor and said, "She has two children. Both in college."

That explained why Beth needed the job so much.

"I'm lucky that Natasha hired me." Beth speared a piece of asparagus. "The job is different every day—never boring."

I struggled to imagine what Beth and Humphrey might have in common. Matchmaking for two shy people wasn't easy. I steered the conversation to books and movies, but in the end, Beth had a real interest in cooking and decorating, and Humphrey was still as bland as rice pudding. I wondered if he was comparing mild-mannered Beth to vibrant

Posey, but didn't understand that Posey would run him over like a bulldozer. Tara wouldn't have given him a second look, either. Poor Humphrey.

We adjourned to the living room for dessert, decaf coffee and tea, and after-dinner liqueurs. I handed Beth a cup of coffee, and when she reached for it, she said, "Thank you for including me tonight." She seemed to have relaxed considerably, and I got the impression that she was comfortable with my friends. The only problem was that she sat in conversational proximity of Bernie and Francie, while Humphrey chatted with Mars near the fireplace.

Emmaline jumped onto the sofa next to Beth. I reached out to remove her, but Beth said, "She's fine. I like dogs. Especially cute little ones."

Nina eyed Beth with new interest. "How do you feel about kittens? Would you like to see some?"

"Sure," said Beth.

"Humphrey, wouldn't you like to see the kittens, too?" I asked.

Bernie and Mars both rose as though they intended to follow Nina up the stairs for kitten show-and-tell, but I snagged the two men by their sleeves and hissed, "Doesn't anyone here realize that we're trying to throw Beth and Humphrey together?"

They acted sheepish and sat down, and I returned to the kitchen to slice the pound cake and arrange it on a platter. I had made the first cut when Natasha stormed in and asked, "Do you think he despised me?"

That was a loaded question. Plenty of people didn't care for Natasha. "You mean Mordecai?"

"Why would he do something so . . . so . . . barbaric? Why didn't they just bury him like they do everyone else?"

"You're looking at this all wrong. You should be honored. He trusted you to take care of him. Obviously he thought very highly of you."

"You think so? Oh, Sophie, what on earth am I going to do with those ashes?"

"Why don't you plant a tree in his backyard and bury the ashes there to nourish it? That way, he'll always be around."

Natasha hugged me from behind. "You're not much of a decorator or a cook, but sometimes you say just the right thing. I'll do that."

*Gee, thanks.* I picked up the platter of cake and carried it into the living room. On the way there, Natasha confided, "I've figured out what I'm doing wrong in the eyes of the Design Guild. They like fussy rooms, and I've been doing very clean, modern rooms. I'm changing my style for them. Do you think romantic country with lots of roses and shabby chic notions will impress them? I can do that, you know."

I had no doubt that she could.

"Posey and Iris do a much more cluttered look." To the entire assembled group, she announced, "I phoned Camille today. She's putting pressure on the police to release Mordecai's house to us. Maybe as soon as tomorrow. And Camille has enough clout to get what she wants in this town. We have to rush or we'll never finish the house in time for the spring tours."

The rest of the evening went well. The Grand Marnier cake proved so moist and delicious that we devoured most of it. But in spite of my efforts to bring them together, Humphrey and Beth clearly didn't have the right chemistry for a love attraction.

My guests left around midnight, with Natasha reminding everyone to check in with her in the morning, because we might all be back to work. Humphrey walked Francie home, and Bernie offered to see Beth to her car.

I tackled the dishes while Nina put Hank to bed in the cage in my sunroom and saw to the needs of the mother cat and kittens. I cleaned up, glad that I could offer some comfort to Nina, who was clearly still anxious about the murders, but the news about the flowers Wolf sent to Tara hung over me like a rain cloud. He could deny being involved with her, but it would be impossible for him to explain away the flowers.

We were tucked into bed by one, and awakened half an hour later when we heard Hank screaming "Kurt! Kurt!" followed by an ominous crash.

# THIRTY

From *"Ask Natasha"*:

*Dear Natasha,*

*I love color. I'm devoted to your show and have learned so much that my rooms are gorgeous. But my stairs are so plain and boring. Any suggestions?*

*—Boring Stairs in Staunton*

*Dear Boring,*

*Stencil the risers. If you're artistic, you can paint them freehand. Select four designs you like and add one to each riser, then repeat. Or stencil a different saying or inspirational word on each riser. Your stairs will be anything but boring.*

*—Natasha*

I stumbled down the stairs in haste. Emmaline nearly tripped me in her eagerness to get to the sunroom. I could hear Nina seconds behind me. I flicked on lights as we hurried along the hallway.

In the sunroom, we found a very disgruntled Wolf sitting on the brick floor. Hank's cage had fallen and lay on its side. My little scamp, Mochie, sat atop it, dipping his paw between the cage wires, trying to reach Hank.

"When did you get a bird?" demanded Wolf. "And why don't you lock your door?"

I helped him up, protesting that I always lock the sunroom door.

He flashed me a reproving look. "If the door had been locked, I wouldn't be inside your house."

Good point. "I must have overlooked locking it. I had company tonight, and we were pretty tired."

"Did you knock over Hank's cage?" Nina set it on the table where it had been.

"Somebody screamed Kurt's name, I opened the door, there was a crash, and I fell over the cage."

I had a sneaking suspicion that Mochie hadn't been as worn out as me, and that he'd paid a middle-of-the-night visit to Hank with fiendish feline motives. "Maybe Hank should sleep in a room where we can shut the door."

Wolf dusted off his hands. "I'll carry the cage into the den if you two will turn off the lights before Kenner sees me here."

I froze, thinking about Wolf and his deceptions. Did I dare confront him? Nina scurried around closing drapes and turning off lights, and we met up with Wolf in the living room. I still harbored doubts, but decided it would be best to play along and pretend I didn't know about the bouquet he'd sent Tara.

"I don't know what you said to Kenner, but it appears to have done some good," said Wolf.

Nina laughed. "You should have seen Sophie in action, making a fuss about how the two of you aren't a couple."

"Have you had dinner?" I asked. "I have leftover lamb."

"As a matter of fact, I had dinner, but I'll have a bit of my Valentine Black Forest cherry cake if there's any left."

Nina amused Wolf with her version of our encounter with Kenner while I fetched the remaining cake. Working fast, I made decaf coffees with Irish Cream liqueur, topped off with dollops of whipped cream.

When I returned, Nina and Wolf had revived the fire in the fireplace and lit the candles on the coffee table.

"I came by to update you on what's going on, but this is just what I needed." Wolf took the mug of coffee I offered him and allowed his fingers to graze my hand.

"So spill the news already," pleaded Nina. "I can't stand thinking I'm going to be the next victim."

"We found Kurt's car in long-term parking out at the airport."

"Were there security cameras? Did you see anyone's face on the tapes?" I asked.

"No such luck. Whoever deposited the car wore a baseball cap with a hood over top of it."

Nina gulped her coffee. "I don't know how long I can go on like this. I'm scared all the time."

"The good news is that we have a tape of someone following Tara. The bad news is that it's Humphrey."

"You know he didn't kill her. He's meek as a mouse." I knew I shouldn't eat more cake, but I took a bite anyway and savored the chocolate and cream.

"We don't know any such thing. I know Humphrey attended the banquet because I recall him helping with

CPR. But it's kind of scary that a guy like Humphrey can blend into the woodwork so well. Almost no one remembers seeing him there."

"He took Francie. I bet she can tell you if he left her side for even a second," I said.

"There's one other thing." Wolf swallowed a bite of cake. "Tara received no less than three Valentine bouquets. Two dozen long-stemmed red roses with a note that said 'I need you,' a pink tea rose arrangement with baby's breath from an anonymous admirer, and, apparently, the flowers that were meant to be sent to you from me." He sucked in a deep breath. "Which contained a card with my name. From what I gather, Tara manufactured a story about our relationship, which she shared with the florist, who thought your address was a mistake and sent the flowers to Tara instead. Unfortunately, that doesn't help my claim that Tara and I didn't have a relationship."

"Oh no!" I groaned, feeling immense relief that Wolf hadn't sent flowers to Tara after all. "So instead of being off the hook, it looks worse for you."

Wolf nodded.

"Wait," I said, "do you know when the 'I need you' roses were ordered? That might exclude Kurt."

Nina gripped her mug with both hands. "How long was Kurt dead? Sophie thinks he was dead when she saw him in the window seat. She may be right but I think he couldn't have been dead long or he would have smelled. If I'm right, Kurt would have been alive and could have killed Tara at the banquet."

"I haven't heard any autopsy results yet. But Mordecai planned ahead for those paintings and artifacts. He installed a climate control system that kept his little gallery at sixty degrees with limited humidity, and that probably slowed Kurt's deterioration. I suspect Mordecai didn't realize that the vent under the porch had broken and that cold air was seeping in."

"The vent?" asked Nina. "The hole where Emmaline and the cat got in and out?"

"How are the kittens?" asked Wolf.

"They're doing fine. Francie and I are taking them to the vet tomorrow for a full checkup." She frowned at Wolf. "Aren't you prohibited from sharing police information with us? Or is this some kind of clever cop maneuver to get me to confess?"

Wolf laughed aloud. "I haven't told you anything that won't be in the morning paper. Well, except Humphrey's name, but you would have figured that out from the description."

I didn't want to pooh-pooh Nina's theory that Kurt could have killed Tara, but his appearance in the window seat was still fresh in my mind, and he had seemed dead to me. "I think we can count Humphrey out. Of all the people I know, I can't imagine that he would be brave enough to shoot a nail gun."

"Then the killer had to be Tara's new lover or her old one," said Nina.

Wolf whipped around to look at her. "Since she told everyone I was the new boyfriend, I certainly hope you don't mean me."

Nina nudged him with her bare toes in a conciliatory gesture. "It could have been the lover's wife. What about Earl? She attended the banquet, and there's something very suspicious about her. Kurt said she was out of town, visiting her mother. But either she never left or she returned early. And she wasn't behaving like someone whose husband was missing."

"What about Posey?" I asked. "She acted like she was

torn up over Tara's death, but I heard she tried to sneak a nail gun out of the convention hall."

"Where's her motive?" said Wolf.

"She and Kurt were an item when they were in college. Maybe she still loved him and flew into a jealous rage."

"This is terrible," blurted Nina. "The cops must think I had a motive. I'm sure they think I was seeing Kurt behind my husband's back."

"Wolf, do you think Kurt was murdered before or after Tara?" I asked. "Is it possible that Tara killed Kurt, and then someone, maybe Earl, killed Tara in revenge?"

"Once again, I'm the prime candidate," Nina announced. "I could have knocked off Kurt and then gone after Tara."

I tried to suppress a grin. "There's only one little snafu with your bold theory—I don't think you knew how to open the hatch to the stairway where we found Kurt."

Nina tucked her feet underneath her. "I'm smart enough to have figured that out." When neither Wolf nor I spoke, she added, "Okay, I didn't know how to open it. I didn't even know it could open."

Wolf rubbed his face. "Don't worry, Nina. Soph and I are right up there with you as prime contenders. Apparently everyone thought Tara and I were an item. It astonishes me how many people believed her when she told them that we were close to getting engaged. I can't imagine what she was thinking."

"*Aww*," cooed Nina. "She had a big old crush on you, you teddy bear."

I ignored their banter because something had been bothering me. "If Mordecai murdered someone and buried him or her under his house, then why would he have wanted his students to find the grave?"

"*Huh*?" Nina squinted at me.

"He arranged the bequest party and gave his former students clues that would lead them to open the wall unit, find their inheritance and, consequently, the grave. Why would he do that? Why not hide their bequest in the attic and leave the grave undiscovered?"

Wolf finished his piece of cake. "Dying confession, in a manner of speaking? Maybe he wanted someone to have some closure and know what happened to a loved one. Or maybe it was his way of clearing up his guilt over the murder."

Wolf's words reminded me that his wife had gone missing. No wonder he thought about closure.

"Maybe it's his wife and he didn't want her body to remain undiscovered for heaven knows how long," suggested Nina.

"Sort of a mean thing to do to a bunch of students whom he apparently liked," I said. "Finding a grave would come as a big shock."

Wolf shook his head. "Poor old Mordecai. Just goes to show what guilt can do to a person. He withdrew from life after that murder and lived the rest of his days in fear of being discovered."

Although it seemed like I should have felt better after talking with Wolf, I felt unsettled. Was there a connection between Kurt's death and Tara's murder? And why would Mordecai lead his students to a grave?

When Wolf was ready to leave, we stole to the kitchen and looked out at the street to see if Kenner was watching. In the wee hours of the night, it lay quiet and calm. A few porch lights glowed in the night. My neighbors slept, no lights shone in the windows.

It was a peaceful scene, except for one small matter that most people wouldn't have given a second thought. Smoke rose from one of Mordecai's chimneys.

# THIRTY-ONE

From "The Good Life" :

Dear Sophie,

My husband and I are living with his parents while we save money for a house of our own. My wicked mother-in-law told me I could decorate our room any way I wanted, but when I did, she had a hissy fit and stole my glue gun. I can't stand her perfect house where everything is too special to be touched or used. What do I do?

—In Agony in Apopka

Dear In Agony,

For the time being, you're really like a tenant, so treat your room that way. Change the linens and the drapes, taking care to hand over the old ones to dear mother-in-law for safekeeping. Use slipcovers that suit your style on the upholstered furniture, and buy accent pieces to replace ones that you return to your mother-in-law. A few little changes and the room will feel like it belongs to you, but can be easily restored to its previous style when you move out.

—Sophie

"Do you see the smoke?" Wolf gripped my arm, and his voice was low and rumbling. "Do you still have a key?"

I retrieved the key, and the two of us snuck out the door and bolted across the street.

When we reached Mordecai's front porch, Wolf whispered, "You stay here."

*Not a chance.* He unlocked the door quietly. I slipped through behind him and listened for the sound of footsteps or running water or any clue to human habitation.

I could hear Wolf sniffing, like Bernie had, and I guessed he was trying to determine where the fire might be. The old house had a fireplace in nearly every bedroom. Wolf peeked into the living room, and I assumed that he didn't see anyone, because he headed up the stairs.

They groaned under his weight, and though I knew the sound couldn't be very loud, in the sleeping house each step reverberated with alarming creaks. I debated whether or not to follow him and decided against it. Wolf would hear me for sure, and the additional noise might alert anyone who lurked in the house.

Instead, I watched as Wolf paused at the landing and listened.

I still didn't hear anyone. But someone must have started the fire. I supposed they could have left with the fire still ablaze. We should hear some wood crackling if we got close enough. *We? I wouldn't hear anything if I stayed in the foyer.*

As soon as Wolf turned right, I sprang up the stairs, taking them two at a time, stepping carefully near the wall, on the theory that they might not squeak so much there. I was wrong.

I made it to the landing and expected Wolf to turn around and be mad at me, but the front door squealed open. Nina, making all the noise in the world, shut the door and stomped up the steps. "You left me alone," she hissed. "I thought you were smooching, but you just went off and left me!"

Wolf turned and glared at us. In haste, I clapped a hand over her mouth and held a finger up to my own, hoping she would realize we were trying to be quiet.

Wolf crept farther along the hallway. In the dim light coming through a window, I could see that the door to the bedroom at the very end of the hall was closed.

Floorboards grumbled, but I didn't think the noise came from Wolf's footsteps this time. He was treading carefully on a long Oriental runner.

Wolf placed his hand on the doorknob and turned it slowly. A momentary glint let me know he had drawn his gun. Maybe Nina and I should step out of the line of fire in case the other person had one as well.

But then, in a flash, Wolf was through the door. A commotion ensued with loud thuds and grunts as though he was wrestling someone, and a woman screamed.

What to do? I'd read somewhere that a person could break up a dogfight by throwing a blanket over the dogs. I looked in the closest bedroom and knew instantly that it was the one Iris was decorating. I snatched the spread off the bed, raced to Wolf's aid, and threw the huge cover over the people on the floor. Hoping my plan would work,

I flicked on the overhead light—and found Beth, wearing a man's shirt that hung loosely on her, holding a lamp over her head as though she planned to crash it down on Wolf.

She screeched and jumped back when she saw me. "It's the killer, Sophie. Be careful!"

*The killer?* "Wolf," I yelled as two people struggled under the bedcover, "it's the killer!"

Beth lowered the lamp. "Wolf? Isn't he a cop?"

I nodded, wondering what I could do to help him.

"Stop!" Beth threw the lamp onto the bed and rushed at the people writhing on the floor. "Stop, Mike. It's the cop!"

Mike? Nina and I grabbed corners of the cover and yanked, revealing Mike and Wolf in a death lock. Somewhat sheepishly, they released their holds and stood up, badly mussed and with the beginnings of what I suspected would become impressive bruises.

"What are you doing here?" demanded Wolf.

Mike looked at Beth, who flushed bright pink. With her new hairstyle pushed out of her eyes and some color in her cheeks, Beth looked the best I'd ever seen her.

"We, um, well, I live with my parents, and Mike is staying with Ted, so . . ."

Wolf's eyes narrowed, and I guessed he wasn't buying it. "Then get a hotel room."

Mike wrapped a protective arm around Beth. "Do you know what a hotel room costs in this town? We don't have that kind of money."

Well, that certainly explained Beth's lack of interest in Humphrey. But how did Mike and Beth hook up so fast?

Wolf wasn't through with them. "This house is a crime scene. There's police tape across the door."

Mike shook his head. "They took it down tonight. Beth

noticed when she left Sophie's house. Both of us have keys. It's not like we're not allowed to be here."

Wolf turned to me. "Did you see police tape?"

I shrugged. We came over so fast, I hadn't paid attention.

Nina giggled. "*Aww*, Wolf. It's so romantic. Cut them some slack."

A fire crackled in the old fireplace. The designer redoing the room had used a blend of country and shabby chic. An old white wrought-iron bed was loaded with ruffled pillows and a sumptuous, barely pink comforter. I recognized pieces of furniture that had been deposited on the porch by other decorators. This decorator had repurposed them, including a very clever reuse of an old arched mirror over the fireplace mantel. Almost everything in the room was white, with random touches of the softest pink.

"Who's doing this room?" I asked. "She won't be happy that you're using it."

Beth turned scarlet.

"Natasha thinks someone else is decorating the room, but Iris said Beth could do it." Mike hugged Beth to him.

I'd heard of sleeping together on a first date, but there was something about the way they acted, as though they knew each other very well, and almost moved in unison. "Good grief! You're Hot Lips!"

I didn't think Beth could be more embarrassed.

Wolf pointed at them. "That's it. Everybody get dressed and meet us downstairs in the living room in three minutes."

On the way down the stairs, Wolf asked, "Who is Hot Lips?"

"Mike's old girlfriend from his college days." I stopped and raised my eyes to meet his. "And Mordecai's niece."

Mike and Beth followed us to Nolan's turquoise living

room and sat primly side by side on the sofa, as though they expected to be reamed out.

Wolf paced. I wanted him to sit down, but he didn't seem capable.

"So you're Mordecai's niece. Did you come to claim the estate?" asked Wolf.

"I'm only related by marriage. His wife, Jean, was my aunt. I moved back here to help my parents and landed a job with Natasha. I had no idea that it would involve coming back to Mordecai and Jean's house."

"That's why you were so hesitant that first morning here," I said.

Beth nodded. "It all came rushing back to me. So many memories. Some wonderful, but some bittersweet. We left in such haste that day. I never dreamed I would return to this house. And then, to walk in and see the love of my life after all these years—I was mortified."

Mike gave her a little squeeze and Beth said, "I was scared to death that he would recognize me. I'm not the cute little Hot Lips I used to be. Two children, more than two decades, and way more than twenty pounds—I always thought if I met Mike again, I'd be svelte and successful, not fat and broke."

"Aren't women silly?" Mike said to Wolf. "I'm no prize anymore, either. But for all Beth's efforts to hide, I couldn't help noticing this very attractive woman sneaking around. And then one day, I was watching her when she didn't realize it and"—he snapped his fingers—"it clicked. I knew she was my Hot Lips."

"What do you mean, you left in haste? What happened?" Wolf appeared unmoved by their love connection story.

"It was such a gorgeous day. Even though it was more than twenty years ago, I remember it so well." Beth twisted the hem of her shirt. "Perfect spring weather, no humidity.

The lilacs were in full bloom and the backyard smelled heavenly."

"Mordecai and Jean threw a party for the whole department," said Mike. "We were celebrating the successful construction of our straw cottage. We'd been in the paper and on the local news, and school was almost out for the summer. Everyone was pretty giddy."

"You were here, too?" Wolf asked.

"We all were. Posey and Kurt and Ted and Nolan. We all worked on the straw cottage."

Beth picked up the thread of the story for Mike. "Everyone was outside in the garden, and then Mordecai wanted to show all of his students something inside, and when we came in, Mordecai caught Aunt Jean and Mr. Ledbetter in a serious lip-lock"—she pointed toward the fireplace—"right there. Well, you can imagine all you-know-what broke loose. Aunt Jean pushed Mr. Ledbetter away, and he fell and hit his head on one of those andirons."

# THIRTY-TWO

From "The Good Life":

Dear Sophie,

We bought a new house, but I adore a vintage look. How can I bring a romantic, old-fashioned feel to boxy modern rooms?

—Hopeless Romantic in Lovejoy

Dear Hopeless Romantic,

Use a soft color scheme on the walls and upholstery. Gauzy or balloon curtains will soften hard edges. Draw the eye away from modern lines by hanging sparkling chandeliers nearby. Replace sleek handles with antique glass knobs, and add those important accessories—mirrors, silver, and a few shabby chic pieces to complete the look.

—Sophie

Nina jumped up. "Just like Kurt. The same thing happened to me. Those are deadly andirons."

Wolf ignored Nina's outburst and prompted Beth. "And?"

"They helped Mr. Ledbetter into the family room to lie down. But you can imagine the fight between Mordecai and Jean."

"And then we got the news that our cottage was on fire," said Mike. "We took off to see it, and our group of friends began to fall apart because we all blamed each other."

"I helped Aunt Jean pack her car, and we left right away. What I remember most was the search for Aunt Jean's insulin. She was diabetic and had to have it, but the refrigerator was packed with food and so many people were milling around and Aunt Jean was just hysterical about it. We didn't even stick around to clean up the food or anything. I've never eaten another blondie since that day."

*Blondies? And lilacs?* "Did they serve strawberry daiquiris and quiche?" I asked.

Mike shrugged, but Beth smiled. "How did you know?"

"The bequest party—Mordecai tried to re-create that day with the food and the lilacs. And he specifically instructed me to set it all up in here." I sat back on one of Nolan's fancy chairs, perplexed.

"Why would he want us to relive that day?" asked Beth. "That doesn't make any sense."

"He wanted to bring his students back together," I theorized. "He meant for you to work together again, that's why the wall unit would only open if all five keys were present."

Wolf had stopped pacing. "Did you find the insulin?"

"No. We took off without it and went straight to her pharmacy."

Wolf's eyes narrowed, as though he was thinking. But then he stifled a yawn.

"Are you going to turn us in?" asked Mike.

Poor Wolf looked exhausted. He stepped out to the front porch and returned a minute later. "No police tape. If you have keys, I don't know that it's any of my business what time you come to work."

Mike smiled and planted a kiss on Beth's forehead.

Wolf motioned to Nina and me, and walked us home. Nina latched a leash on Emmaline and took her out back while Wolf said good-bye.

"It was nice of you to let them stay there," I said.

Wolf massaged the side of his face with his hand. "With all the weird stuff going on, maybe it's a good thing that someone is keeping an eye on the house at night. Unless they're the killers."

"What?"

"C'mon, Soph. They'd clearly practiced that story. In spite of Nina's theories to the contrary, I'd lay odds that one of Mordecai's other students killed Kurt." He threw his hands in the air. "And who knows? Maybe Tara's death had nothing to do with Kurt's death. There's something else that you don't know. There was an old bottle on top of the grave in Mordecai's basement. A little glass bottle—the kind insulin comes in. It was dirty, as though it had been buried."

A chill ran through me. Had Beth inadvertently expanded the implications against her aunt and uncle? "It was on the grave? Like Mordecai wanted us to find it?"

"Looks like it." Clearly distracted, Wolf dispensed a perfunctory kiss, said good night, and strode away.

Nina must have seen him, because she walked up to the kitchen door clucking. "The bloom off the rose already?"

"They found a bottle that might have contained insulin on top of the grave in Mordecai's crawl space."

Nina took off Emmaline's leash. "Jean's missing bottle of insulin!"

"That's what I thought. It was dirty, like it had been buried." I poured each of us a glass of sherry, and we sank into the comfy chairs by my fireplace.

Nina sat up, excited. "Just like my husband's high-profile case—the murderer injected the victim with an overdose of insulin. Do you think Mordecai killed his victim that way? It can't be a coincidence that he left the bottle in the crawl space."

I bit back a grin. Curious Nina was the perfect spouse for a forensic pathologist. "It's kind of hard to imagine how an insulin bottle could have made its way to Mordecai's basement otherwise. But Wolf said it was dirty, like it had been buried."

"So he buried it to hide it, and later changed his mind and left it on the grave, like a confession."

I sipped the sweet liquid. "I don't know. . . . If I had killed someone with a drug, I think I would prefer to dispose of it far from the body. Throw it in the river or something."

She nodded. "That would be the smart thing to do. Then why did Mordecai leave it where it would be found?"

"That's the question. I suspect that's what was distracting Wolf. The two murders have been a big strain on him."

"Everybody in town is talking about him."

"What do you mean?"

"I didn't want to tell you, but with the rumors about his wife, everyone is speculating about whether he could have killed Tara."

I must have shown my shock, because Nina stroked my shoulder and said, "It's just idle speculation."

"That means they're speculating about me, too, doesn't it?"

Nina sighed. "I didn't want to tell you, honey. Look, in the morning, when we're fresh, we'll put our heads together and try to figure this out. I can't go on being afraid, and you and Wolf deserve to be cleared."

We trudged up to bed. In spite of the early morning hour, I didn't think either of us would sleep well—not until the murderers of Kurt and Tara were in custody.

Nina and I slept in the next morning. I'd barely opened my eyes when the phone rang, and the irate convention hall manager at the hotel informed me that the police had removed the yellow tape, and he expected all the exhibits to be removed immediately so they could accommodate the next group.

I skipped a shower, pulled on an oversized denim shirt and stretchy jeans. I woke Nina, who grumbled and flipped over. Fine by me, she could sleep all day. But before I made it to the bedroom door her brain must have engaged, because she sat up and shouted, "Don't leave me alone!"

"Nina, I have to go."

"No, no, no, no." She reached for her cell phone and made a quick call. "Francie is on her way. Please wait until she gets here."

I agreed and hustled downstairs to feed Mochie, who prowled the sunroom as though he thought Hank might be hiding there. I dashed out the door the moment Francie showed up.

As I walked on the other side of the street, I could see Natasha holding court on the porch at Mordecai's house. "We're behind schedule," she announced. "But if we all work very hard, we can still pull this off."

Iris sprang up the stairs and said rather loudly, "Who

made you queen of the world? Do you not understand the meaning of co-chair? You've been ordering everyone around, and I've had about enough of your superior attitude."

I was sorry I couldn't stick around to see how their spat turned out, but work called. During my walk to the hotel, I started phoning the exhibitors. Most were thrilled that they could pick up their belongings, but some had other plans for the day, and I anticipated the worst.

Shortly after my arrival, local exhibitors started turning up. Natasha sent Beth to dismantle her exhibit, and I couldn't help noticing that Beth seemed like a different person. She'd pulled her hair out of her face, and moved with confidence, giving directions to a helper.

I hurried in the direction of Ted's glass house, crossed the bridge, and stepped inside. A couple of guys I'd never met were packing up the curtains and furnishings.

"Is there a problem?" asked one of them.

I smiled reassuringly. "No. How are you going to dismantle this?"

"The panes come apart pretty easily. Some lady bought it, so we'll be reassembling it as soon as the weather improves and we can pour concrete footings."

I gazed around, trying to imagine what had transpired. Tara's killer must have lured her inside. She was looking for Wolf when I saw her. It wasn't hard to imagine that he could have called her into the glass house—or that I could have, for that matter. No wonder we were suspects. It would have been easy to draw the hazy curtains closed. And then Tara's killer shot her with the nail gun while her back was turned.

I couldn't help thinking it must have been someone she knew. Or someone who overheard that she was looking for

Wolf. Why else would she have entered the little house? Unless she thought someone needed help. She was a cop, after all.

Surely she'd seen that her killer held a nail gun. They were too big to conceal. But at Rooms and Blooms, no one would have given a nail gun a second thought because so many people were using them. Even on the last night, it wouldn't be unusual to make a quick fix to something.

If I was right, then Wolf was the least likely culprit. I didn't believe he had killed Tara, but she would have wondered why he was carrying a nail gun. That meant the killer almost had to be an exhibitor.

"Yowza!" exclaimed one of the workers.

I followed his line of sight to Earl, who apparently thought displaying excessive cleavage was appropriate for exhibit dismantling. She looked around, her hands on her hips, as though she was miffed.

I left Ted's house and walked over to Earl. "I'm so sorry about Kurt."

"You," she sputtered in an ugly tone that left no question about her feelings toward me. "I've heard all about your friend with the bird who screams Kurt's name."

# THIRTY-THREE

From "THE GOOD LIFE" :

Dear Sophie,

I'm decorating my first house on a budget. I'm thrilled that I have lots of windows, but I can't afford curtains for all of them. Any clever suggestions?

—Window Woes in Waldo

Dear Window Woes,

Make your own! Use antique tablecloths from the flea market, or fabric remnants from the budget bin. Anything can be used as a curtain rod, including a straight branch or pole. Sew coordinating ribbon along the top of the fabric, leaving a four-inch loop at regular intervals. Slide the loops over your rod and you'll have curtains. Don't cut fabric that's too long, let it puddle on the floor for a romantic, billowing look.

—Sophie

Earl continued in a scathing tone. "Talk about incriminating. I hear she can't shut that bird up. Tara told me how your friend, Nina, killed Kurt and you cleaned up the crime scene. I suppose you thought no one would ever discover your clever hiding place, and that we would never know the truth."

"Tara told you?" I'd dismissed Nina's theories about Kurt and Earl, but maybe she'd been right. How could I find out more without sounding like I suspected her of murder? "You knew Tara?"

"Our shop is—was—in her sector. She used to stop by to dream about the kitchen she would have in her house one day."

I had to take a chance if I wanted useful information. "Did you know she was seeing a married man?"

I expected Earl to be angry at my intimation that the married man might have been her husband, but she seemed sad. "Why do women have to go after married men? Why did your friend, Nina, have to take my Kurt from me? She has a husband, a filthy rich one from what I understand. She didn't need Kurt. She should have left him alone." Her demeanor changed, and she poked a finger at me. "I've told that nice Detective Kenner all about you and your friend. He knows everything. You won't get away with this."

I figured she'd get huffy, but I asked anyway. "Have you been calling Nina from Kurt's phone to torment her?"

She laughed maniacally.

"So it was you!"

Earl didn't deny it, and strode away smiling. At least she'd inadvertently explained one other thing. I now knew how Tara found out Kurt was missing. I had an inkling that if she hadn't pursued it as a favor to Earl, Tara might be alive today. If that were true, then it meant Tara had discovered something that made Kurt's killer very nervous.

I wished the coffee bar hadn't managed to shut down and move out so fast. I needed a jolt of java—and a Krispy Kreme doughnut, which I figured I deserved since I'd been under so much stress. Didn't stress burn calories?

I took the escalator up to the lobby and ran into Camille DuPont. "How's Nolan?" I asked.

Camille looked terrific, as always. Her cream-colored suit nipped in perfectly to accent her waist, and her hair brushed her shoulders in a natural, unsprayed way. "Milking the mugging for everything it's worth. I left him with the nurse, who"—she checked the time on her watch—"is probably cozying up to him at this very moment."

I forced a little laugh. "You don't mean that?"

"Unfortunately, I do." She tweaked the bridge of her nose like she thought it might ease some sort of discomfort. "Listen, Sophie, I'd like to unload some of the furniture in the store. You and the other designers can take anything you want on loan for Mordecai's house. Maybe we'll be able to sell some of it that way."

"That's very generous of you. What I need, though, is a huge sofa."

"No problem." She pulled out an elegant leather-encased notepad and scribbled an address. "Ask for Victor and tell him I sent you."

I thanked her again and asked, "Is there anything I can do for you? Are you here about Rooms and Blooms?"

She sighed. "I'm here to meet with the man selling the bulldozer. Nolan was the idiot who bought it, and now

I have to beg to get out of the contract." She tucked the notepad into her purse. "Just between the two of us—I'm through cleaning up after Nolan."

I watched Camille ride the escalator to the exhibit level and couldn't help thinking that her wealth didn't protect her from problems.

Posey passed her, going in the other direction on the escalator. They nodded at each other, but from what I could see, Posey didn't ask about Nolan. She arrived at the landing and said, "Do I file a claim for my losses with you or the Guild?"

"Losses?"

"The police confiscated my cordless nail gun."

"I'm sure you'll get the nail gun back."

"What am I supposed to do in the meantime? If you recall, I have a dining room to finish."

I should have been nicer, but I blurted, "As I recall, you weren't nailing anything."

"I have to do something about curtains. I was going to build valances." She stalked off in a huff.

Okay, so that wasn't kind of me, but she could use a hammer, couldn't she? I chalked my rudeness up to hunger. But my caffeine-deprived brain went one step further. Why hadn't Posey asked how Nolan was doing? She'd known him for a long time. It was common politeness if nothing else. Unless Posey feared the answer. Or feared she'd been seen. Surely Posey hadn't clobbered Nolan in an effort to obtain his key?

I could understand her eagerness to find the bequest. Mordecai had made a game out of it, and his heirs had fun looking for it. But even Posey wouldn't have attacked Nolan to steal his key—would she? I followed Posey out and headed in the same direction, trailing several yards behind her as she made her way up King Street. She paused to peer in Nolan's shop window, and I wondered if she'd been eager to find the bequest because she needed money. My own business had suffered when people cut back on events. I could well imagine that her trompe l'oeil business wasn't in great demand. But she would have to be in dire straits to have conked Nolan over the head just to obtain his key and speed things up.

Posey continued on her way, and I ducked into a store that I thought might have a Krispy Kreme doughnut. But I darted out to the sidewalk again. I could still see Posey, not that it mattered, really. What if her objectives in obtaining the key had nothing to do with the bequest? What if she knew what we would find behind the wall unit and she needed the key so we wouldn't have enough keys to open it?

Reeling from that revelation, I staggered back into the shop and said to a saleswoman, "I am in urgent need of coffee and a Krispy Kreme doughnut, preferably with chocolate icing."

The woman smiled at me as though she understood completely. "All the way in the rear." She chuckled when she said, "They're fresh."

"The back? You should put them out here where everyone can see them. You'll sell more."

"Are you kidding? This way we force you to walk through the store, so you'll see other merchandise and buy more."

Her gleeful explanation of how they manipulated customers brought Mordecai and his bequest to mind.

"Hon? You okay?" she asked. "It's not a big deal. Even department stores do it."

I nodded and made my way to the doughnuts, where I selected two with chocolate icing and the biggest coffee they offered. Something was bothering me. Consequently,

I didn't see a single other item the store offered as I paid and left. I made my way to the fountains at Market Square and sat down, steam rising from my coffee in the cold air.

I had been looking at the murders all wrong. I never considered Mordecai as a possible killer of Tara or Kurt because he was dead. But through his bequest he had reached back from the great beyond to manipulate us. Had Mordecai provoked a chain of events that resulted in Kurt's or Tara's murder?

He set up the bequest to remind his students of the party they'd attended in his home more than two decades ago. The food, the lilacs—he hadn't wanted substitutions because the tastes and scents were supposed to trigger memories. And someone, Mike maybe, had suggested that Mordecai built the opening in the wall unit to operate only when all five students were present with their keys. Mordecai wanted them together. That made perfect sense. And it seemed clear to me that the paintings and other treasures beneath the house were the bequest.

But what struck me as very peculiar was that Mordecai had intentionally led his students to a grave. Just like the store that manipulated people and forced them to find the doughnuts in the back, Mordecai had wanted his students to discover the grave. What would possess him to want his students, or anyone, for that matter, to find the grave he had hidden so carefully for so many years? If he had wanted to clear his conscience, he could simply have left a note with his attorney regarding the grave. But he hadn't done that. Instead, he wanted his students to find it. And he'd left the bottle of insulin there, too. A shudder ran through me. Surely the students hadn't killed the person who was buried there? Had there been a sixth student? Perhaps the one who had sabotaged the cottage they built for Mordecai's class?

I looked up to see Ted headed my way. "Gorgeous day for February, isn't it?" He sat beside me and munched on a take-out burger.

To be honest, I hadn't even noticed the weather until that moment. I nodded, though.

"We're supposed to get snow again tomorrow. Who'd have thought it would be sunny today? Like life, huh? The unexpected around every corner."

"Ted, when you guys built the straw cottage—the one for Mordecai's class—how many people worked on it?"

He pulled the top off a cup of coffee. "All of us. Posey, Kurt, Mike, Nolan, and me. Well," he snickered, "Nolan had already perfected the art of looking like he was doing something when he was really just telling everyone else what to do—and we did a lot of griping about that. Mordecai pitched in a little, and his wife helped with decorating decisions."

"No one else?"

"Why do you ask?"

"Just thinking about Mordecai and the body in his basement."

Ted swallowed a bite of his burger. "Blew me away. I've known Mordecai forever, and that's the last thing I expected. Just goes to show that even the smartest person can flip out, I guess."

"You knew Mordecai before you were his student?"

He nodded. "My dad did lawn work for a bunch of people on your street. I was an impressionable kid, and Mordecai was like a magician. He always had a trick up his sleeve or some game in store for me." Ted sucked in a deep breath. "Mordecai is the reason I went to college. My dad had enormous respect for him."

"That's why you know Iris and Bedelia. Your dad worked for Bedelia, too?"

"Yes. Great people, the Ledbetters. They were always good to us."

"Did you know my neighbor, Francie?"

He chuckled. "Francie's husband thought he was a horticulturist and wouldn't let anyone else touch their lawn. But I mowed your grass for Faye when I was a teenager."

As far as I knew, Mars's Aunt Faye, who had left us the house, had never married. It came as no surprise that she had employed a lawn service.

Ted wiped his mouth with a cheap paper napkin and crammed it inside his empty coffee cup. "Gotta check on my men. It wasn't easy escaping from Natasha. She doesn't understand that I have other jobs going on and I can't drop everything for her."

"Mike still there?"

Ted stood up. "I don't know what's up with him. He found another place to stay, and he's acting odd and mysterious."

If Mike had chosen not to tell Ted that Beth was Hot Lips, it probably wasn't my place to spill the beans.

"He's broke, but suddenly he has money to pay for a room somewhere?"

I tried to think of a way to change the subject. "Nina thinks Earl killed Tara and Kurt."

"Earl?" Ted wiped a hand across his mouth. "I never considered her. She's really the one who threw Mike out of the kitchen business, you know. She didn't want to split profits with anyone."

# THIRTY-FOUR

**From "THE GOOD LIFE" :**

Dear Sophie,

I adore my Havanese, so people are always giving me cute decorative items with Havanese dogs on them. My mother says my house looks tacky—like a Havanese shop. How do I display all these items?

—Happy Havanese Mom in Havana

Dear Happy Havanese Mom,

Instead of spreading everything around, place clusters of three or five items together. More than five items on a horizontal surface can be a bit overwhelming. You might consider selecting one wall where you can display similar items as a group. Walls can absorb a greater number of similar objects without being overpowered.

—Sophie

Ted bit his upper lip. "Do you think Mike is trying to get revenge? His entire life might have been different if Earl hadn't ruined it by kicking him out of their kitchen business."

Mike and Beth? Was it possible that the lovebirds had planned this? If Wolf and I hadn't spotted the smoke from their fire, would they have continued to pretend they didn't know each other?

I searched for an innocuous answer to Ted's question. "You know Mike better than I do."

Ted acted like the garbage receptacle was a basketball hoop and launched his trash at it with dead-on accuracy. He wiped his hands, displaying his satisfaction. "I never dreamed that Mordecai could have killed anyone, and I thought I knew him very well."

Although I needed to get back to the mayhem at Rooms and Blooms, when Ted left, I took a few extra minutes to sort my thoughts about the murders and possible suspects. There was quite a bit to keep straight.

Mike harbored resentment against Kurt, but unless he lied about living in Pennsylvania, I doubted that he knew Tara. So although he might be implicated in the first murder, it was hard to see how he would fit into the second. I thought I understood Beth when I found out she was Hot Lips, but it was possible that she was helping Mike. She had known Kurt, and might have had reason to dislike him since he came on to so many women, but if she'd just moved here, I couldn't imagine why she would want to murder Tara.

Surely Camille hadn't killed anyone. Did she even know how to shoot a nail gun? She did seem put out with Nolan. Had she taken advantage of the murders to try to get rid of him?

I was beginning to think that Posey's temper matched

the dark flame in her hair, and wasn't sure if she had loved Tara or hated her. She'd certainly been involved with Kurt once. She seemed to be one of the few who had a connection to both victims.

Iris had brought charges against Kurt, and didn't want to work on the same project as him. But did she even know Tara?

And then there was Ted. It had to be more than a coincidence that someone had shot nails into his pond liner and that Tara had been killed by a nail gun. I wished I knew how long Kurt had been dead. Maybe Nina had been right all along, and it was Kurt who killed Tara. But then, who killed Kurt?

Kurt had certainly alienated a lot of people. And that brought me back to Earl again. I had to find out where Earl had been the night Nina went out with Kurt. If I had to bet, I'd have chosen Earl as the killer. She knew both of the victims and hadn't acted like a worried wife.

With renewed vigor, probably from the coffee, I returned to the hotel conference hall and took stock of what needed to be done. I walked the hall, making a list of exhibitors whose booths remained. The mini bulldozer chugged past me, and I wondered if Camille had managed to break Nolan's contract. And then I wondered if Nolan was even alive. I felt ashamed of my thought, but Nolan hadn't been seen or heard from since he was mugged.

On my way to the lobby, I swung by the Finkel Kitchen and Bath booth. A couple of young men were loading the last of the cabinets.

"Excuse me," I said. "Have you seen the redhead who worked for Kurt?"

"Do you mean me?"

I turned around to find the redheaded girl who'd manned the booth.

"Do you have a job available?" she asked. "Mrs. Finkel fired me. I came by to see if I could persuade her to write me my last paycheck. I mean, I spent days of my life sitting here. I deserve to be paid."

"I'm sorry, I don't have any employees." She looked like she might drift away, so I got to the point. "Mrs. Finkel went out of town during Rooms and Blooms. Do you know where she went?"

The redhead shrugged, and I couldn't help thinking that if I were hiring, I'd want someone with more spunk.

But the two men snickered, and one said, "Everyone knows that. You'd have to be blind not to figure it out."

Feeling stupid, I said, "Could you be a little more specific?"

"She got implants."

The redhead finally came to life. "Oh yeah. My mom said Mrs. Finkel is a pathetic old crow trying to regain her youth and hold on to her husband. That's why she thought I was after Mr. Finkel. As if! Like I need a geezer?"

In spite of all my suspicions, I felt sorry for Earl. A woman who would go to those lengths to make her husband happy probably wasn't planning to kill him. Or had Earl's efforts caused her to be even more disappointed when she learned Kurt had dinner with Nina?

I thanked them and took my list up to the lobby to phone the people who hadn't collected their belongings. I was in the middle of a heated discussion with a man who claimed he couldn't remove his exhibit until the following week when Francie and Humphrey burst into the hotel.

Francie pointed at me. "There she is!"

They waited politely while I wound up my call, but the second I clicked the phone shut, Francie said, "We have a problem."

Humphrey whispered, “Kurt died from a blow to the head by a hammer.”

*Ewww.* “But that’s good news, in a way.” I brightened up. “That clears Nina.”

Humphrey didn’t look happy. “When Kurt disappeared, so did Bernie’s hammer. And Bernie’s the one who figured out how to open the wall unit.”

“Then it ought to be obvious to you that had Bernie killed Kurt, he wouldn’t have opened the wall unit.”

Humphrey and Francie exchanged a foolish look.

“Where’s Nina?” I asked. “I thought she didn’t want to be alone.”

“We left her at the vet’s with the menagerie. She’ll be okay there.” Humphrey looked at me like a confused puppy. “You don’t think someone is really after her?”

I doubted it. “She’s very frightened, though.” I checked the time. “You pick up Nina. I have to close up here and run a few errands. I’ll meet you back at my house in a couple of hours.”

When I returned to the hall, only one Rooms and Blooms exhibit remained. The hotel crew was already busy setting up for the next convention. Amid the clanks and reverberating sounds of items being wheeled in and assembled, I realized how easy it had been for someone to lurk among the exhibits and kill Tara. No one paid any attention to me, and if I suddenly vanished, I doubted any of them would remember that I had walked by.

I was on my way to find the manager when the guy who’d insisted he couldn’t dismantle his exhibit until the following week appeared, and began packing up his display of tools. Although he shot some nasty glances in my direction, I was thrilled to wrap up Rooms and Blooms.

When I left the hotel, I headed to the address Camille

had given me for a sofa for the family room. Although I went with a buttery color in mind, I chose a deep, cushy sectional in a bittersweet coral. They promised to deliver it the next day.

Nolan and Camille's antiques store was only a couple of blocks away. I stopped in to see if Nolan was back at work yet, and to pick out some items for the family room.

Borrowing from Nolan's store was way too much fun. I didn't have to pay attention to the frightening price tags, and imagined that the extremely wealthy probably shopped with the same gleeful abandon. I found mismatched side tables with interesting wrought-iron bases, and selected a host of colorful urns and decorative items.

Camille appeared at my elbow. "I'm so glad you stopped by. I've been wanting to show you something for your room."

I trailed after her to a huge armoire, painted in earthy Tuscan colors with a surprising touch of bittersweet coral, that would be ideal with the sofa. Out of sheer habit, I turned the price tag and staggered backward at the hefty five-figure price.

Camille laughed. "It would be a huge favor if you would display this. Maybe someone will see it and we can finally unload it. I think it goes with your color scheme and Tuscan feel perfectly. I'll have it delivered tomorrow morning."

"Are you manning the store?"

She beckoned me to a table, sat down, and wrote a receipt for me. "Nolan's still playing the wounded victim." She slid the receipt in my direction. "Sophie, are you still in touch with Wolf? According to gossip, you're not seeing him anymore."

*Oof.* I didn't like to lie to Camille. But I wasn't sure I dared spill the beans, either. There was no telling who might tell Detective Kenner the truth. "We're just friends. Why do you ask? Do you need to talk to him?"

She looked aghast at the thought. "Good heavens, no. Has . . . has he said anything about progress in solving Tara's murder?"

"I think they figured out who was following her."

A little shudder coursed through Camille.

# THIRTY-FIVE

From *"Ask Natasha"*:

*Dear Natasha,*

*I can handle the basics of decorating but I'm lost when it comes to accessorizing. How do I choose what to display? Nothing I do looks as polished as in the magazines.*

*—Accessory Challenged in Cheektowaga*

*Dear Accessory Challenged,*

*Accessories reflect the interests of the owner. Let your inner decorator guide you. Get out the glue gun and adorn the things you love with beads, shells, and crystals. Mount old shutters or trellises on the wall as eye-catching backdrops, and arrange glittery keepsakes in front of them in groups of three.*

*—Natasha*

I thought I heard a tremor in Camille's voice when she asked, "Who was the stalker?"

"My friend Humphrey. But I'm sure he didn't murder her. He's very meek and mild-mannered."

Camille slid a hand across her brows and up her forehead.

"Are you all right?"

"Sophie," she whispered, "what would you do if you thought Mars murdered someone?"

"Mars?" The very idea sent a chill up my spine. "That would never happen."

"Don't be so sure."

"You think Mars killed Tara?" I had to ask, although I knew it wasn't likely.

"Nolan had an affair with Tara." She held perfectly manicured hands to the sides of her face. "I'm the one who was tailing her, trying to catch them."

"Nolan?! So he's the married man she broke up with."

"*Hah*! She might have been blabbing about Wolf, but I caught them at the hotel where we held Rooms and Blooms. They had the nerve to meet in a room upstairs, when they knew I was nearby. Can you imagine? I hardly think it was over."

I sat back, confused. Did Tara tell everyone she and Wolf were a couple to throw them off the truth about her relationship with Nolan? Or had she really broken it off with her married man, as Posey claimed? "You have to tell the police, Camille. It might get Wolf off the hook."

Her entire body sagged, and for the first time since I'd known her, she looked old and tired. "Would you turn in Mars? I can't do that to Nolan. Besides, I don't know that he killed her, only that they were involved. I will divorce him. I will close down this money-draining shop of his, but I can't turn him in."

I hated to admit it to myself, but I did understand Camille. It would be hard to report a husband, even a philandering scoundrel of a husband. And she didn't have any proof that he killed Tara. "Do you think Nolan knew you were on to him?"

Camille grimaced. "Is that a nice way of asking if I think he killed Tara so he could stay with the cash cow?" She moaned and sat up straighter. "I don't know. It's certainly possible. And if I go to the police, we'll both be suspects. I imagine that his mugging wasn't a fluke, though. I'd be willing to bet that it's connected with Tara's murder somehow."

Reeling from Camille's revelations, I stood to leave, but she grabbed my hand. "I know one thing for sure. On the day before the Rooms and Blooms banquet, I was tailing Tara—and she was following Nina."

Snowflakes danced through the air the following morning, and if I hadn't been worried about two murders, I would have enjoyed the short walk to Mordecai's house. Nina still slept, and her guardian, Humphrey, snoozed on the sofa in my family room.

When I opened the front door to Mordecai's house, a chorus of voices cautioned me to enter with care. Bernie shut the door behind me.

Happily, it wasn't Beth standing on scaffolding to install Natasha's wallpaper on the foyer ceiling. Three men had taken on the onerous job. They must have worked the day before, because they were almost finished.

An incredibly ornate cream diamond shape adorned with golden emblems surrounded a new light fixture of opaque glass. Like a fancy Oriental rug, a border around the diamond led to a larger surrounding square with a detailed pattern incorporating the cream and gold and introducing turquoise shells. Another border boxed it in, and beyond that, turquoise became the background color. If Natasha had shown it to me, I'd have protested that it was too busy, but I had to admit that it was very impressive and transformed the dark, dingy foyer into a grand entrance.

Iris watched the workers, her mouth turned down at the corners. "Natasha hired Nolan's men to put it up."

"It's certainly eye-catching," said Bernie.

"*Hmmph.* It's called overdecorating." Iris shook her head. "Does she think this is the White House? That's the problem with people who aren't real designers. They don't understand creating a room that people want to live in. It has to be beautiful but livable. No one wants all that junk on the ceiling. And she took down the best part of the foyer—the chandelier."

I smiled, relieved that she wouldn't be able to make that complaint about the family room. If anything, it was too comfy and not sufficiently high style.

Bernie beckoned to me, and I followed him into our family room. Nolan's guys must have started at the crack of dawn, because the armoire and side tables already waited. Bernie and I shoved them aside to make room for the sofa, and not a minute too soon. When the bittersweet coral pieces were in place, even Iris approved. The three of us nestled into the comfortable seating and discussed placement of accessories.

"There's an old wooden door in Mordecai's garage that Mars and I could beat up a little bit." Bernie gazed around. "Can't work inside anymore with all this nice furniture in here. If it gets warm enough outdoors to stain it, the door would make a great coffee table."

"Very Tuscan. Good idea. Iris, where's Bedelia?" I asked.

"Packing. I hate to see her go. It's been such fun having her here." Iris rose to arrange candlesticks of three different heights together. "I've asked her to live with me, but she doesn't want to leave Florida."

I was making a mental note that I needed cushions for Bernie's window seat when a loud bang thudded through the house, and the lights went out.

The three of us rushed to the foyer, where Natasha's workmen climbed off their scaffolding, looking around anxiously. Voices in the kitchen drew us in that direction.

We arrived in time to see Ted and Mike fly out the back door. We followed them to the garden and discovered Beth consoling a distraught Natasha.

Ted knelt at an electrical outlet and said, "It's okay. Just an electrical overload. This is what happens when amateurs take on more than they can handle."

Natasha drew herself completely erect. "I am not an amateur. It's this house. It's just—old." She stood next to a preformed pond liner.

"You're installing a water feature when it's snowing?" I asked.

"Ted said he didn't have time, so I took it upon myself. Like everything else in this house. I have a co-chair, but all she's done is her own little room upstairs. Meanwhile, I have coordinated the kitchen, the foyer, and a bedroom, and I'm determined to get this water feature in."

I held out my arm to prevent Iris from launching herself at Natasha. "Ted, do you think you can fix it?"

"Probably. Anybody have a flashlight?"

I hurried home through heavily falling snow to retrieve a couple of flashlights. On my return, Mike and Ted disappeared to the basement to repair the damage Natasha had inflicted. Those who lived farther away and couldn't walk home took off before the streets became slick. The rest of us resumed our decorating tasks.

Bernie was helping me hang simple curtains when Bedelia swished into the family room. "Darlings, I'm off to the ancestral manse in the land of the sun."

"Have you called the airport to check on your flight?" I asked.

"It's already tapering off. Don't worry about me." Bedelia waved a hand as though she wasn't concerned. "Iris's master bedroom is gorgeous. If she doesn't win the Guild Award, I'll know that Natasha cheated somehow." Bedelia scooted over to Bernie and waggled a gnarled finger at him. "I want you and Iris to go out to a romantic dinner—on me. Iris is just like me. If only I were forty years younger—I'd stow you in my luggage and take you back to Florida with me."

Bernie laughed and kissed her on the cheek. That appeared to satisfy Bedelia, and she departed with a grand flourish.

A short time later, Bernie was called to the restaurant about an emergency, and I took a break. In the kitchen, Beth was handing Natasha a collection of colorful pitchers to place on a shelf above the window.

"I see you're sticking to your new romantic country idea." I picked up a straw hat with blue and lavender silk flowers attached to the band.

Natasha smiled. "I don't know why I didn't do this before. I'm a natural at it. Did you see that gorgeous bedroom upstairs? Iris won't tell me who decorated it. It's not my style, but there's something so romantic about it."

Beth shot me a nervous glance. She needn't have worried, I wouldn't betray her confidence.

The door to the basement was open, probably for the

small amount of daylight that would be provided. Holding the rail, lest I trip in the dark, I stepped down carefully. At the sound of my footsteps, a flashlight swung in my direction. "It's only me, Sophie. How's it going?"

Ted or Mike grumbled in response. I reached the bottom and realized just how much of the basement Mordecai had given up for his little art gallery on the other side of the wall. I didn't have a light, but I ran my hand over the rough surface of the wall. "Mordecai built this out of concrete block. It must have taken him ages to build everything."

"Hence the amontillado," said Mike. "He didn't build the wall around a live person, like in the Poe story, but it was a clue to the fact that he'd walled off the basement."

"What I still don't understand is why Mordecai wanted five students he presumably liked to find the grave under the house. He went to so much trouble to build this wall, not to mention the ornate wall unit upstairs," I mused. "Then he guarded it, was almost obsessed about leaving it alone."

"I think you're on the right track when you say he was obsessed," offered Ted. "He killed someone, and the trauma caused him to lose touch with reality. He constructed his own world here and imagined things that didn't exist."

"I don't think so, Ted," said Mike. "Beth and I have been talking about it. Sophie's right. Mordecai wanted his bequest party to bring back memories of the party all those years ago. There was something odd about that day, something he wanted us to remember, but we can't put our fingers on it."

"No mystery there," said Ted. "What could possibly be more uncomfortable than finding the host's wife in the arms of another man? I'm sure they'll find that the bones belong to Mordecai's wife. He probably flipped out and killed her, then couldn't live with himself."

The lights suddenly came on. We could hear cheers and applause coming from upstairs.

Ted and Mike high-fived.

I followed them up the stairs, thinking about what Mike had said. Mordecai meant for them to find the grave, and he wanted to trigger a memory. If the students hadn't killed anyone, why would he do that? Why burden them with the knowledge that he had committed a heinous crime?

Unless my speculations the day before had been correct and—it wasn't Mordecai's crime.

# THIRTY-SIX

From *Natasha Online*:

*Mirrors are my very favorite decorating devices. Hang a collection of similar mirrors on a wall across from a window and they'll brighten the entire room. Place a huge vase of flowers on a pedestal, and flank it with two six-foot-tall mirrors to enlarge a room. And don't forget to hang at least one mirror in every room, including the kitchen, so you can check your appearance in a flash.*

"Mike!" We were in the kitchen when I asked, "Is there a possibility that Mordecai wasn't the murderer? That he brought his best students together so you could figure out who had committed the crime?" He'd taught them to solve problems, to figure out his tricks. "Was he relying on you to solve a crime that happened over twenty years ago?"

"Don't be silly, Sophie. What an imagination." Natasha

hung a mirror on the wall opposite the door to the family room. "I think if we place the wreath of silk roses behind the cake pedestal, it will make a darling counterscape."

Natasha appeared to be talking to Beth, but Beth's eyes met mine and gave away her thoughts. She excused herself and hurried into the foyer, with Ted, Mike, and me on her heels. "Those bones have to belong to Mr. Ledbetter."

"Or Jean," I interjected.

Beth's face screwed up as though she was fighting tears. "They're not my Aunt Jean. She lived with me until she died four months ago. With my kids in college on the East Coast, there wasn't anything keeping me in Nevada anymore. That's why I moved back here to help my parents."

"I'm so sorry, Beth," I said. "The bones could actually belong to anyone—a delivery guy, for instance."

Mike shook his head. "This has something to do with us, the five students. I'm sure of it. Beth and I have been wracking our brains going over the events of that afternoon. Ledbetter was also a professor, but I don't think any of us had it in for him. Besides, he was alive when we left."

I shuddered. The circumstances reminded me vaguely of Kurt's death. "Okay, let's think this through. The five students left to go see the burning cottage at the community center. Right?"

Beth nodded. "Mordecai went with them, but he didn't stay long. I was here a little longer, packing the car. Other guests were still here, too, oblivious to the entire drama." She placed a hand on Mike's arm. "Do you remember someone giving Ledbetter a pill? Like Valium or something? We shut the doors to the family room so he could rest."

"What about the gang of five? What happened when you saw your cottage on fire?" I asked.

Ted winced. "Lots of accusations, of course. Everyone blamed it on someone else. But there was a theory that Ledbetter was responsible for the sabotage. Mordecai had received some kind of prestigious award, and we all thought Ledbetter was jealous. Think about it—Mordecai's wife left, the cottage burned, and the man responsible, his archrival, was in the family room on the sofa. Mordecai went in there and killed him."

"Or one of the students might have come back here and killed him. One of the students who thought Ledbetter set the cottage on fire," I said.

Mike nodded. "I'll call Posey and Nolan and get them over here. I'll tell Nolan someone wants to buy one of his overpriced antiques, that'll roust him. Two o'clock okay with you?"

Ted looked at his watch. "I may be a little late. I have to check on another job, and I have a crew reassembling the glass house for the woman who bought it. But it shouldn't take too long."

"Two o'clock is fine for me." I'd no sooner said it than Natasha waltzed out of the kitchen.

"Am I the only one who ever does any work around here? Beth, take a lunch break, I'll be back in two hours. Sophie, you'd better get cracking on cushions for that window seat. Do you even know how to sew?"

Ted, Natasha, and I pulled on jackets and walked out into crisp, cold air. A layer of snow dusted our street and the sky was ominously gray, as though more snow was on the way. Natasha hurried toward her house, muttering something about Beth and employees. Ted shivered and hopped into his truck, but I crossed the street slowly, still thinking about Mordecai and his students. If the body was Ledbetter's, and Mordecai thought Jean had killed him, what changed his mind? What made Mordecai think one of his students killed Ledbetter?

The minute I opened my kitchen door, Francie and

Duke bounded out. "Nina is going to have to hire a bodyguard. I can't keep babysitting her." Francie hooked a leash on Duke, who pranced delightedly in the snow.

I didn't make it into the house because Nina thrust a coat at me. "Francie bolted without it."

I rushed after her, caught up on the sidewalk, and helped her slip it on. Duke dug in the shallow snow, tossing it in the air. A little mound of snow stuck to his black nose. Francie and Duke continued their walk in the direction of Natasha's house, and I turned back.

My hand was on my gate when the words of Mordecai's lawyer came back to me. Mordecai had told him his little dog dug up something that made him realize he'd labored under a misconception. Could Emmaline have dug up the insulin? The killer would have wanted to be rid of it, but since it would implicate Jean, maybe the killer buried it in the crawl space. When Emmaline uncovered it, Mordecai realized Ledbetter hadn't died from a blow to the head. Jean could have killed him with her insulin, but she needed it and wouldn't have left it behind.

And crafty old Mordecai found he had a new puzzle to solve. He came to suspect one of his students, since they'd been present when he found Jean with Ledbetter. He set up the hunt for the bequest secure in the knowledge that the person who buried the body wouldn't want the others to find it, and thought the killer would finally be revealed.

He just hadn't realized how desperate that former student would become, and that other lives would be lost in the unveiling of the killer.

I shivered and gazed at Mordecai's house, imagining the horror of that day, when I noticed that Ted's truck hadn't left. I studied it for a second. No one was inside, the engine was off, and snow still clung to the windshield. Had he changed his mind?

I walked closer. Maybe his truck wouldn't start. And then I realized *his men couldn't be pouring concrete in the snow.* They'd told me the weather had to improve before they could work on reassembling the glass cottage. I approached the truck cautiously and looked down at the footprints in the snow. Ted's large footprints left little confusion about which direction he'd gone. I could see that he'd gotten into the truck. But another set of his footprints led down the sidewalk, as though he'd gotten out again. I followed them around the side of the house to the gate in back, where I'd met Tara the night I thought I saw a light in the house. The footprints continued in the direction of the house and the pond liner that Natasha was trying to install. I followed them up to the back door and looked through the window.

Nothing seemed amiss. To be on the safe side, I pulled my cell phone out of my pocket and called Wolf. I knew I shouldn't phone him because of Kenner, but this was surely an exception. When Wolf answered, I said in a low tone, "I'm at Mordecai's and something's not right."

"Can you be more specific?"

"I believe I've caught Ted in a lie." I snapped the phone shut and tried the door. It swung open easily, though it did creak a bit.

I stood in the English Country kitchen and listened for voices. The door to the family room stood ajar, and unless I missed my guess, I could hear someone talking softly.

I hadn't moved when Ted called out, "Sophie! Please join us."

How had he known I was here? I swirled to hide or leave, and realized that he could see my reflection in the mirror Natasha had hung earlier.

"I have a gun, Sophie. Don't make me use it."

I gazed around the kitchen for a weapon. Beth and Natasha had cleaned out Mordecai's knives, and the straw hat wouldn't do me any good. My only chance was to drop to the floor and hustle outside—fast. I crouched and waddled to the door. Before I could open it, I heard a mechanical click behind me, and looked up to see a perfect round hole in the glass of the door. In the few seconds it took me to register what had happened, fissures spread in the tempered glass. It crackled as they grew and filled the door window, and a moment later, I covered my head as the entire window crashed to the floor in tiny square shards of thick glass.

"Now get in here and don't make me shoot you." Ted's tone had taken on an unfamiliar hard edge.

The pile of tempered glass glittered in front of me. It was all I had as a potential weapon. Thankful that they didn't have the razor-sharp edges of regular broken glass, I scooped up handfuls of the prickly shards and dropped them into my pockets. Gulping hard, I rose and walked very slowly toward the family room.

Beth and Mike sat on the beautiful couch, holding hands and looking very frightened. Each of them held a small glass filled with liquid. An unpleasant, pungent odor wafted over to me—turpentine?

"Pity that you showed up. I thought I might be able to spare you once the lovebirds killed themselves over their dirty deeds."

I hoped Wolf was on the way. I needed to keep Ted talking, so I feigned stupidity. "Beth and Mike killed Mr. Ledbetter? Mike, was it you and Beth who were in Mordecai's house a couple of days after he died?"

Ted laughed. "That was me. Making sure old Mordecai hadn't left some kind of message about the body in the basement."

Mike seemed confused. "We didn't kill anyone, Sophie. It was Ted."

Ted tilted his head: "And that's why they're drinking turpentine. They'll be dead by the time their two o'clock appointments arrive. I hadn't counted on you, though, Sophie. You don't fit in this plan at all. I guess I'll have to take you with me and dispose of you somewhere."

I needed to stall him. "You buried Mr. Ledbetter in the basement? Mordecai must have known."

"He was so distressed about Jean's infidelity that he was hardly functioning. Jean had been planning to leave with Ledbetter, and when Mordecai learned that, he threw her out of the house. I think it broke him. I remember him sitting in the garden like a statute surrounded by guests who hadn't a clue about what had transpired." He sounded angry when he added, "Mordecai didn't deserve that kind of treatment from either of them. He was a decent and giving man."

"So you came back to the party." I took a chance. "With Kurt?"

"He helped me carry Ledbetter's body to the basement. I thought I could trust him. But when I showed up that night, after Nina pushed him into the andirons, he'd opened the wall unit. We hid in the stairway while you and Nina searched the house." A smile turned up one side of his mouth. "Kurt thought that was hilarious. When you left, he found a bottle of booze in the kitchen. I never knew he was such a talkative drunk. He was a danger to us, a loose link who had to be silenced. The best place for him was with Ledbetter, under the house. But Kurt had closed the wall unit, and I couldn't figure out how to open it."

In horror, Mike said, "You kept him alive until he showed you?"

"It took the whole night. Drunk men don't focus well. We finally figured it out, and I'd just slammed him in the head with a hammer when Sophie came in to clean. Who cleans that early in the morning?"

"So he might have still been alive when you stuffed him into the window seat?"

"If he wasn't dead, he was unconscious. I waited in the closet and had to hustle when you left. I threw him down the steps and applied the hammer again, then hid there with him while you brought the cop inside."

"Then you're the one who moved his car and returned his cell phone to his booth at Rooms and Blooms."

Ted frowned. "Perhaps it's a good thing you happened along. You know too much already."

"I don't know who shot nails into your pond."

He sighed. "It seemed prudent at the time. In case anyone tried to blame Kurt's death on me, I wanted it to appear that I was a victim. But then when I followed Tara back to the convention hall, I didn't have a weapon and had to improvise. Posey's nail gun happened to be handy. I wish I hadn't killed Tara in my own exhibit, but it was the only place with a degree of privacy."

"You didn't have to kill Tara. She didn't know anything," I protested.

"Mordecai would have loved her. She kept dropping a feather on the floor in front of the wall unit. She figured out there was a draft and that it opened. It would only have been a matter of time until the cops swarmed the place. I had to prevent that at all costs. As long as the cops didn't find out about the stairwell behind the wall unit everything would be fine."

"You should have allowed them to find my husband's corpse to begin with, Teddy." We all turned to see Bedelia standing in the doorway. "If you'd only left well enough alone. Mordecai's students would have found the grave, everyone would have thought Mordecai killed his wife's lover, and that would have been the end of it. But you've gone and told the whole story to these people—three of them. I'm so disappointed in you. I thought you would keep our little secret. And now the best place in Old Town to hide corpses has been revealed." She *tsk*ed. "What to do, what to do?"

# THIRTY-SEVEN

**From** "The Good Life" :

Dear Sophie,

My wife and I are furnishing our new Arts and Crafts-style home. We have some artwork we'd like to hang in the foyer, but it seems like all the frames are too ornate or too plain. How can we make them stand out without going the gilded route?

—Frameless in Fruitville

Dear Frameless,

Use inexpensive square or rectangular frames in the Craftsman style. But cover them with bright, one-inch-square glass tiles. Your artwork will pop, no gilding necessary.

—Sophie

"I have everything under control, Mrs. Ledbetter," insisted Ted.

"Teddy, I've been so worried about you. I'm afraid you've lost control. Sweetheart, you never kill a cop. That's a fine way to make sure the rest of the men in blue get agitated. You're such a dear, but now you've gone and gotten us into a terrible mess."

"You knew your husband was buried under this house?" I blurted.

"Darling, he was a worm. He announced his intention to leave me for Jean. Leave me without anything. No house, no money, no savings. I would have been penniless. There was only one way to save myself."

"You hired Ted to kill him?" Beth asked, aghast.

"Some things you have to do for yourself. Jean's insulin worked quite nicely. He was woozy and barely noticed the injection. But I paid Teddy to get rid of him for me. I had no idea what he might have done with his will and couldn't take the chance his body would be found. So much easier to divorce him in absentia and simply keep everything." She *tsk*ed. "Poor Mordecai. I hear he never came out of his funk. I do feel a bit guilty about that. I started the rumor that he'd killed Jean to frighten people. I guess it worked. He must have wondered who carried the body to the crawl space and buried it for him. I imagine he lived in fear of being blackmailed. He knew he and Jean would be prosecuted if anyone found out." She shook her head in disbelief. "He spent his life protecting a woman who cheated on him."

"It's sort of romantic. If only Aunt Jean had known how much he still loved her." Beth wiped a tear from her face.

"Drink your turpentine and you can tell her when you see her in heaven. Now drink up," demanded Ted.

"Wait!" I cried. *Where was Wolf?* "Beth, did Jean know Ledbetter had died?"

"I suspect she did, because she refused to ever step foot in Virginia again. She cried all the way to Nevada. I remember trying to console her by saying that Mr. Ledbetter could join us in Nevada. Little did I know . . . she just sobbed."

"Ted, if you didn't kill Mr. Ledbetter, why did you try to prevent the discovery of the grave?"

Bedelia shuffled over to Ted and planted a kiss on his cheek. "Teddy has been doing odd jobs for me since he was a little boy. I knew he needed seed money to get his business off the ground. All he had to do was bury my dear dead husband where he wouldn't be found."

"Ted, I thought you loved Mordecai," I said. "Why would you do this to him?"

"To him? I did it for him. Don't you see? The insulin, the public argument, Jean's affair—everything pointed to Mordecai and Jean as the killers. Kurt and I did the only logical thing. We got rid of the body to save Mordecai, Jean, and Bedelia. It was the only way to protect all of them."

"Then you were the one who mugged Nolan?" asked Mike.

"We were short one key." Ted grinned. "And I knew Nolan had it in his wallet. I had to keep Posey from getting it and opening the wall."

The front door slammed open. Thank goodness! Wolf had finally made it. But it was Nina's voice that echoed through the house from the foyer, "Sophie! You left me alone again."

Things happened very quickly after that. A green blur shot through the air, aimed directly at Bedelia's oversized glasses. Hank latched onto them with his beak and Bedelia shrieked, trying to beat the bird away.

Ted looked on in surprise, and I figured the commotion was our only chance. I lunged at Ted and smashed handfuls of broken glass into his face. Beth jumped up, ran behind him, and doused him with the turpentine in her glass, and Mike tackled him at the knees.

Nina was trying to rescue Hank, who beat his wings wildly. Bedelia threw her glasses to the floor and Hank landed on them, screaming, "She's a witch!"

At the top of her lungs, Beth yelled at me, "Duct tape?"

I thought there was a roll in a box of painting supplies we'd shoved in the corner. I dumped the contents on the floor and grabbed the duct tape.

I hoped Bedelia was too old to do us much harm, especially without her glasses, and hurried toward Ted and Mike, who wrestled on the floor. When Mike almost had Ted pinned, Beth sat on Ted's legs in an effort to hold them so I could secure his ankles with duct tape. It worked.

We flipped him over, but it wasn't easy pulling his hands behind his back to wrap duct tape around his wrists. When we succeeded, I was out of breath.

I gazed up at Nina and Bedelia and saw that Nina had cleverly used one of Bedelia's necklaces to bind her hands together.

It must have seemed chaotic to Wolf, who barged in with handcuffs. He nodded his approval and looked over at me. "You're bleeding."

I looked down at my hands. I hadn't even noticed.

# THIRTY-EIGHT

From "THE GOOD LIFE" :

Dear Sophie,

My new husband and I are retiring to the mountains. We'd love to have a bedroom for each of our grandchildren, but it's not financially possible, and they would be empty most of the time anyway. Bunk beds seem too childish, and we'd like them to have some degree of privacy. Any suggestions?

—Newlyweds in New Port Richey

Dear Newlyweds,

Consider built-in beds. Each bed can be painted to reflect the child's personality. Build bookshelves at the head and the foot and they'll have plenty of room to stash their gear. Plus, the drawers underneath the beds eliminate the need for dressers. Make sure everyone has a closet space and you'll be set!

—Sophie

Four days later, the family room of Mordecai's house showed no signs of the drama that had taken place there. The turpentine had eaten the finish off the floor in one spot, but Bernie and I had sanded, buffed, and applied polyurethane, so it was only visible to those of us who knew where to look.

I strolled into the living room, where Nolan cast a critical eye at his turquoise walls.

"Feeling better?" I asked.

"You heard about the divorce, I suppose."

I nodded. "What are your plans?"

"Thankfully, my share of Mordecai's bequest should enable me to buy Camille out of her portion of the antiques store."

"You know the value of Mordecai's paintings?"

He huffed. "I *am* in the business. I knew they had to be here somewhere. For years an absentee bidder had been outbidding me at auctions. I always suspected Mordecai. He had a good eye." He bowed his head. "My only regret is that Tara isn't with me."

"So she hadn't broken it off with you?"

"She had—but she would have married me, I'm sure."

Posey emerged from the dining room. "Don't believe him, Sophie. She wanted nothing more to do with Nolan and had her sights fixed on Wolf—someone who wouldn't have to cut the cord with his wife's bank account."

Posey and Nolan glared at each other, and Nina broke the

tension by arriving with a basket of kittens. She handed two to Posey. "Where's Bernie? He's taking the other two."

Natasha must have overheard, because she barreled in from the kitchen. "No way. Bernie lives above my garage, and I won't have animals there."

Beth followed Natasha into the living room. "I'll pick up Hank and Mom Cat when I leave this afternoon."

"Hank?" I was delighted that he'd found a home. "I didn't know you liked birds."

"Mike and I are taking Mom Cat. But when my dad heard that Hank sings Hank Williams songs, he had to have him."

Nina nodded. "He's retired, so Hank won't be so lonely and get into mischief."

The front door opened and voices drifted to us. Natasha patted her hair. "Nolan, you should have hung a mirror in here. Everyone to your rooms." She clapped her hands like a schoolteacher. "The Guild judges have arrived." Natasha started for the foyer, turned around, and said, "And get those animals out of here. I don't want the judges to see them."

Nina and I scooted through the foyer, past the judges, to the family room, and I peeked from the doorway. Natasha was in her element, wearing her TV face to welcome them. Camille carried a fluffy little dog wearing a pink collar embellished with rhinestone hearts.

I beckoned Nina. "Is that Emmaline?"

She grinned. "I thought the two heiresses might understand each other."

I hugged my friend. "Good call." Bernie stepped in from the kitchen. "Reporting for inspection duty with team Sophie. Are those my kittens?"

"Natasha doesn't want cats on her property." I hated to break the news, but it was better for him to find out before he bonded.

Too late. He lifted the squirming kittens from the basket and cuddled them. And then he grinned at me. "If I can't keep them at Natasha's place, I suppose we'll just have to move."

"Did your husband finally make it home?" I asked Nina. "Are you still married?"

"We never even got around to talking about Kurt and Mordecai. You know the woman I was worried about? The one who had the hots for my husband? Someone pushed her overboard!"

"Not your husband, I hope."

Nina snorted. "He's far too proper for that. If he were to kill someone, he'd drop something toxic into the victim's martini. It seems one of the other wives had enough of the trollop and tossed her over the rail. Turns out it's a good thing Detective Kenner has records of my presence here at home—I have a perfect alibi!"

Natasha whispered loudly in the foyer. I thought I'd better make sure she wasn't expelling Posey's kittens, but I needn't have worried.

Natasha glared up the stairs at Beth. "Where do you think you're going?"

"To the room I decorated."

"You? *You?*" sputtered Natasha.

Beth took advantage of Natasha's surprise and sprinted up the steps.

"Iris gave her a room," I said.

Natasha was not amused. In a dead voice, she said, "Don't tell me. The pretty romantic one."

I smiled.

"I can never get ahead. Why does everything happen to me? I never should have hired someone who seemed knowledgeable. Let that be a lesson to you, Sophie." She retreated to the kitchen, still muttering.

After the judges viewed the family room, which they appeared to like, we waited impatiently for them to finish looking at the upstairs rooms. At long last, the judges and decorators gathered in the foyer.

"Ladies and gentlemen," said Camille, "I'm delighted to announce a unanimous decision. The room we'd all love to have, that showed ingenuity and love, the best room in the Show House, was decorated by Beth."

Applause broke out, but not before I heard Natasha release a disgusted sigh.

Camille sidled up to me. "Did you see my little darling, Emmaline? She's such wonderful company. We're both in the same boat, you know. She lost Mordecai, and I lost Nolan."

I stroked Emmaline's head.

Camille leaned in and whispered, "Iris is winning the Guild Award this year. Mostly for managing to pull off this house in spite of Natasha."

After the judges departed, I took one last look at Mordecai's wall unit, thinking about how much he must have loved Jean to hide their secret all those years. I heard giggling, and found Mike and Beth in an embrace behind me. They opened their arms to include me in their hug.

"Natasha fired me," said Beth with an enormous grin.

"But it doesn't matter, because we're opening Country Kitchen Designs together." Mike looked as happy as Beth. "We're in the market for a house. Wish we had the money for this one. It's big enough, don't you think?"

Beth explained, "My parents are moving in with us. And Hank and Mom Cat."

"And we need room for our three kids when they're home from school," added Mike.

I had no doubt they would have a big, noisy, happy household. I followed them out and down the steps. An uncontrollable shiver climbed my spine when I saw Detective Kenner standing on the corner.

A florist's van slowed in front of me and parked, blocking my view of Kenner. The driver got out and handed me a vibrant red gerbera daisy plant in full bloom. "Sorry, Ms. Winston. This was supposed to be delivered to you on Valentine's Day, but we had a little mix-up. Hope Wolf won't be in too much trouble. It's our fault it's so late."

I assured him Wolf would be forgiven. When he drove away, Kenner still watched me.

My heart beat faster, even though I knew I was innocent and that the killers were in custody. Giving him a polite nod, I crossed the street at a fast pace, but he caught up.

He stopped me on the sidewalk, and all I wanted was to get away. Where was Wolf when I needed him? Surely Kenner no longer suspected me of anything criminal.

I dared to look him in the face—what else could I do? The skin under his cheekbones, on both sides of his mouth, sunk in. I wondered if he was capable of happiness.

"Sophie, now that you're not dating Wolf anymore, I wondered if you would like to go out with me? Say this weekend?"

*And Natasha thought she had problems.*

# RECIPES & COOKING TIPS

## Strawberry Daiquiris

*1 15.5-ounce package frozen strawberries*
*1 6-ounce container frozen lime juice*
*5–6 ounces rum*
*3 ounces triple sec*
*2 cups ice*
*corn syrup (optional)*

Place the frozen strawberries and the lime juice in a blender or food processor. Using the empty lime juice container as a measuring cup, add 5–6 ounces rum and pour it into the blender. Add 3 ounces of triple sec. Add enough ice (about two cups) to fill the blender to the top. Blend and pour into wide-mouthed glasses. If it's too sour, add a bit of light corn syrup.

Makes about four cups of daiquiris.

## Blondies

*2 cups dark brown sugar*
*1 stick (8 tablespoons) unsalted butter*
*4 tablespoons heavy cream*
*2 large eggs, lightly beaten*
*1 teaspoon baking powder*
*¼ teaspoon baking soda*
*pinch salt*
*2 cups flour*
*2 teaspoons vanilla extract*
*¾ cup large semisweet chocolate chips or chocolate chunks. (optional)*

Preheat oven to 350 degrees. Butter a 9x13 baking pan.

In a medium size pot, melt the butter with the cream and the brown sugar over medium heat. (It does not need to boil.) Set aside and let cool for about 10 minutes. Drop a spoonful of the mixture into the eggs and whisk to temper them, then add them to the warm mixture and mix well. (You can stir the remaining ingredients in by hand but Sophie gets better results using her mixer at this point.) Pour the mixture into a mixing bowl. Using an electric mixer, stir in the baking powder, baking soda, and salt until thoroughly mixed. Stir in the flour and the vanilla. It makes a fairly thick batter. Pour half of the batter into the prepared pan and smooth. Sprinkle the chocolate bits over the batter. Pour the remaining batter over top to cover the chocolate and spread. Bake for 25–30 minutes. For easiest cutting, cut while still warm, but leave in pan to cool.

Makes about 35 blondies.

## Gruyère Onion Tart (Quiche)

*1 crust for 9-inch pie or quiche pan*
*2–3 tablespoons grainy mustard*
*6 ounces Gruyère*
*2 medium onions*
*1–2 tablespoons olive oil*
*3 medium eggs*
*1 cup milk*
*½ cup cream*
*¼ teaspoon thyme*
*½ teaspoon salt*
*¼ teaspoon pepper*
*1 package bacon, cooked (optional)*

Line the pan with the pastry and, using the back of a spoon, spread the bottom with the mustard. Refrigerate for 30 minutes.

Preheat the oven to 375 degrees. Slice and cook the onions until translucent. Set aside to cool.

Using a cheese slicer or a vegetable peeler, slice the Gruyère into thin strips. Whisk together the eggs, milk, cream, thyme, salt, and pepper.

Assemble by spreading the onions on the bottom of the pan. Lay the strips of Gruyère over the onions (and crumble in the bacon). Pour the egg mixture on top. Bake for 40–45 minutes. The top should be set and slightly golden.

## Sophie's Brine Spice Mix

*¼ teaspoon black pepper*
*1 teaspoon Hungarian sweet paprika*
*1 teaspoon salt*
*½ teaspoon dried thyme*
*2 teaspoons dried rosemary*
*1 teaspoon garlic powder*
*olive oil*

Pour all the spices into a plastic zip top bag. Add two tablespoons to ¼ cup of olive oil, depending on how much meat you have. Mix the spices with the olive oil by mashing the bottom of the bag a bit. Slide in the meat, zip the top closed, and turn over a few times to coat the meat. Refrigerate for about 45 minutes before cooking.

## Mudslide Lava Cakes

*⅓ stick butter*
*3 ½ ounces unsweetened chocolate*
*1 ½ cups sugar*
*3 medium eggs*
*3 egg yolks*
*1 ⅓ cups flour*
*dash of salt*
*¼ cup Kahlua or other coffee liquor*
*¼ cup Baileys Irish Cream*

Grease six ramekins thoroughly with butter. If you don't have ramekins, ovenproof teacups can be used instead. Melt the butter with the chocolate. Beat the eggs and egg yolks with the sugar until thick and lemon-colored. Mix in the melted chocolate and butter. Add the flour and salt slowly and mix thoroughly. Add the liquors. Pour into the ramekins. Bake at 450 degrees for 13 minutes. Gently loosen the edges of each cake and turn it onto a serving plate. Flip the cake right side up. Serve plain, dust with powdered sugar, or add a dollop of vanilla ice cream for a sinfully delicious treat!

NOTE:

The batter can be made a day ahead. Pour the batter into the ramekins, then cover each with plastic wrap and store in the refrigerator. Bake at 450 for 13 minutes just before you want to serve them. They're at their best straight from the oven.

# Cozy up with Berkley Prime Crime

**SUSAN WITTIG ALBERT**

*Don't miss the national bestselling series featuring herbalist China Bayles.*

**LAURA CHILDS**

*The Tea Shop Mysteries are the toast of Charleston, South Carolina.*

**KATE KINGSBURY**

*The Pennyfoot*

*series is a te*

**For the**

**detectiv**